BREAKFALL

BREAKFALL

ZHANNA SLOR

Copyright © 2023 by Zhanna Slor
Cover and jacket design by 2Faced Design
ISBN 978-1-957957-05-0
ISBN 978-1-957957-29-6

Library of Congress Control Number: available upon request
First hardcover edition April 2023 by Agora Books
an imprint of Polis Books, LLC
62 Ottowa Road S.
Marlboro, NJ 07746
www.PolisBooks.com

MARCH

CHAPTER ONE

It all started because of the car. Well, not actually the car itself, which was an unremarkable used Chevy Passenger van, but the bureaucracy surrounding the purchase of it. Mina's friend Dylan was a reformed felon, and told her he couldn't register a vehicle himself, so it seemed a simple thing, offering up her name, her good credit, her help; these were things in life she could still offer. She wasn't sure how long even these simple realities would be hers to give; she had been spiraling a bit since her separation. Grasping at air. Between her two jobs and her daughter, she hardly had time to guess what it was that she kept missing, but she knew she was missing something, every day, a little more. Maybe it was happiness; maybe it was the entire idea of herself and who she was. Maybe it was nothing at all. Sometimes she thought about it at night, when she was supposed to be sleeping but couldn't. But most of the time, she tried not to think. Thinking was what had brought her here, after all. Thinking could only bring you down, not up. Obviously, she should do less of it, not more.

Mina had never been great at moderation.

Which was how she ended up allowing Dylan to register a car in her name; by not giving it too much thought, or any thought at all, really. She probably should not have been friends with a felon, but she liked Dylan. He was a nice guy for a former drug-dealing thief, and supposedly an honest law-abiding citizen now; most

1

importantly, he had offered to drive her in exchange for the favor, when she needed it, and she did often need it. It was a brutal winter, and the streets and sidewalks of Chicago were a constant slippery blockade to her ability to maneuver with a toddler and stroller. So she could hardly say no to a free car, especially one she didn't have to actually drive. Plus, it saved her from having to take the CTA so much, which really had been adding up, at five dollars a day every time there was inclement weather and she couldn't walk Amelie to daycare. Paying the mortgage and utilities on her own, plus the credit card debt she and her ex had acquired, which had all ended up under her name somehow, had rendered her more broke than she had ever been in her life.

Therefore, it had seemed like a good idea at the time, to let Dylan drive her to work or help pick up her daughter, being as she needed so desperately to do both; they were the only things keeping her afloat these days, away from the abyss that always threatened to consume her entirely.

Admittedly, the abyss had seemed much closer to swallowing her when she was married, and the one main improvement in her life after splitting up with her ex was indeed her mental state. It was a rather incremental improvement, but improvement nonetheless. Irreconcilable differences was the official reason for their parting, though everyone knew the real reason was that she'd slept with someone else. Everyone knew because they'd all gone to the same Jiu Jitsu gym, and people who did Jiu Jitsu gossiped like excitable girls in middle school. Now, she could hardly recall all those months last summer when she could hardly think straight, consumed as she was with this overpowering, endless need to be with this man who was not her husband.

Her therapist believed she had only been so sex-crazed because she was unhappy in her marriage and looking for a way out. She was probably right, though at the time she didn't believe that. At the time she thought her body was betraying her, wanting something it shouldn't have, wanting it so much she couldn't stop herself from getting it. She thought it was just her body, just sex. But it was never just sex, was it?

This confusion about her recent past was the main thing keeping her from having sex with Dylan now—that and the fact that he still went to her former Jiu Jitsu gym—though she knew she could if she wanted to. He definitely wanted to. But she was not mentally capable of sleeping with anyone new, and wasn't sure she ever would be. Her divorce wasn't official yet; technically they were still separated, and would be for a few months longer at least, long enough for Dimitry to get his citizenship. They'd been lazy about applying for it when they were married, and had waited until they were eight years in, which happened to be around the time their marriage had started to fall apart. Considering this was the average span of a marriage these days, it was pretty typical Dimitry, who was in so many ways an average person.

For the next two years, they tried in vain to keep the relationship alive, during which his application had gotten stuck in the system for some ridiculous yet vague reason that was still not entirely clear to her, and he didn't get the notice to come in for an interview until things had already gone to hell between them. Now they were just waiting for the final notification. After everything she had done, it was the least she could do to wait. Not that he was entirely blameless in what had happened, but she still felt bad about it all. She still wondered if there was some way she could have found her way back to him, found a way to love him again, even though in her gut she was pretty sure there was not. Once you were gone, you were gone. No amount of marriage counseling or forcing yourself to touch someone who repulsed you could help in the end. She wished it could, but she had tried and tried and tried and only ended up a ghost of a person by the end. Whatever she was now, at least she wasn't a ghost.

During the several months of therapy she'd endured before making the final decision to leave him, it was this sense of selfhood that had come up more often than not. Before the marriage counseling, before the breakup, but not before the cheating, she was struggling with what she had deemed a three-pronged midlife crisis, albeit a tad early at thirty-two. One: her daughter had turned two and become a monster. Two: her career as a writer felt like a failure. Three: she could no longer stand her husband. The first two she understood would likely be temporary situations; a toddler didn't stay a toddler forever, and she was often prone to feelings of failure in her career, being as it was not the easiest path in life to write and sell books.

It was the third problem she couldn't quite get a grasp on, especially as months passed and it only got worse. She kept trying to pinpoint what it was she couldn't stand about Dima, if they were small, fixable things, or if it was just him as a person she could no longer be around. It was the fact that he left town so frequently, left her alone with the tiny beautiful monster they'd created, left her alone with the books she wrote that no one read. It was the fact that they were always poor, and never seemed to be getting less so, despite his long absences for work, the exact absences which had initiated the process of her hating him. It was the fact that he could talk about little else than their daughter's speech delays—some of which she believed to be his fault, for talking to her only in Russian and being so absent. That he had long ago stopped being fun, that she could no longer stand to hear the sound of his voice.

So many small reasons, but not a divorce-able offense, nothing big she could point to and say, yes that is the problem, the one unresolvable thing. They all seemed like unresolvable things, small as they were. Added up together, they felt like a whole.

"It sounds like you might not be in love with him anymore," her therapist January had suggested early on in her treatment. It may have even been her first appointment, it had been so obvious.

"But what does that even mean?" Mina had asked. She had of course considered this option before, but couldn't decide if it was true or not, because she couldn't quite figure out the definition of what they had felt for each other, then or during the years prior. It was, after all, a rather philosophical question. And the problem with philosophical questions was that they didn't have answers. This was why she had never been able to finish any courses in philosophy in college, maybe it was even why she wrote mysteries—they always required an answer. When a person was murdered, there was always a murderer. In real life, you didn't always find out who that was, but in a book—in a book, there needed to be a definitive solution. An answer with a bow and ribbon, handed to the reader like a present, payment for sticking it out. "What does it mean to love? We're married. He's a good dad. I love him in some capacity."

January didn't have an explanation for her. She was a half-retired psychologist who accepted Medicaid. How could she unpack such a complex idea as love? How could anyone? The word was too heavy with meaning, and yet no one could really say exactly what it meant. The feeling was a chameleon, always morphing and re-morphing, just out of reach. This was why she could never write a romance novel. Romance felt far more mysterious than a mystery. If it wasn't, half of all marriages wouldn't end in divorce.

"What does it mean to you?" January asked. Typical therapist response, but it was a good question. She really had to think about it for a long time. It was what made her like January, what made her decide in that moment that she would keep returning. She loved when people asked questions that actually made her have to think. It didn't happen often, and when it did, Mina noticed.

"That you care about someone almost more than yourself," she finally decided. "That you know them."

"Do you love this other man you've been seeing? The one from your gym?" she asked.

She considered this for a long time too. She loved fucking him, that was for sure. They'd been sneaking around for months at that point and the desire for him had not abated. It was honestly the best sex of her life. But she didn't know how deep her feelings ran, and she didn't have the mental space to really understand what they were doing or why. And he was not much of a deep thinker, so he had even less access to his own feelings. The few times he had told her anything remotely vulnerable was when he was completely wasted. Not that he needed to tell her he cared for her to know; she could see it in his eyes, in the way he touched her leg, both absently and with ownership, when they talked. She just had no idea how deep the feelings went, if they were real or merely a mirage created by sharing so many intimate moments. If she didn't know, how could he?

"I care for him, and I like him a lot, but I don't know him. Not really." She paused, trying to reflect on it further. "I don't think I trust him enough to love him. He's kind of…a mystery. But that is part of what intrigues me, I guess. He's the opposite of Dima."

"Hm," January said, writing something down in her notebook and underlining it. "That's an interesting word to use. You said you write mysteries, yes?"

She nodded. She could guess where January was probably headed with that line of questioning. It was not something that had escaped her attention either.

"Do you see this man as…a mystery that needs to be solved?" she asked her.

Mina almost laughed, hearing it said aloud. "No, nothing like that," she said. "I don't want to solve this one. If I solve it, it stops being fun."

"Fun. You used that word before too. So, that's all this is to you… fun?" she inquired.

"It's definitely the biggest part, yeah. We have a lot of fun. And we have insane chemistry in the bedroom. I've never experienced anything like that before."

"Well, sex isn't everything. Is he someone you can see yourself being with? Long term?"

"I try not to think about that. He's never going to leave his wife," she said. And, knowing how cliché it sounded and still unable to keep from saying it, added, "Not that it makes any sense to me at all. He doesn't even like her. She's boring and never wants to have sex with him."

January swallowed, looking at her. She understood then that it had been a mistake to bring up the wife. It's always a mistake to bring up the wife. She had learned this the hard way.

"I think it's important to understand what you're getting from him that you're not getting from your husband," January said. "It sounds like the two of you have been under a lot of stress. Maybe you could find a way to have fun with your husband again?"

The answer was no. No, there was not. She had spent months trying to figure that out. Even at the time, she was pretty sure the answer would be no, but she still said she would consider it.

"Maybe you can go on a date," January had suggested. "Rekindle that spark, the one that's missing from the bedroom."

"We never had that spark," she said.

"Never?"

"No. Never," she admitted. This was likely the root of the problem, the one with her body, that she had buried away her sex drive in a box so deep she had forgotten it was even there. Until she met Matthew. And although she had forgotten about her vagina, her body had not. Suddenly that box she had buried opened up and shot its way out like a bullet, trying to make up for lost time, not caring who got hurt in its way.

And it had hurt people. A lot of people. If she hadn't spent so much time thinking about the collateral damage, she might have been able to find a way to be single again, or to even date. But her mind was still too mired in the guilt and shame of it all. Or maybe it was too mired in him. She still wanted Matthew, even after everything. She still got excited when she saw the model of his truck driving past in the street, even while knowing it wasn't his. It was some kind of reflex she really needed to unlearn if she was going to regain her sanity one day. Same with the desire to have sex with almost any tattooed man she talked to more than five times. This was why she was going to stay far far away from Dylan, her only remaining friend from the gym. The guilt probably had something to do with her letting him register the car under her name too.

Unfortunately for her, whatever she'd set into motion when she had agreed to register Dylan's van—perhaps what she had put into motion that past summer when she'd started sleeping with Matthew—was about to come crashing down on top of her.

CHAPTER TWO

Mina was giving Amelie a bath when she first heard the knocks on her door. She ignored it at first, thinking it was UPS or FedEx leaving her a package. But when they got more insistent, she finally understood it was no delivery driver. She grabbed a towel and dried off her squirmy daughter, only managing to put her in a *Frozen* pull-up before placing a blanket around her and heading to the front door.

That was when she saw two uniformed cops standing on her well-lit porch. One was tall and rail-thin, the other short and stout, possibly Hispanic. Both of them seemed a little out of breath, like the hill of steps that led up to her house had winded them.

"Mina Banksy?" the tall officer asked her when she opened the door, toddler on hip.

"Yes?" she asked. She tried to act surprised, but she wasn't, not really. Somewhere she must have known this thing with Dylan would be trouble. Dylan had trouble written all over his chiseled, tanned face. He had promised her he was done with that old life, the one that had led him to prison and then to rehab and then back to prison again. Part of her had believed him, but mostly she didn't. She knew people were not very capable of changing, not in a positive direction anyway. You could get worse easily enough, but not better. To get better you had to be capable of being better, and not everyone was. Some people just lived in the muck. Ten years of marriage and motherhood had tricked her into thinking she was one of those people who

9

could change for the better, but you could only trick yourself for so long, could only bury those parts of you so deep. They were always bound to resurface. She understood that now. But Dylan had a PhD in philosophy and the bluest eyes she had ever seen, so she had put this knowledge away into yet another box in the back of her brain.

When she saw those two grizzly cops standing on her porch that snowy March evening, she instantly knew she had been, once again, wrong to trust him. Correction: to trust anything that required a box. Because what she had learned, and had to keep relearning, was that everything you put in a box will have to be taken out again. Sometimes forcibly so.

The tall cop looked down at a form he was holding, then at her, the warm orange glow of her office lamp behind her reflecting into his glasses. "You related to that graffiti artist?"

She tried not to roll her eyes at hearing this question yet again, and from a cop no less. "No. That's not really his name, you know."

The second cop, the short one, cleared his throat and looked down at a piece of paper. "You have a car registered to this address. A white Chevy Passenger van, correct?"

She swallowed. "Correct."

"Do you know where your vehicle is, ma'am?"

Mina pressed her lips together firmly, then inhaled despite herself. "I do not."

The cops exchanged glances. She took the time to check the badges on their breast pockets; the tall one read Miller, the other Conner. Instinctively, she wondered if either of them trained at Open Guard. There were a lot of cops who did Jiu Jitsu; most of them went to the gyms farther north in the city or in the suburbs, but her former gym had plenty too, especially the location downtown. There were too many people who trained to keep up with them all, or even know their names. Between all the Open Guard locations, and the fact that injuries required months of absence at times and that half of all new members would quit, it was pointless to keep track.

"Did you report the car stolen? It's not showing up as stolen in our records," the one called Miller said. Amelie began to fidget on her hip, and eventually Mina let her down, hoping she would manage a few minutes without a tantrum. This was difficult enough as it was.

"No," Mina said. She shook her head, watching as Amelie hopped into the other room and began pulling out all her books from the shelf, the books she had just finished putting away. Having a toddler was possibly the most Sisyphean task she'd ever encountered. Like most things in her life these days—work, love, old house—nothing ever seemed to get resolved, it only seemed to get bandaged temporarily. This tedium had been largely responsible for the impetus to destroy her life the previous year, the oppressiveness of it, of everything suddenly becoming not only repetitive but difficult. Matthew had been the only thing that felt easy and simple, albeit a tad unpredictable. It had been hard to let that go.

"Then why don't you know where it is?" Miller asked once her attention had returned to them.

"Um, I lent it to a friend."

"A friend. This friend have a name?" asked the one named Conner.

"What's this about?" she finally asked.

"There's been some…activity relating to the vehicle that's of concern," Miller replied.

"What activity?"

"Why don't you just tell us your friend's name, and we can go sort it out with him?" said Conner. "Or would you rather come down to the station? You got a sitter for the little one?"

She shook her head, and could feel her entire body turning pink. "No. It's just us."

"So do yourself a favor, ma'am, and tell us your friend's name. This little girl needs her mama around, and we don't want to charge you with aiding and abetting."

"Unless you give us reason to," interrupted Miller, his eyes darkening a little, as if he was expecting her to give him a reason.

She sighed. Well, Dylan never said anything about her having to lie for him, or go to jail, she told herself. He was sometimes vague about his whereabouts and what he was up to, so she figured some of it was no good, but she didn't really know anything. He needed to sort it out himself. "His name is Dylan," she said. "I don't actually know where he lives, but he's at the gym a lot. The Jiu Jitsu one down the block, Open Guard."

Neither officer showed any signs of recognition, but Miller looked down the street to see if the gym was indeed there, then realized it was too dark to make out from her porch and turned back around. "This Dylan have a last name?" he asked.

She tried to remember. They didn't really use last names at the gym unless it was someone's nickname because they had such a surplus of common American male names there; Davids, Johns, and Andys abounded.

"I think it's…Nash? Maybe?" She paused, thinking on it more. "No, that's not it. But it starts with an N."

"Are you telling us the truth, ma'am?" asked Miller, his brows furrowed.

"We're not that close."

"You're not that close, but you lent him your car?" Conner asked, incredulously.

"What about a phone number? You got that?" Miller interrupted.

She shook her head. "He didn't have a phone. They weren't allowed at the rehab he was living in." Mina licked her lips, which felt suddenly parched. Of course, Dylan did have a phone, he got one shortly after the car, but it was hidden somewhere, as they were strictly forbidden where he lived. But she didn't want to get him into even more trouble so she left that part out. She'd gotten good at that, leaving things out. She could do it now without even blinking. "He just kind of showed up sometimes."

Officer Conner gave her another onceover, followed by a severe frown. "Can I give you some advice, ma'am?" he asked, and before she could answer, said, "Maybe stay away from men who live in rehabs and don't own phones. Lotta red flags right there."

"He's a nice guy. And—"

"And what? He told ya he was reformed? An upstanding citizen?" She flushed again, even pinker. "Yeah."

Now both men were chuckling. "There's no such thing as reformed," Officer Miller said. His brows furrowed like he was a father disciplining a child. "The guy was just trying to get in your pants."

"Well, that much I figured out," she said, crossing her arms over her chest. Either having the door open was making her cold, or just the mention of getting into her pants had made her nipples hard, and she wasn't wearing a bra under the thin sweater she had thrown over her shirt on the way to the door.

"And he probably thought, innocent girl as you are, no record, that he could use you for this car too," Miller said. The two of them looked at her as if expecting a response to this.

Mina cleared her throat. "Is it illegal to loan a friend a car?" she asked.

"Actually, yes. Did you put him on the insurance? Or registration?"

"No."

Another look was exchanged between the two men, one she was very familiar with, being that she was a woman who lived in the world. Some sort of combination of exasperation and pity. She straightened up and stared them both dead in the eye, as if to explain she was not as naïve as they were painting her out to be. She did not subscribe to the idea that all women were just scared little girls who needed men—first fathers, then husbands—to protect them from the world's ills. If anything, it often felt like it was the other way around. Men needed women in a way women did not need men. A deeper need, one that was much harder to give and to get, one that could drain you entirely if you let it.

"Okay," Miller sighed, turning away from her gaze. "When was the last time you saw the vehicle?"

She had to think about this for a while. It had been some time since she had seen either Dylan or the van. "Maybe a couple weeks ago?"

"A couple weeks ago," Officer Conner repeated. "And it didn't occur to you to report it stolen?"

She shrugged. "I figured it would show up eventually. I don't really like to drive."

Officer Miller sighed again. It really was starting to feel like a conversation with her father; they often went a lot like this too, the rare times she even spoke to him these days. A lot of sighing and frustration on both ends. Miller looked at his partner. "Let's go to that gym, see if they have his contact info. If not, we can call all the nearby halfway houses."

Officer Conner handed her a business card. "If he…drops by, please give us a call. I'd rather not see you get in trouble, but that will be up to you, darling."

Mina pocketed the card. Already her mind was thinking about whether or not to call Matthew. Just to ask him if they were bluffing, if she really could get arrested or fined for loaning out the car. She wasn't sure he would answer if she called, though. They hadn't spoken or seen each other in quite some time, not since he and his family moved to Arizona the previous autumn.

"Is there any way I can help?" she asked, suddenly nervous about her own level of involvement in whatever Dylan had done this time. What if he really could get her into trouble?

Conner just looked at her and shook his head. "Get better taste in men."

She swallowed a laugh. "Yeah. I'm working on that."

CHAPTER THREE

Her hands were shaking so much after the cops left Mina went straight to the liquor cabinet above her sink and poured herself a very stiff brandy Old Fashioned. She ignored the cloud of sadness it brough on to look at it. That was the drink of choice she always had with Matthew when they were...whatever they were. It took two of them to calm her nerves, by which point her anxiety had mostly abated. Her body ached for a cigarette, like it always did after two drinks, but she had tossed them all out on her fourth and final attempt to quit smoking, which she had only picked up again during their affair. If not for her daughter, she might have walked to the nearest gas station and bought a new pack. But it was her bedtime, so she distracted herself from the need for nicotine by brushing Amelie's teeth and reading her a story, then finally placing her into bed and shutting the door. After which, she took a long, shaky breath and poured herself a third drink.

Finally, the brandy emitting a cool buzz throughout her system and her daughter's little squeaks and ramblings petering out, she was ready to call Matthew. It was nearly nine by then, so he would probably be awake, even with the two-hour time difference. For as long as she'd known him, he'd always worked night shifts, and she figured he was likely still working night shifts, which meant he slept during the day and didn't wake up until his daughter was often already in the middle of dinner and bedtime routines. Which was probably around now. Amelie and Dallas were almost the same age; they'd even gone to the same daycare, had been friends. Sometimes she missed all the playdates they'd had, fucked up as the situation was, the two of them with their big secret acting like they were practically strangers, even though he knew every inch of her body and she knew his darkest desires—which were pretty dark, truth be told.

It had been oddly easy to hide from their spouses, which was how it went on so long. They'd both married rather unobservant people. Or maybe they were both just really good liars. Either way, it had gone on far too long, almost a year if you included the months of flirtation. It was a relief now to have it all out in the open. She missed his company, but she did not miss the days of having this secret hanging over her head, the stress of it getting out sometimes too much to bear. Not that the consequences of their outing had been easy; quite the opposite in fact. Some days she wondered how different her life might be had they just stopped sleeping together earlier. She could still be at the gym, she could have her old friends back. She wasn't naïve enough to think her family would still be intact—that ship had already sailed. But the rest of it would have been nice to hold on to. She was so isolated without the gym's familial community, her actual family spread across the country like scattered pieces of a puzzle that no longer fit together. Even her dad had up and left to New Jersey after he retired, which happened to coincide with the year Amelie was born. By the time she'd turned two, Mina had no idea how to explain to her daughter what family even was. Now she was three and she was probably less sure. It was usually just the two of them.

Once Mina had gotten the nerve to finally dial the phone, she had worked herself up into such a frenzy she could hardly hear it ringing over the sound of her manically beating heart. She was so busy listening to the sound of her blood pumping through it that she hardly registered it when Matthew picked up.

"Who's this?" he asked gruffly, jarring her out of her stupor.

"Uh, hello to you too."

There was a pause on the other end of the line, as if he was registering her voice. She'd gotten a new number since he'd moved, and she had never updated him, as it didn't seem necessary. She didn't think they would ever talk again.

"You shouldn't be calling me," Matthew said. His tone had an edge to it, but it didn't actually sound like he was upset to hear from her. It was more matter-of-fact, or occupied, like he had been in the middle of something.

"I know," she said.

"If Ariel was around, she would already have a gun to my head," he grumbled.

"Well, I'm glad she's not home, then," she said. "It would be quite the mess to clean up, considering the size of your head." She drained the rest of her drink in one gulp, feeling the burning of the alcohol travel all the way down to her empty stomach. There was another pause, a shift, followed by Matthew's deep laugh.

"Sorry," Matthew said, his voice softening. "I didn't—"

"I know," she said. "It's fine." Suddenly she was fighting back tears, so surprised by them she didn't realize it until her cheeks were damp. "I'm…" She struggled to compose herself. He had never seen or heard her cry, and she wanted to keep it that way. It was a pet peeve of hers, overly emotional women. So much so that she sometimes could come off as robotic and unfeeling, even though this wasn't the case at all. She just preferred to be in control of the situation, feel her feelings alone, when no one was watching. "Sorry, I'm just calling because I…might be in some trouble, and you were the only one I could think to ask about it."

"Hm. What trouble?" he asked. She heard him crack open a beer. It must have either been his night off, or she had really stressed him out by calling. He never drank before work. At least, he never did when she knew him. She decided she wouldn't ask about it. No reason to put him on edge any further.

"Well, I sort of let Dylan register a car under my name—"

"You did *what?*" he asked. "Why the fuck would you do that?"

"I don't know, it didn't seem like a big deal at the time. He gave me rides sometimes. I didn't pay for it or anything..."

Even though she couldn't see him, she imagined him sitting at his kitchen table, a palm over his pale forehead, thinking how could he have ever gotten involved with such a complete moron. She expected some long diatribe in this vein, but instead, he cleared his throat. "Let me guess. Some cops just showed up at your house asking where your car is."

She blushed, glad he wasn't around to see her face. Before she could respond, he continued, "And you told them you don't know where it is. Am I correct?"

"You're not incorrect," she mumbled.

Matthew sighed. "I told you to stay the fuck away from that guy," he said.

"You told me that about every guy at the gym, Matthew."

"Because they're all a bunch of degenerates."

"So I should have stayed away from you too, then?" she asked, rolling her eyes. She didn't like to be infantilized.

Matthew grunted. "That would have saved us both a lot of trouble."

"Great. Build me a time machine then, so when you stick your hands down my pants outside the gym, I can go tell you to fuck off."

Matthew laughed. "As if you could. You were practically throwing your panties at me."

"You wish." Mina had to stop herself from smiling. She'd somehow managed to forget this odd turn of phrase. "Seriously, though. Who says *panties?* What are you, sixty?"

Matthew laughed again, then exhaled. "Look. My point is, I

don't say things just to say them."

"Yeah. I know. You barely say anything at all."

"That's not true," he said. "You're just pissed things didn't work out the way you wanted."

"Did they work out the way *you* wanted?" she couldn't help but ask, another layer of tears rushing to her eyes. She wiped them away quickly with one hand.

Matthew was silent again. She took his silence as an invitation to talk more. "How is it out there, anyway?" she asked quietly. "Arizona, I mean."

"Arizona is fine," he said after a moment.

"So you hate it," she said, a smile forming on her lips.

"I said it's fine," he snapped.

She waited until she could tell he had calmed down a bit to continue, refilling her drink. She was now well on her way to drunk, but she didn't care. It had been so long since she'd heard the sound of his voice, and just hearing it made her whole body buzz. Suddenly, she felt her sex drive return with a vengeance for the first time in months. It was all she could do to ignore it.

"Did you find a new gym at least?" she asked.

"Yeah, I did."

"Not as good as Open Guard?"

"No, of course not."

"Yeah, I miss it too," she said. "I think about going back sometimes."

"You should," he said.

"I can't," she said. "I'm always gonna be that…girl," she said, without finishing the sentence. The girl who had an affair right under her husband's nose, at his own gym no less. Mina knew she was this kind of girl, of course, but it was another thing to have the whole world know it.

"Well, that's your own fault," Matthew grumbled.

"How can you still blame me, after all this time? You were there too."

"But I know how to keep my fucking mouth shut," he said. She heard another can being cracked open and wondered how many he'd opened before she'd called, because he was sounding far drunker than someone who'd only had one beer. It also reminded her what a complete dick he was most of the time. Even after all the therapy she'd gone through, she hadn't quite figured out why this was so attractive to her. It was definitely not an insecurity problem; doing Jiu Jitsu every day had molded her body into the best shape it had ever been in. It was part of why she had gotten so much attention from the men at the gym to begin with.

"I told you we'd get caught eventually," she said to Matthew, her mind wandering to that horrible moment where everything had collapsed on them, then blocking herself from thinking about it. "Everyone always does."

"You also said we deserved it," he said. "So how can I even believe you that it wasn't your fault?"

"We did deserve it," she mumbled. "And it wasn't."

Matthew grunted. "Yeah. This is so much better than sneaking around a little."

She wanted to correct him—it wasn't sneaking around a little when you met up several times a week for over six months to have sex—but since she knew they didn't have much time, she figured it would be better to stop rehashing the past. It wasn't like they could change it. They had done what they had done, and they were living with the consequences. Truthfully, it still surprised her that Ariel had given him another chance. They had both assumed she would file for divorce immediately. Instead, it was like she had wanted him even more afterward. From what Mina had gathered, she'd blamed Mina for the entire affair and used it as a bargaining chip to get what she wanted, which was apparently to move somewhere warm and far, far away from her.

"Matthew…" she started. "What's going on? You sound…weird."

"You need to tell those cops you lent Dylan the car and it was your mistake but you'll never do it again, okay?" he ordered. "Give them all his contact info. Don't reach out to him again. They probably won't charge you with anything, but it depends on the cops."

"Okay, I got it."

"Say you didn't know Dylan was a felon. You have that innocent look about you, they'll believe you."

"All right. That's basically what I did already."

"Basically?"

She swallowed a lump in her throat. Anyone else would have ignored that "basically," but not Matthew. He was always paying attention. "I mean, I didn't say I had no idea he was a felon, because that's not true," she said. "You know I'm not good at lying under pressure."

Matthew chuckled at this, unamused. "Oh, is that right?"

Mina clenched her fists, her nails biting into her skin sharply. "For the millionth time, I never lied to you—"

"Bullshit."

She inhaled a long, deep breath. It did her no good to go down this road again. All their arguments about their past, or their relationship while they were still having one, ended up going in circles. He didn't trust her. And how could he, considering? She didn't trust him either, but not in the same way. "I just wanted to know if I could still get in trouble for something."

"You might," he sighed. "But I doubt it. CPD has more important shit to do than arrest you, that's for sure."

"Why do you even care so much?" she couldn't help asking. Because it sounded like he did, and it was hard to wrap her mind around, being that she'd spent the last six months convincing herself that he didn't care about her at all and never had.

"Stop fishing," was all he said. "Just do what I tell you."

She shook her head. "I always do what you tell me," she said quietly. "That was kind of the main problem."

Matthew let out a laugh that sounded like half grunt. "Yeah, that's what I liked about you," he said, his voice lowering an octave. "You used to be a very good girl."

"I still am," she said.

"Are you?" he said flirtatiously. She was starting to get confused. This was not where she imagined the conversation going. The last they'd spoken, he had made it very clear that he was team "stay with the spouse and work it out." He'd blocked her on Facebook and Instagram. He may have even blocked her old phone number—she had never tried to use it, so she didn't know for sure. As much as she had once longed for him, she was not into chasing people who wanted nothing to do with her, and Matthew had made it pretty clear where he stood on that front. Plus, there was Ariel's vengeance to consider, which seemed to be an endless fountain only directed at her. It hadn't been worth the risk. She wanted to put the whole thing behind her.

Mina squeezed her hands together, mentally challenging them to stop shaking. "Matthew, what are you doing?"

"What do you mean?"

"Why are you drinking before your shift?" she asked.

"Sorry, are you my mother now?" he said.

She sighed. "I don't know why you're so angry with me," she said, finally sitting down on the couch. The alcohol, the conversation with the cops, and Matthew's bizarre energy were getting to her now. Plus, Amelie had been a nightmare all day—she was probably developing yet another cold from daycare. Her body felt like it could melt into the couch, that's how tired she felt. But she was also very present in the moment; the hum of the furnace beneath her, the splash of every car that drove by in the snowy streets. Her heart in her stomach like she was a teenager again. That was always what Matthew did to her; he was like a drug that way. He made her feel alive. Too alive, maybe.

"I'm not angry with you," he finally said.

"You sound angry," she said.

"That's not directed at you specifically."

She heard him breathing, weighing which words to use, what to tell her. She tried to picture him, the way his clear blue eyes could bore into her, how he was always so present when they were together, so watchful of everything. She could still remember the smell of his sweat and peppermint nicotine gum like he was standing right in front of her. And here she'd thought she'd gotten over the whole thing.

"I miss you," she said before she could stop herself.

Matthew was silent.

"Sorry," she mumbled, feeling stupid all of a sudden. "I shouldn't have said that."

"It's okay," he said eventually. "I miss you too."

"You do?"

"I just fucking said I do, Jesus Christ," he said. This made her laugh, because it was so typical Matthew, to offer up something about himself then get mad at her afterward.

"Okay. Well, thanks for talking to me," she said, assuming he was likely anxious to get off the phone. But he didn't hang up right away. So she waited. Maybe he would tell her to never call him again. Maybe he would tell her he regretted ever meeting her. She really had no idea. She never had, with him. It was part of the fun. It felt like a game.

"What are you wearing right now?" was what he ended up asking her.

She looked down, confused, but also a little turned on. "Tank top and leggings," she said. "The usual."

"No bra?"

"Nope."

He exhaled. "Fuck."

When he didn't continue, she asked, "Matthew. Where's Ariel?"

"She's in Oklahoma, with her parents."

"Where's Dallas?" she pressed further.

"Oklahoma."

She thought about this, trying not to guess what it meant. She didn't want to get her hopes up. "Where are you?"

Matthew cleared his throat. "Me? I'm in the doghouse."

"Well, you're always in the doghouse. You fucking live in the doghouse," she said, remembering how it used to be, all the fights and tension and threats of divorce that passed between him and Ariel back when they were still living just down the street. Back when she thought their marriage was ten times worse than hers. It used to drive her nuts, because she was sort of friends with Ariel too, and had to hear about it from both sides. Not that she could complain, since she knew she was probably contributing to their issues quite a bit. But she could never wrap her mind around why Matthew refused to leave. They always seemed so miserable together. Anytime she had asked about it, he always said it would be too expensive or too difficult for Dallas.

"Well, it's gotten...smaller," he said, cracking open a third beer.

"I meant where are you physically?" she said. "Are you still in Arizona?"

Silence on the other end of the phone. "No," he eventually admitted.

"So *where are you?*" she pressed again. Why was it so hard for him to answer a specific question? He must have not wanted her to know where he was.

He sighed. "In Chicago."

Suddenly, it felt like she was in an elevator that had descended too quickly. Her heart began thumping loudly again, a million miles a minute. "You're in Chicago."

"Yep."

Matthew. In Chicago. Breathing the same air as her, walking the same slippery concrete sidewalks. It was enough to turn her entire body into a nervous wreck. "Why?"

"You know why. You know or you wouldn't be asking."

"I don't. I'm not a mind reader."

She did not miss this part, the part where she had to extract information from him like a damn surgeon removing a tumor. He kept everything so guarded, like it would cost him to share what was in his head, or cause him actual physical pain.

"I thought that was why…Never mind."

"I really had no idea, Matthew."

"Okay. Ariel is divorcing me, and we still didn't sell our old house, so that is the only place I can afford to be at the moment. Happy?"

Truthfully, she was a bit happy. For several reasons, and not just because it made Matthew available. It felt like finally they were in the same place again. They had tried to see each other a few times after she and Dima had split, but he was still with Ariel, and it had felt too unbalanced, somehow more wrong.

"You're telling me you're at your old house? And that you and Ariel are separated?" she asked. How could he be three blocks away from her and she hadn't noticed it, felt it, something? How had no one told her? Oh right. Because everyone at the gym thought she was a whore. No one had said this to her directly, but she had heard things. She had been surprised, but she probably shouldn't have been. There had never been a time in which women weren't blamed for things. You could go all the way back to the Garden of Eden, and that was a woman's fault too. But Mina knew better than to say any of this out loud. If there was anything worse than being perceived as a whore, it was a bitter one.

"Yes, that is what I'm telling you," he grumbled.

"Well, then why aren't you over here right now?" she asked, half confused and half furious.

Now it was Matthew's turn to laugh. It was the mean laugh he had, not the one where he actually thought something was funny. "You said you never wanted to see me again. Or am I remembering that wrong?"

He was not. But still. He was Matthew. She had never been so drawn to another person in her whole life. If she hadn't been, she would have never done what she had done, would have never cheated, not once. But from the moment they'd met, she had never been able to stop thinking about him.

"You threatened to kill me," she explained.

"That was a fucking joke," he said.

"No, it wasn't," she said. "You meant it. I could see it in your eyes."

Matthew inhaled. "I apologized for that. I was mad."

"So was I. But I didn't take it out on you," she said.

"That's because you're a nice person. I told you from the start that's not what I am."

She paused. He had told her this, more than once, a long time ago. "Yeah, well. I guess I didn't believe you at the time."

Matthew laughed again, but this time, with amusement. "And now?"

"Now I believe you," she said.

"And you still want me to go over there?" he asked, still laughing.

"Maybe I don't care about being nice," she said, finishing her fourth drink, finally relaxed. "Maybe I never did."

She suddenly felt very tired again; that was the problem with relaxing when you were a mother. It turned instantly into exhaustion. Normally, she would be cleaning the house right now, getting it ready for another day of destruction, but now that she had gotten comfortable, she didn't want to get up. She could hear her daughter snoring from the other room, and snow was beginning to fall outside. The clock read 9:30 p.m., which meant she should be getting herself ready for bed soon. But, tired as her body was, her heart was still beating rapidly, and her mind kept going in circles, thinking about how she and Matthew were both single at the same time. She had never considered that possibility as an option. Or maybe she had; maybe she had been waiting all this time for his marriage to inevitably fall apart. Because how could it not? But she had underestimated Ariel's need to stay married. And his too, perhaps.

"Now that's what I like to hear," Matthew said, his voice lowering another octave. She could practically feel his erection from there.

"Why? Not like you were ever nice before," she said, rolling her eyes.

"As I recall, that's how you like it," he said.

"In the bedroom," she said. "Real life is different."

"I told you I liked your hair," he chuckled.

She couldn't help but laugh. "Yes. One time you told me you liked my hair."

"I told you I liked your tits too. More than once."

"That doesn't count. Everyone likes my tits."

Matthew was quiet for a moment, and she thought she could hear him sigh. "So when you say nice, what exactly do you mean? What is it that you want me to say?"

She swallowed. It was a good question, not one she had a good answer for. "Right now?" she asked. "I want you to say you're coming right over."

Matthew laughed again, amused. "All right. I'll be there in ten minutes," he said. "You better be ready for me. Do you understand what that means?"

Mina was already unlocking the back door and taking off her tank top and leggings. It had been a while, but not that long. She knew what he meant.

"I'll see you in ten minutes," she said, hanging up the phone.

CHAPTER FOUR

"Jesus, I missed that," Mina said, lying in a sweaty heap on her bed, not bothering to get dressed. Matthew, however, was already putting his clothes back on, as always. He was not a fan of his own nudity, she had noticed early on. He was one of the few guys at the gym who wore a rashguard top under his Gi instead of leaving his tattooed chest exposed. She attributed this to the fact that he was a little overweight and sensitive about it too. Not that it had bothered her. "Are you leaving already?"

"Relax, I'm just grabbing a drink. You got any beer?"

She shook her head. "Just seltzers, I think. And brandy."

He sighed, but retrieved a spiked seltzer from the fridge anyway. Then he returned to the sweaty room already half done with the can. He didn't even ask her if she wanted one, which she did. But she was afraid to get out of bed, afraid that if she did he would just disappear, like he did before. She could still barely wrap her head around the fact that he was here, in Chicago, in her bed, of all places. She hadn't been able to take her eyes off him once since his arrival, worried he was a mirage she had conjured up in a drunken haze.

"What's this look?" she asked, catching him wincing as he sat down.

He shook his head. "Just weird being back here."

"Yeah, but doesn't it feel better without the lying?" she asked. "Or did that part actually turn you on?"

He shook his head again and glared at her. He only ever looked at her that way when they were having sex or having a serious conversation, like he could cut into her soul with his eyes. Like he could murder her. It was haunting and possibly terrifying and she kind of loved it. "Don't," he said. Meaning: don't start.

She shrugged. "Fine, I won't," she muttered. She stood up and went to the bathroom to rinse off in the shower, then put her clothes back on to sit in the bed. They weren't what they were before, so she couldn't put her head on his shoulder or rest her feet on his lap like she might have a year prior. She didn't want to think about what this interaction meant and she definitely wasn't going to ask him when he was clearly very conflicted about his being there. Mina watched as he opened a new pack of Nicorette gum and took out a piece.

And then she decided, fuck it. They hadn't seen each other in months, and why wasn't she allowed to ask him about what the hell was going on? He always knew what was going on with her, and she hardly knew anything about his home life. It was always a little unbalanced that way. "I thought you guys got divorced," she said, watching his blank stare.

Matthew sighed again. At this point she could make a drinking game out of it, except that she would probably get wasted within the hour. "Separated."

"Okay, but that is basically divorced. Or are you still trying to work it out for some inexplicable reason?"

Matthew turned to her, his eyes on the verge of anger again. "We have a child."

"Yeah, I know," she said. "So do I."

"Not everyone is as cool as you about living in a broken home."

"Excuse me? You think I like this for her? Amelie cried for, like, the first two months after he moved out."

Matthew just shook his head, then drank the rest of the seltzer in one gulp. "You're the one who kept wanting to tell them," he said.

"Yeah, because it was wrong," she said. "I was sick of feeling like a bad person. But I didn't tell them, did I?"

Matthew looked like he was going to respond, but he didn't get the chance, because there was another loud knock on her door. They exchanged glances. There was no way for him to leave without being noticed by the police, if that was who was at the door. "Uh, just stay here for a sec. I'll see who it is," she told him. Already she could tell he was regretting his decision to come over, and she couldn't help but be annoyed by the timing. Usually, she was totally alone in her house at night, no interruptions. Why did he happen to be here on the one night where something was going on? Mina slipped on a bra under her tank top and went to the front door, her heart back in her stomach, worried about Matthew leaving as well as Amelie waking up from all the commotion. Could she ever catch a break? It was a miracle Amelie hadn't woken up the first time.

But it wasn't police at the door this time. It was Dylan.

She looked at him, confused and furious at the same time. "What the fuck, Dylan?" she asked. "The cops were just here asking about your van." She looked behind him to see if he had driven up in it, but all she saw was a bike leaning against the porch.

Dylan looked behind him too, farther into the street, like the cops might still be there. For all she knew, they were. "Can I just come in? I'll explain everything."

"Just for a second. Then go deal with whatever it is you got me into," she said, pulling the door open. Dylan slipped inside, and for the first time she noticed he was limping a bit, that his clothes were ratty and spotted with dark stains she really hoped weren't blood. She looked to the clothes, then to him, a question in her eyes.

"Look, this needs to stay between us," Dylan started saying, but he was interrupted by the door of the dining room swinging open.

"What are you doing here, man?" Matthew asked, his arms crossed over his chest, his pale legs sturdy against the cold hardwood floor.

As understanding dawned on him, the creases of Dylan's face

went suddenly flat. "Uh, hey Matthew. Didn't realize you were…
back," he said, looking at Matthew, then at Mina, for a moment
too long.

All he did was blink, but he was the type of man whose blink
contained multitudes, and it made her entire body blush. Dylan, of
course, knew all about the shit show that was Matthew and Mina.
Everyone did, but he knew details, because they were friends. An
awkward silence wrapped around them, until Matthew stepped
forward to break it.

"You need to leave," he ordered. She wished he wasn't wearing
only an Open Guard t-shirt and shorts, because there was going to
be no way to convince Dylan later that he had only stopped by under
platonic circumstances, and that kind of gossip was sure to spread
around the gym like wildfire. Not that she should care anymore,
but she did. "Whatever dumb shit you got yourself into, leave her
out of it."

She was surprised by his level of protectiveness; flattered, even.
But she did wish he would stay out of it. Dylan had wanted to tell her
what was going on, and she really wanted to know now.

Dylan raised his hands, looking perfectly aloof. "I didn't do
anything, I swear."

Matthew, performing a dramatic once-over from Dylan's wet
hair to his muddy boots, shook his head. "Who do you think you're
talking to?" he said, moving closer, and eventually holding onto
Dylan's shoulders. For a moment it looked like they were going to
fight. "I can make the call myself. But since we're friends, I'll do you
the courtesy of allowing you to turn yourself in."

Dylan shook his head. "I can't do that, man."

"Why, because you're still on parole?" Matthew asked, pushing
him out the way he came. "Ask me if I give a fuck." He craned his
neck around to give Mina another disappointed look.

Dylan stopped and turned around too. "Mina, I'm really sorry.
I know you were doing me a huge favor, and I—"

"Time to go, Dylan," Matthew said, still pushing him. They were all by the front door now.

"Anyway, the van is gone," Dylan said. Matthew forced him outside with an aggressive shove, but he didn't leave. "That's what I came here to tell you."

"Gone?" she asked, holding the door open and letting in a frozen gust of air that made her shiver.

"Yeah. Sorry. That's all I can tell you," he said.

"Should I report it stolen then?" She watched his face for clues. Matthew was pulling her back into the house, but she refused to budge.

"Of course you should fucking report—" Matthew started.

"That's not a great idea," Dylan interrupted. He was all the way outside on the porch now, picking up his bike.

"Why not? It was stolen, wasn't it?" she asked.

Dylan hoisted the bike over his shoulder as if it was weightless. The muscles in his neck tensed as he looked at her. "Just don't," Dylan said. She knew if Matthew wasn't there, he would tell her the whole story. But he barely knew Matthew, and he certainly didn't trust him.

"What exactly were you doing with it?" she asked, her concern for him suddenly melting into a worried frown.

"It's better if you don't know," he said, this time looking at Matthew, as if he might agree with him for once.

"Is someone after you?" she asked. "You look spooked."

"Eh, maybe, but I don't think it has to do with that," he said, nonchalantly. Dylan was always insanely indifferent when speaking of his criminal history and time in prison. She had never met anyone so fearless before, but maybe that's what became of a person when all the worst things have already happened to them. Before she could ask him to explain, he had mounted the old purple Schwinn and started heading west, towards a heavily trafficked street that led to the nearest El stop.

If she knew it would be the last time she saw Dylan, she would have run after him, found out what he had to say, told him to crash on the couch, even. But Matthew was there, waiting for her to close the door, watching her. She knew he didn't want her to chase after Dylan. In fact, he was probably waiting for her to call the cops.

"Are you going to do it, or do I need to?" Matthew asked, his jaw clenched, once Dylan had turned the corner. She lost sight of him quickly in the snow, then turned back inside, closing the door behind her.

She shook her head, rubbing her arms up and down for warmth. "I'll do it. Just…give it a few minutes."

"Why, so he can get away?"

"I'm sure whatever it is, it's probably not a big deal. It's not like he's a criminal mastermind." Mina shivered and went back inside to the living room, wrapping herself in a blanket. She was suddenly freezing.

Matthew followed her but continued standing. He chewed on his cheek, thinking.

"I'm sorry," she said. "I'll call. I swear my life is not usually so exciting."

"The one thing I learned from our time together, is that where there's Mina, there's drama."

Her jaw dropped, as if he'd told her she was a serial killer. "Dramatic is the last thing I am," she said, offended. "You had it so easy with me. I never asked you for anything."

He shook his head. "I didn't say you were dramatic. That's not what I meant. You're just incapable of being invisible. That's different. Drama finds you."

Her brows straightened, but she couldn't help but smile a little. It was a pretty good insight, and she wasn't expecting him to notice. "A lot of that drama had to do with you wanting to have sex with me, let's not forget."

"I know," he said, leaning over to put on his ratty Vans. "Not denying I enjoy having sex with you."

She rolled her eyes. "Well, if you did deny it, I would know you're lying," she said. "I can't see Ariel letting you choke her so hard she passes out. Not to mention all the other stuff."

A flicker of amusement passed over his face before turning into rage. He shook his head back and forth. "Stop bringing her into this."

Now she felt herself getting angry. Why was she the one always needing to step around his feelings? She had rarely brought up Ariel when they were sneaking around all summer because he would always get so quiet, and she knew it bothered him. But now they were past that, and she was over his whole fragile tough guy act. "Why not, Matthew? She exists, does she not?" Mina asked.

Matthew spit out his gum and started chewing a new piece, not looking at her. Now he was getting his coat on too, his too-thin winter hat. "It's not a game, okay? You don't win because we have better sex."

"Oh, is that what I'm trying to do?" she said, brows furrowed.

He finally looked back up at her, his blue eyes locking with hers. "That's what you've always tried to do."

"And what about you, Matthew? You're just totally blameless in all this? No masculine competitiveness with Dimitry?" she said. "Because that's not what you told me back in summer."

Matthew took a deep breath in, his eyes narrowing, before putting a heavy hand on her shoulder. She could tell he was trying to fight off his temper, but she no longer cared. "The reason I understand it, Mina, is because I've had similar feelings. I've also had a lot of time to realize how dumb it is."

Mina shook her head and stepped back. "Fine. Just go," she muttered. "That's what you're good at."

Matthew blinked, his mouth curling up into a sneer. He was frustrated with her. But the upside of not seeing him for so many months was that she no longer cared about his feelings. She didn't care if he found his way back to her house, to her bed. She had gotten used to being alone, and it wasn't that bad. It was easier, at least.

"As usual, you've got things all mixed around," Matthew said, deflating. He looked more tired than she had ever seen him. Maybe even a bit sad.

"What does that mean?"

"You're the one who's mad," he said. She realized as he said it that it was true, and he must have seen it all over her face, because his expression softened a little more. Before he could say anything else, though, his attention fell to the patio, his brows narrowing into confusion, followed by annoyance. She sighed, preparing herself to deal with another round of cop interrogations or Dylan's vague warnings. But when she turned to find who Matthew was looking at, her heart dropped into her stomach. It wasn't cops or Dylan.

It was Ariel.

CHAPTER FIVE

Mina turned to Matthew, wondering what to do. He just shrugged, as confused as she was. It was snowing and twelve degrees outside, so she couldn't exactly leave Ariel out there. Mina opened the door. Which was how the three of them ended up standing in her chilly office side by side, staring at one another blankly. They hadn't been in the same room together since...well, since the day everything had blown up in their faces. Although it was etched into her mind for eternity, Mina did not ever think about that day, that moment. It was the single worst moment of her life. She hadn't been able to face Ariel since.

Ariel couldn't look at her either, turned out. "I just fucking knew you would be here," Ariel said to Matthew, the first to talk. She was shaking her head, her arms crossed. She looked pale and thinner than the last time Mina had seen her. Her dark brown hair was down to her shoulders, a stripe of purple running through the middle, and she had put her gauge earrings back in. "You're so predictable."

"Ariel, what the hell are you doing here?" he asked, looking truly concerned. "Where's Dallas?"

"She's fine, don't worry," Ariel said.

"That doesn't answer my question," he growled.

Ariel shook her head. "You don't get to play worried father now, Matthew."

"I'm not playing," he said, grabbing her wrist and squeezing.

Mina backed up, getting suddenly uncomfortable. It reminded

her far too much of how they used to be, before anyone knew about their affair. They would fight right in front of her, like it was nothing, like they didn't even notice they were doing it anymore.

"Look, why don't the two of you—" Mina started.

Ariel turned to her abruptly, her eyes colder than frozen earth. After she'd found out about them, Ariel had wished death upon her, and that was putting it nicely. Mina could see now from that look that she had meant it. "Oh, now you want to stay out of it? A little late for that, Mina."

"I just mean…we're not…" She stopped herself. No reason to add to the pile of lies they'd already thrown at Ariel. There had been a lot. But she really wanted the woman out of her house. Adrenaline was pouring through her body and making the little hairs on her arms stand on end. "He was just leaving, was what I meant to say."

Ariel turned back to her husband. "Well, I don't know where the fuck he would go, since according to our lawyer, that house technically belongs to me, and I'm staying there."

"Since when?" Matthew asked, narrowing his bright blue eyes.

"Since today," Ariel said, her voice breaking a little. "Since my dad fucking died and I couldn't stand to be in Oklahoma one more goddamn second."

"Oh," Matthew said, blinking. "Why didn't you just go home?"

"You mean our shitty condo in Phoenix? That's not home. Fuck that place."

Matthew chewed on his lip, watching her every move carefully. "I'm sorry about Dave," he mumbled. "He was a good guy. When's the funeral?"

"It was yesterday," she said, her eyes tearing up. "Everyone asked where you were and I…" She shook her head. "I just couldn't even tell them."

He put a hand on her shoulder. "That's okay. You don't have to do that right now. Or ever, really."

Ariel shook her head back and forth, then pushed his hand off her shoulder. "Don't fucking be nice to me right now, Matthew. I can't take it," she said, her eyes wet.

Mina was deeply uncomfortable now, looking at the floor as if there was a magnet that stretched from there to her eyes. Their conversation felt far too intimate for her to bear witness to. And she still really, really didn't want to be anywhere near Ariel. Even before they'd moved, she'd made sure to never risk being in the same physical space as her, temporarily switching daycares for Amelie until they'd left town despite the extra cost.

"Okay, where exactly do you want me to live, then?" Matthew finally asked her.

"I don't give a shit," Ariel said. "That's the saddest part, I guess. You can live here for all I care."

Uh, no he can't, was the first thought to come to Mina's mind. But she didn't say anything because this conversation didn't have anything to do with her, not really. It just happened to be taking place in her office, which was only the entryway to her house where she had placed a desk and half of her books. She really did wish they would both leave. She wanted to collapse into bed and not think about anything that had happened that night. It was already getting to be too much. And while her body had wanted desperately to see Matthew, her brain was still miles behind. Plus, her body had gotten what it wanted, for the moment. Her body was done calling the shots, as far as she was concerned.

"Okay, Ariel. Whatever you want." Matthew shook his head, exasperated. He always got this way when the two of them were both in close proximity to him, like it was too much female energy for one person to take. This was the worst she had seen it though, like he couldn't take either of them anymore, like he wanted to go live in a cave in the woods, leave it all behind. *Well, too bad*, Mina thought. He wasn't exactly blameless in all this. He had pursued *her*.

"Great. And Mina?" Ariel asked. Mina finally looked up from the floor to see Ariel's eyes directed at her, still filled with hatred and rage.

"Yeah?" Mina asked.

"Fuck you."

JUNE

CHAPTER SIX

If she wasn't so sensitive to smells, the whole thing would have never happened. But the first time she got a whiff of him—a strong mix of sweat and cologne, or possibly aftershave—her entire bottom half was practically buzzing for the entire week. She couldn't stop thinking about it. Not so much him, at first, as his smell. Matthew was not a man she would normally look at twice; since her wedding nearly ten years earlier, she hadn't looked twice at any man, not really. But now, when she wasn't looking at him, she was actively avoiding it, which was probably just as bad.

It was all her nose's fault. Despite growing out of most of her hippie tendencies in her twenties—now a skinny-jeaned mother with a rambunctious two-year-old, gone were the days of tofu scrambles, dumpster diving, and American Spirits—Mina was still a hippie where it counted. She continued to be drawn to things that were on the natural side: biking, camping, growing her own vegetables. Her laundry detergent was the expensive hypo-allergenic kind, and she couldn't remember the last time she'd used deodorant—probably sometime in the last century? She preferred to take a hot shower instead, using bath soap that was just a purple bar with flakes of patchouli.

Mina loved patchouli; that was another hippie tendency she couldn't be rid of. It reminded her of her misspent youth, which she had wasted in a drunken haze of parties with artists and hipsters in a very rundown neighborhood of Chicago that at the time was full of nothing but car jackings, coffee shops, and punk houses. (It had, in the intervening years since, been gentrified into endless blocks of condos and yuppies, like most artistic neighborhoods tended to do in Chicago.) Her nose was nearly canine-level acute; she was known to locate cherry blossoms from a block away and detect a dirty diaper from across the room. Normally this did not get in the way of her general life; normally, it was not people that her nose was attracted to, but coffee beans and piles of autumn leaves. It was laundry drying in the sun. It wasn't...sweat. And yet, sweat was what started the unraveling of her long-fought-for stable life.

On its own, the one-time brief smell of a man she didn't find physically all that attractive might have passed with hardly a thought. But there was another, more problematic factor, which was that Mina was very actively—like, generally six days a week for at least an hour—practicing Brazilian Jiu Jitsu. So was her husband. And so was Matthew. There was some combination of the three of them at the gym nearly every night. If she hadn't constantly been thrown together with Matthew—quite literally on top of the guy, although, because he was a brown belt, more likely under—she would have never looked twice at him, despite her nose.

A bit stocky, pale, with a thick black beard, he was not her type at all. Before she had started Jiu Jitsu, and it was only her husband who went, they had socialized together with some of the other couples with young children from the gym and she had hardly noticed him. He had been quiet then, and because it was the natural thing to do with couples, she had become friends with his wife, Ariel. She was not the most interesting person to talk to but since they had a kid the same age, Mina forced a connection with her over their teenage obsession with punk rock.

Ariel was a nurse and more of a yoga person, and did not ever come around to Jiu Jitsu, so although they still met up a couple weekends a month, she now saw her the least often. Matthew, she saw almost daily. Most people didn't go to the gym that frequently, but Mina and Matthew did. Jiu Jitsu could be addictive, and she already had an addictive personality, so it was easy to let it take over her life, partly because it frustrated her to no end to be bad at something (but everyone new was bad, that was just the law of the land), and partly because it was really fun. It certainly didn't hurt that it was only a few blocks away. Now she liked it so much if she had to miss a class it would ruin her entire day.

Having spent years only fighting a heavy bag prior to starting Jiu Jitsu, she hadn't expected to like such a hands-on and violent martial art. She was constantly covered in bruises and nursing minor injuries. Her rib cage especially, after its first couple of sprains, felt permanently out of whack. But she had fallen so in love with the place that none of it mattered. It really had felt like falling in love; she thought about it all the time, and it was practically all she and Dima talked about some days. The people who went there were also among the coolest (albeit the oddest) she had ever met. Jiu Jitsu attracted a very certain kind of person, one that she liked far more than your average citizen, though she hadn't quite figured out why yet. A combination of drive and humility? An interest in self-sufficiency? Competitive inclination combined with a need for community?

Or perhaps it was her fascination with broken things; as much as it attracted people who committed to difficult tasks, it also attracted those prone to depression, anxiety, and addiction too. Some people needed Jiu Jitsu like they needed to breathe. Those were the ones you saw most frequently, and also the ones Mina most connected with, perhaps because there was something broken in her too.

In some ways going to Jiu Jitsu was like going to church, a church of misfit toys but a church nonetheless, one where you felt a sense of belonging the second you walked in the door. Except instead of sitting down and listening to Bible stories, you tried to murder each other. Well, not really murder. But she did know at least a dozen ways to make a person pass out, which was not a bad thing to know.

Unfortunately, there were some less desirable side effects too. The main problem being her sensitive nose. It didn't help that the entire exercise involved constantly sandwiching together two sweaty bodies, and you could not always control where your hands ended up. Everyone she had discussed it with beforehand told her there was nothing sexual about the sport, but this was not entirely true. Sure, most of the time it felt entirely platonic, if not a little enjoyable, to get thrown around by grown men twice or three times her size. But it sort of depended on where your mind was at. If you weren't vigilant about keeping it sexless, just one little movement, one little touch that felt just a tad too gentle, one look of misplaced hunger, could turn that theory right on its head, and that's what had happened with Matthew.

Or maybe it was just a vibe of his that she had intuitively picked up on. She really had no idea where it came from. But almost right away, it felt different when they were paired up in class, which was most of the time since it was better for Mina and Dima to go separately so someone could stay home and put Amelie to bed on time. It felt like flirting. Flirting very violently.

It was never acknowledged, and some days Mina convinced herself she was imagining the entire thing, but her body felt it, somewhere deep down, like a kernel of truth that was so far buried it was almost as if it didn't exist. But it did, in fact, exist. And she didn't feel this way towards anyone else there, not even the more objectively attractive guys, the ones with eight-packs and perfect golden bodies slathered with tattoos. Only with quiet, dark-eyed Matthew.

Except, as she was starting to learn the more she frequented the place, Matthew was not actually so quiet. He was practically a different person at Jiu Jitsu. He was in his element there, friends with just about everybody, helpful and easygoing, unlike at home, where he mostly seemed tense and annoyed. And somehow, without ever planning it aloud, a few months into her new obsession, she was almost always partnered with him for class during the first half where they learned new ways to break arms or legs or choke someone out.

Every time she ended up in some new entangled position around him she was reminded yet again of the lower half of her body—something she had basically forgotten about after having Amelie. It was beyond frustrating. Why was her nose doing this to her? And why Matthew? Matthew whose wife she was friends with? If you had put him side by side next to Dima, there would be no question her husband was more attractive; Dima was over six feet tall, thin, and olive-hued, with finely shaped biceps, long thick hair, and a nice smile. He was genuinely nice, and funny; the happiest person she'd ever known. It was part of why she had married him. After the endless chain of depressed musicians she had dated throughout high school and college, Dima's natural happiness level was a shock to the system. One that had buoyed her own depressive tendencies.

But it wasn't aesthetic, this attraction to Matthew. It was something else; something…animalistic. Matthew had a darkness inside him that she hadn't seen in so long she forgot what a pull it had over her. (There was a reason she had dated so many depressives after all.) It was clear, to anyone with eyes, that he had a temper. This temper repelled her and attracted her in equal measure. Though he was, for the most part, very nice to her and Dima, rage often simmered in the tight features of his face. They witnessed pieces of it come out when he was around Ariel, and sometimes with his daughter too, when he would spank her for some small infraction. Mina did not like how he treated his wife or his daughter. Nothing about what she saw made her want to get involved with him. She didn't want to get involved with anyone at all. She was married, and their little family was an island, one that, until recently, she had believed to be strong and impenetrable.

But the problem remained: he smelled really good. Hadn't she read somewhere about the power of another person's smell? Something about natural pheromones, how you couldn't be with someone whose smell repelled you. This was the case with most of the men at the gym, some of whom repelled her so much she avoided them in class; but not him. Because of this, some kind of invisible, irresistible pulley had inserted itself between them.

For a while, she tried to ignore her attraction to him. This would have been impossible in her early twenties, when she was known to get obsessive about her crushes, but she was a working mom and barely had time to eat dinner some days let alone imagine all the things she wanted Matthew to do to her. For months, she only really thought about it late at night when she was trying, but failing, to fall asleep, a hormonal problem she'd had since giving birth. She would replay their interactions from the gym and then attempt to fantasize about what that could turn into were they to ever be left alone in a room together. The fantasies didn't usually get very far because the logical part of her brain could not ever picture a situation where this might happen—they were always in a crowded gym or socializing together with their spouses and other friends. It was too impossible, even if he did feel the same, which was a whole different question.

She was in pretty good shape, better than some of the women at her gym, but she was no spring chicken anymore. She was already in her early thirties and had given birth naturally in a bathtub at home. There was no guarantee Matthew felt the same about her. Once or twice, she caught him looking at her during parties, but that could have meant anything. Maybe he was only looking at her because she was talking. She did do a lot of that when drinks were involved. He, on the other hand, talked less and less the more he drank. It was another reason to avoid getting close to him: he was obviously a bad drunk. She didn't have to ask Ariel to know this about him; it was written all over her body whenever he surpassed three beers. Her shoulders would tense up, like she was expecting a debacle, and when they left, she looked relieved. She remembered the feeling from college, and it gave her a flush of satisfaction that her husband was a happy drunk, if he even drank at all. He generally abstained.

Somehow half a year went by like this. Her crush fluctuated from obsessive to forgettable depending on the week, but it never entirely went away. She was stuck in an endless loop; unable to do anything about the crush, but also, for some reason, unable or unwilling to let it go. It made no sense; she and Dima had a really good relationship, as far as she was concerned. They never fought, at least. After ten years together, this was no small feat. Matthew and Ariel, on the other hand, were more and more at each other's throats as time went on; half the time they met for drinks now, you could practically feel the tension in the air, like she and Dima had come over just as the two of them had ended an argument.

It didn't help that they almost never saw each other; Matthew worked night shifts and Ariel worked day shifts, and Mina was pretty sure she talked to him at the gym more than Ariel did at home, since he spent most of his free time there and didn't have much of it. She understood a lot about their marriage, perhaps too much. It was becoming more and more clear that a door had opened in their relationship, and he had opened it. But had a door opened in hers?

Apparently, it had.

Things began to shift in a dangerous direction that summer, when Dima, a long-haul truck driver, was out of town more and more due to employee shortages. In retrospect, there were a combination of factors that led to the shift. Partly it was because of the isolation; being a full-time mom to a toddler was the hardest thing she had ever done, and a few days into it, she already felt like pulling her hair out. Additionally, though she had stopped breastfeeding Amelie when she was two, it had taken her body six months to get the message. Once her milk finally dried up, her hormones got wacky. For the first time since she had met Dima, she felt on the verge of a bottomless pit of depression. Because of her troubled youth, sadness had somehow become linked with sex for her. She could go days without eating more than a piece of bread and eggs, but she could hardly go an hour without thinking about sex. She and Dima had more sex in the week before he left town than they had in months, when she had felt about as a sexless as a bean bag.

Going to Jiu Jitsu every day did not help. Sometimes she felt she was wearing a neon sign, the way some of the men looked at her, like they could tell she wasn't satisfied in the bedroom and they wanted to fix that for her. Other times she worried if everyone there could tell that she spent the entire hour as focused on Matthew as she was learning the moves. Probably not, but it really began to feel that way. Two days into Dima's long June trip, Mina had to start avoiding classes entirely. She didn't trust herself around him with an empty house, and she was so distracted with thoughts of him and sex in general that she could hardly focus on class anyway. But it ended up having the opposite effect as she had intended; she thought about him more and more when she didn't actually get to see him. So on the third day she decided to get a sitter and go to class, if only to feel less anxious, since Jiu Jitsu was, in addition to everything else, a great exercise. If Matthew was there, fine. If he wasn't, even better.

Of course, it was a Tuesday, so Matthew was there. And Tuesday nights were no-Gi, which basically meant everyone was wearing spandex. Matthew was in shorts and a short-sleeved rashguard top; his tattoos, which covered his arms from his biceps to his wrists, as well as his calves, all visible.

She tried not stare at Matthew's biceps while they practiced the new move, which was a Judo-style takedown that started from standing and required him to grab her neck and arm before tripping her with his legs. The way he looked into her eyes—like he enjoyed the violent act a little too much, that it maybe even turned him on—while he did it made her knees weak, and she was almost glad he had to throw her down, because otherwise her legs might have buckled under her. When she stood back up, he was laughing.

"What?"

He shook his head. "Nothing," he said.

"What's so funny?"

"Your neck is just so small," he said.

"Well, I'm small," she countered. She was, after all, only five foot three.

He smirked. "Most of you, yeah," he said with a quick, barely noticeable glance at her chest.

She rolled her eyes, but she was getting all tingly again. This had been a bad idea, probably. But she felt drawn to him like a siren song, like she didn't have any control over it at all. Plus, there was nothing inherently wrong with what they were doing. They were practicing Jiu Jitsu, in a room full of people. So what if there was tension between them? That wasn't entirely in her control. It wasn't like she could make his eyes stop looking at her like that, if she was even seeing what she thought she was seeing in them.

She put her hand on his neck, as it was now her turn to trip him with her legs. Her other hand had to go over his bicep, which was like a rock, and didn't help the situation at all. She tried to ignore how good he smelled. God, what was it about him that her body wanted so badly? Objectively, without Jiu Jitsu, he would have been totally unnoticeable to her. In fact, he had been before she'd started spending so much time getting caught in his leg-locks and armbars.

"You like throwing little girls around, huh?" she asked.

Not for the first time, she imagined how he was in the bedroom; she knew deep down in her bones he would be rough and full of demands, and every time she considered this it made her insides flutter, because that was exactly the sort of thing that turned her on but that Dima was too nice to ever do. Probably after ten years together she should have discussed this with him, but she could tell it wasn't in his nature, that if he tried to be rough in the bedroom it would feel like they were playing pretend. And she didn't want to play pretend. Plus, if he hadn't figured it out by now, he never would.

"I don't hate it," Matthew joked.

They were maybe crossing the line into actually flirting now, but she didn't care in that moment. There was nothing illegal about flirting. Plus, it was too loud in the gym for anyone to hear them; the fans were on, and Felix, the brown belt who often taught class when the owner got too drunk or hungover to show up, had The Smiths blasting. Unlike the owner, Felix did not have children, and was just as obsessed with Jiu Jitsu as he was drinking. He never missed a class.

"Yeah, I bet you don't," she said with a wink.

Matthew only let out another deep laugh and let her sweep him onto the floor. Somehow, they managed to get through the class without any more borderline-inappropriate comments, but then, since Felix was basically an alcoholic—a lot of the guys had drinking problems at the gym, and the back room was often stacked with cases of beer and hard seltzers—a bunch of them ended up staying after class to hang out. As usual, she was outnumbered by testosterone, and as usual, she enjoyed it more than she should have. In class it was easy to ignore any sexual tension, because there really wasn't that much of it, focused as everyone was on the actual sport. But when they were drinking, she sometimes felt like she was wading in a shark tank, covered in blood.

She could feel Matthew's eyes on her as she drank several cups of wine that had been left there after a recent party, though they didn't directly do that much talking until most of the other guys had left. Eventually it was just them and Felix, and she was very drunk. She hadn't eaten dinner, plus they'd all done Jiu Jitsu for an hour, and it was a pretty difficult workout. There had been plenty of times she had stayed at the gym for drinks, but now that she thought about it, she wasn't sure Matthew had ever stayed so long before. He always had to run off to work or pick up dinner. Now, he was in no rush at all, and it made her want to stay too. Was he staying for her? She pushed the thought away. So what if he was? They were friends. They were allowed to hang out.

"Don't you have to work?" she asked him finally, when Felix disappeared into the changing room. She looked at the clock on the wall, which was a bit blurry to her now, but she could at least see it was past nine o'clock. "It's so late."

"Nope," he said. He was being a gentleman, avoiding looking in her direction, where her bra was so soaked with sweat from class it had dampened the clean shirt she had changed into. He was always a perfect gentleman around her. It was partly how she had managed to convince herself the crush was not a two-way street, even though her body was not ever in total agreement with her mind about this. "Weekend starts today."

"Oh. Nice," she said. She could never keep track of his weekends, which changed constantly due to the odd scheduling of night shifts. Her heart was drumming in her ears. They were barely two feet apart but it felt like they were somehow already touching.

His eyes were drinking her in, hungry for something, hungry for something a part of her desperately wanted to give him. It reminded her of a wolf, spotting its prey. She had no idea what her face was doing, but she knew whatever it was, he understood her. They must have understood each other in that moment; they had locked eyes and neither of them was breaking the spell. But they were at the gym. And Felix was still there. If he didn't intend on leaving, then whatever was going on between them would have to end when he returned from the men's room. When he did emerge, a moment later, they both turned to him, the spell broken. Felix was dressed in his street clothes now, sunglasses on despite the fact it had long ago gotten dark, and a bag strung over his shoulder.

"All right, can one of you lock up the gym?" he said nonchalantly, not even looking their way. "I need to eat something before I pass out." He seemed oblivious to what was happening, which was not totally unusual for Felix. He lived in his own world, which was mostly Jiu Jitsu. It took years of commitment to the sport to become a brown belt. Once you got to be that high-ranking, it became a big part of your identity, she had noticed. Many of the guys there had tattoos of the gym's logo somewhere on their body, like being marked. People thought CrossFit could get cultish, but Jiu Jitsu was even more extreme, perhaps because it wasn't as solitary. To do it, you needed other people. And once someone had sweat droplets into your eyeball, it was much easier to do away with the small talk and get to know each other on a deeper level. Which was how she ended up being friends with so many guys from the gym in the last six months; practically her entire social life now revolved around the place.

"Sure, I have keys in my bag," Matthew said, finishing his beer and crushing the can.

He and Mina exchanged glances before she picked up her gym bag and slid across the damp mats to the front of the gym. By the time she reached the door all the lights were off; the darkness of it made her heart rate speed up. Or maybe it was who she was with in that darkness. As she headed outside behind Felix, Matthew locked up quickly, then they lingered in the parking lot of the gym, several feet apart, as they watched Felix drive away. She didn't say anything because she had no idea what to say. What if this was still in her head? And yet, he was lingering too. If he wasn't interested in her, he would probably not be standing there alone with her in the parking lot.

It was seeming more and more unlikely by the second that she had imagined anything. The tension in the air was like a balloon ready to burst. But she wasn't going to be the one who burst it, just in case it went awry.

"I should probably get back," she said. "My sitter is getting anxious." She didn't mention that her sitter was her niece on Dima's side, that she was thirteen, and it was way past her bedtime. She'd already told Maya she would be home really soon and would make it up to her with an extra five dollars.

"Yeah?" he asked, popping a piece of gum into his mouth. It was Nicorette gum—she'd seen him with the case before. She was a former smoker too, so she understood the compulsion to have nicotine in that moment. She certainly wanted some herself, if only to slow down her rapidly beating heart. It felt dangerous to be there alone with him. They'd never really, truly been alone. Maybe they should have never been alone.

"Yeah," she said. But she didn't move. "Don't you have to go too? Your phone keeps buzzing."

"Probably," he said. Then he spit out his gum, where it landed on the cement. A plane flew by overhead, its rumble making her heart pound even faster. "Should I?"

"Well, isn't that up to you?" she asked, biting her lip. He was still watching her, and though he didn't move, she felt him wanting to. No, this probably wasn't in her head at all.

"Maybe," he said, moving closer to her. Just a few steps, but close enough that she could smell him again, almost touch him. "What do you think?"

Mina stepped back a little, too nervous to talk to him when they were so close physically. "I think…we probably shouldn't be out here," she mumbled.

"Why?" Matthew asked with a smirk. He had that look again, the hunger in his eyes, made even hungrier after several hours of drinking. It was unmistakable. Some people could hide that hunger, or stop themselves from sharing it for an extra moment too long; she had witnessed similar versions of this look from other men at the gym before, especially since she had lost her baby weight, but these were generally only flickers, passing through and getting shut down. Not Matthew. He was someone who could look straight into the eye of the storm and not turn away. She wasn't like that; she was the kind of person who turned away, even now.

"I don't know," she finally answered. "I don't think our spouses would like it. Or how much we talk when they're not around."

"Why's that?" he asked.

She looked past him, towards the dumpsters, wondering how to answer this, and not being able to come up with an honest answer that didn't betray her secret feelings for him.

"Hey. Look at me," Matthew said, not letting her get away with it.

She looked at him, hunger meeting hunger. Maybe that was what he had wanted to see, why he had told her to do it. You could deny all sorts of things, but you couldn't deny what was very clearly in front of your face.

"Why?" he asked again.

"You know why," she finally said, eyes boring into his. Because of course he knew why. He knew or he wouldn't be asking her, wouldn't still be standing there, so close she could smell the peppermint on his breath.

Matthew took another step forward, turning her chin with his hand so that she couldn't look away again. Suddenly his body was nearly pressed up against her. They had just spent half of class on top of each other, but this was not Jiu Jitsu; this was real life. She took in a deep breath, so quick it was like a gasp. Were they really going to do this? Right there, outside of the gym, where anyone could find them? She could almost see the light from the windows of her living room, they were that close to her house. Gingerly, he placed his hand on the small of her back, pulling her even closer to him. Then his hands meandered down her leggings, and she didn't stop them.

"This is maybe the worst idea in history," she finally said. Her body had started trembling, but she didn't move away.

"Probably not the *worst…*" Matthew mumbled, his eyes sparkling. His hands remained where they were. Then, he kissed her. And kept kissing her. And she let him, for a moment. It felt like the greatest release, like when you've been without water for too long and finally find a bottle. That's how much she had wanted this. For months she had wondered what it would be like to have his lips on hers. But she could still see her house, the gym, directly in her line of sight. Drunk as she was, she managed to eventually pull away. It was far too distracting, even if it may have been the best kiss of her life.

"We can't do this here," she whispered, waving her hand towards the street, the lights, the group of people outside a bar down the road. Her mind was swimming, and she was still pretty drunk, but she wasn't so drunk that she didn't understand the danger of what they had just started. "Anyone could see us."

"Where do you want to go?" he asked, quietly, squeezing her backside again.

She turned and pulled him towards the back door of the gym, which was at least semi-hidden behind a few dumpsters. Matthew pushed her against the cold brick of the wall and started kissing her again, biting her lip, his hands moving up her shirt. They kissed like that for a long time, their desire growing and growing until he was practically trying to tear her clothes off right there. She felt his hard-on through his pants, pressing against her thigh, getting more and more insistent. She hated that her body had been right all this time. But she was also very glad, because this was the most alive she had felt in years.

"I have to get back," she finally said, shaking her head. "Maya has been texting me for the last ten minutes."

"She can wait a little more," he said, kissing the side of her neck, nibbling on her ear. Damn, he was a good kisser. She was really hoping he wouldn't be, that they would have zero chemistry were they to ever actually hook up, but she could already tell it would be the exact opposite situation. "I've been waiting much longer."

"Oh. Really?" she asked. She was surprised, but she also wasn't surprised at all.

"Yeah," he said into her ear, his voice low, like an animal's. "I've been waiting so long." His hand dove back into her leggings, from the front this time. He let out a little groan that sounded almost like a laugh, like he was pleased with his discovery down there.

"Me too," she admitted breathlessly. His fingers started moving and her limbs began to burn like her body was a fire only he could put out. Lost in the moment again, she forgot about the street lights, the parked cars, the rowdy bar crowd down the road.

"Oh yeah?" he asked, kissing her again, then biting her lip.

"Yeah," she said. She swallowed. Her throat was as dry as a desert.

"Well, fuck. Why didn't you say something?" he asked.

She pulled away and looked at him. "What was I supposed to say?"

"I don't know," he mumbled, his hand still sliding around, like he was playing an instrument, one he knew how to play expertly.

"'Hey Matthew, even though we're both married and go to the same gym every day, I've been fantasizing about you for months while I'm in my husband's bed'?"

Matthew let out a low laugh. He had a deep, manly voice, one that seemed to lower another octave when aroused. "Okay, I see your point," he said. He angled his head back a bit to look at her. "You thought about me in bed?" he asked. "While you were getting off?"

"Yeah," she said. "A lot of times."

"That's so hot," he said. He took his other hand and wrapped it around her throat before kissing her. It kind of surprised her, but also, it turned her on. She could feel her pulse pressing against his thumb, like the beat to a song.

He took his lips off hers. "You like that?" he asked, looking her in the eyes with an intensity that surprised her even more than the rest of it, the corner of his mouth curling. Like his inner wolf wanted to eat hers.

"Yeah, I like that," she said, breathlessly.

His other hand was still deep into her pants, and suddenly a finger went inside her. He let out another pleased low groan. "Hmmm. Yeah. You really like that."

They continued on like that for a while, his hand squeezing harder and harder around her throat, but the entire time she couldn't stop thinking about her house, about the very public street. "We can't do this," she said again, catching her breath. Things were escalating too quickly. She felt lightheaded, either from the lack of oxygen or the situation itself. "I really have to go."

"God, you're wet," he said, not letting her go. He squeezed her neck even harder. "I want to be inside you right now."

"But, Matthew..." she started, not even shaking her head free because she enjoyed the way he was holding on to her neck. She wanted what he wanted, of course; she had never wanted it more in her life. But they were still outside in the gym's parking lot, and turned on as she was, she was not a complete idiot. She wrapped her hand over the top of his. "This is a bad idea."

Matthew frowned at her like she had told him the sky was blue, but he stopped squeezing her neck. "Yeah. It's a very bad idea." For a second, they exchanged a look that would haunt her for a long time afterward. Some kind of combination of regret, lust, and determination. Because she had only ever dated when she was single, or very briefly, in college, within open relationships, she was very unaccustomed to all the various ghosts in the air with them.

Furthermore, she was not an impulsive person anymore. She thought and thought and thought about everything. She had thought about this, but mostly by forcing herself not to think about it. Never had she gotten this far in her fantasy. Because of that, she didn't know what to do. She was a mom now, a planner, the kind of person to have a never-ending to-do list on her phone. If she let this happen without any contingency plan, she felt like her whole life would explode into an instant fireball.

"I'm married," she explained again, as if he might have forgotten. "So are you."

"I am aware."

"I'm friends with your wife," she said. "We just…we shouldn't. Right?"

He frowned. "No, we shouldn't. But this was kind of inevitable, don't you think?"

She looked at him and realized he was right. It was inevitable. As much as she had tried to convince herself that it wasn't happening, it had been happening this entire time, right there, under the surface of things. Just because you don't admit to the darkness doesn't mean that darkness doesn't exist, after all. And that's what this was. They both had something wrong with them. If not, they wouldn't have been standing there right then, covered in each other's smells. She'd spotted it in him the moment they'd met, because she was the same. But it was one thing to fantasize, and quite another to act. Already, her mind was reeling, trying to undo the events of the last five minutes, to erase history. How on earth was she going to live with this tomorrow, when it was no longer just a harmless fantasy?

Matthew kissed her again, resuming the very capable things he was doing with his fingers, but now that she had said all of that aloud, she knew she couldn't keep going with it.

"I just…" she started. "I need to think. I'm sorry. I gotta go home."

"Okay," he said, nodding, still looking at her right in the eyes. He took his hand out of her leggings. "I'll see you tomorrow."

"Yeah. Maybe." She pulled away from him and quickly started walking, relieved he didn't follow her, if not a little bit disappointed too. She could feel him watching her walk the entire way back, her mind spinning, her body buzzing with so many mixed emotions she almost wanted to puke. But she had to deal with sending Maya home in an Uber first, and then take a shower, before having time to consider what on earth had just happened. And even as she lied there in bed, thinking about Matthew like she always did when she was in bed, it was too big a thing to grasp. Her mind went in circles, and it always ended with her wanting to see him again, to finish what they had started.

That was the problem with darkness; once it got a hold of you, it would only pull you farther and farther down into it. She had already learned this, and relearned this, several times throughout the course of her life. Now, it seemed, she would need to learn it yet again.

CHAPTER SEVEN

Because she was a woman in her thirties, Mina was constantly battling a war, not only with her body, but also with her own house. She thought after installing a new furnace, repainting the outside fence, and replacing several cracked windows that she would, in the grand scheme of home ownership, catch a break for a while. A few months at least. But the very next morning, a pipe broke in the basement while Amelie was at school, and without thinking, she had immediately texted Matthew. It felt like a sign, the pipe breaking like that. He seemed like the kind of man who could fix things. Correction: he seemed like the kind of man who broke things. Then fixed them.

She had never messaged Matthew before, although they had been Facebook friends for a while. Like most couples, all their plans were made between the wives. After what had happened the night before, she wasn't even sure he would respond. Surely, he had arrived home and realized they'd made a mistake, a drunken mistake that they should have probably forgotten ever happened. Maybe he too was relieved they hadn't let it get any farther than it had. Maybe he was ruing the day he ever met her. But he did write her back. And she was right to contact him, at least on the fixing front. Within minutes of his arrival the water had stopped erupting, leaving a pool on the floor about an inch high. Matthew had even brought a sump pump, which he connected before heading back upstairs. Her dog, a consistent terror to tradespeople and strangers, didn't bark when he came into the kitchen to wash his hands; Isabelle had always loved Matthew, which was a bit strange for her, considering it generally took her several visits to get accustomed to their friends, and even then she barked at them. But Mina understood this, because Matthew did have this way about him that made you feel safe. It was another thing about him she tried to ignore but couldn't help but find attractive. Plus, he really did smell good. If anyone other than Mina would see that, it would be her dog. Crazy as she was, she had good taste.

Mina hadn't slept well, so she was in the middle of making another pot of coffee when Matthew emerged upstairs. She asked him if he wanted some, but Matthew declined. He said coffee didn't do anything for him, and he avoided drinking it because of his odd sleep schedule. Instead, he went to her fridge and opened a spiked seltzer he'd left there when he and Ariel had been over last.

She blinked, suddenly nervous it had become a social call. She had been so busy worrying about the pipe and making coffee that it took until now to realize that they were alone again. Without Amelie, without their partners, without the gym. Almost immediately, the air took on a tightness that hadn't been there before. Part of her wondered if that was truly why she had texted him and not a plumber. Was she secretly making an attempt to be alone with him again? Hadn't she been waiting for an opportunity the entire time they'd known each other? Hadn't she wanted to talk to him ever since she had walked away from the gym last night?

No, no, no. They were friends, and he lived nearby. That's why she had texted him. Surely, now that he was sober, he would realize what they did was a mistake. Now that she was sober, she was more nervous than turned on. Her heart was beating manically.

"Sorry," she said, almost as if to herself. She was very flustered suddenly. "I am a little out of it today. I shouldn't have texted you."

Matthew drank half the seltzer in one gulp, never taking his eyes away from her. "You apologize too much," he told her after letting out a burp. He had straightened up a little, as if he had also just noticed they were alone again. But he didn't go, either. He seemed in no rush to go. If anything, the opposite. "Has anyone ever told you that?"

"Yes, actually," she said, turning her gaze to the floor. He was so close she could smell him now—the same mix of sweat and cologne she'd been drawn to for more than half a year already. She was so distracted by it that she didn't turn and walk away from him. She felt compelled to get closer, like his smell was a siren song that she could not avoid. Now that they'd kissed, it felt so difficult not to touch him again.

"I'm glad you texted me," he said.

"You are?" she asked, nervous.

"Yeah. We didn't get to finish what we started. I don't like that."

So he wasn't regretting it after all, she realized. She was so busy trying to hide her nervousness, she barely noticed he had come around to face her. He reached out and lifted her chin so that she was forced to look right at him. His eyes were focused and fierce. There was no shame or regret in them at all. Just the same look she had witnessed before: an unambiguous, magnetic attraction. An animal, hunting. He licked his lips. Then he kissed her.

Outside, an ambulance siren wailed, followed by a police siren. In Bridgeport, the sound was so normal she usually hardly registered it; it was a neighborhood filled with retired cops, old Irish families, and hipsters, but it was still the south side, after all. Now, the noise made it feel like her head might explode. There were too many senses on high alert, too many feelings and sounds and tastes for her brain to process at once. She felt like she was short-circuiting. Matthew was here in her house, alone. His body was touching hers. She couldn't move. But also, most importantly, she didn't want to. They kissed again, for longer this time. It had been a long time since she wanted to kiss someone that much, so much you feel as if you could do it forever. More than a decade, at least.

She shifted back against the counter. But Matthew drew in closer, closing the space between them until their bodies were connected from every point and angle. Because they had often been in the same position, only on the floor in the middle of the gym, in some ways it felt totally natural. But, of course, it wasn't. It was not the same at all.

"I was thinking about you all night," she admitted, a little breathlessly.

He let out the same little grunt-laugh that had so turned her on the night before and smiled. "Yeah?"

"What, you didn't?" she asked as his hands moved from her pants to her hair. He pulled on it as he kissed her again.

"Oh, I've thought about all sorts of things to do to you. Not only last night."

It was the exact right thing to say, and she could already feel her resolve melting away. Matthew, who was already used to throwing around her body into various uncomfortable positions, lifted her into the air like she weighed nothing and placed her on top of the kitchen counter, which was still covered with spilled coffee grounds and cereal crumbs. She ignored it and wrapped her legs around his hips. She felt like a completely different person; or, more accurately, like a different person had invaded her brain. This wasn't her, talking like this, behaving like this. It was some kind of parasite she'd picked up at the gym. The whole thing felt so surreal that if someone told her she was dreaming she would have believed it.

She paused to catch her breath, then looked him in the eye. "What...things?" she asked.

His eyebrows raised. "You don't want to know," Matthew said.

She did want to know, actually. She could feel his erection through his pants, digging into her thigh. Now that they were safely hidden indoors, she didn't think she could walk away from it again.

"Show me," she said. Matthew groaned, then lifted her again and carried her into her bedroom, dropping her on the bed and starting to unzip her jeans with an authority that was so perfectly intrinsic it felt like the essence of manliness. But it was also so unlike Dimitry, who always seemed to be silently asking for permission, that her body seemed to instantly turn cold.

"Wait," she said, so quietly she wasn't sure he could hear. It was reality check time. Combined with the smell of her bedroom, her brain went from sexy-fantasy-world to emergency-stop-bad. She had spent many hours in that bed thinking on this exact moment, but this was, after all, the bed she shared with her husband. And, in some ways, it made the betrayal feel worse, the fact that it wasn't spontaneous. Not that she had planned it, of course. But it didn't come out of nowhere. It wasn't some stranger at a bar. There was a deeper level to the attraction that made it not only more wrong but more difficult to stop. The fact that they had been fighting it for so long—it was like a dam ready to burst. Last night had only made it worse, knowing it went both ways.

Still, she did have to stop it. Right? Yes. She did. After Matthew, who seemed oblivious to her sudden coldness, pulled down her pants until they were lying on the floor, Mina quickly shifted away so that she was out of reach. The man could easily break pretty much any limb of her body in two seconds, but he stopped instantly. They were not in the gym anymore, and the power imbalance was all off.

"What?" he asked.

"This is a bad idea," she said, when she could catch her breath. She sat up on the bed and hugged her knees like a shield.

They remained close, but not touching, and he kept the distance that she had insisted on a moment earlier. "You texted me, Mina."

She swallowed, turning pink. "I know. I'm not very…handy."

"That's okay. I am," he said, putting a hand between her legs again. He inched closer until he was on top of her again.

"It's one thing to—I mean, I've thought about it more than I should have," she started. "I never planned to actually…" She couldn't finish the sentence because she could not admit how much she had been wanting to sleep with Matthew. Not to him, or to herself.

"Look. We tried our best," Matthew said. He began kissing her again. First on the mouth, then on the neck, then further down. Her body was buzzing again, but her brain, her brain—it was still telling her there was a chance to stop things before their lives got ruined.

"Did we, though?" she asked.

Matthew sighed, rolling over onto his back. "Do you want me to go?" he asked, his hand lazily resting on his chest. She really did not. As if to explain they were both on the same side, she took off her shirt. Matthew drew in a pained breath before putting his hands over her bra.

Then under her bra. Then her bra was off.

"Fuck," he said, pinching her nipples between his fingers. "Okay, I'm rescinding that offer to go."

They started making out again, more aggressively this time. She still felt hesitation, even knowing there was little chance she'd stop anything at this point. Matthew was kissing her stomach all the way down to her underwear line. They had already royally fucked up. But for some reason she couldn't stop talking. Maybe she was nervous. She hadn't been with anyone but Dimitry in more than ten years. Or maybe she really was trying to stop it. Her body and brain were in conflict.

"Everyone will know," Mina said. "They'll think I'm a slut."

"What, you think I can't keep a secret?" he said from between her legs, where he began sliding down her striped underwear with his mouth. "Ariel doesn't know half the shit I do in a day."

This was true, but that was more related to the fact that Matthew was a cop. Another reason she really should not be getting involved with him. Everyone knew to be a cop you had to have a few screws loose.

"They'll know at Jiu Jitsu," Mina said. "They'll figure it out."

Here, Matthew stopped to laugh. "You're thinking of actors," he said. "The only thing people think about at Jiu Jitsu is Jiu Jitsu."

Mina frowned. "I think that's just what everyone tells themselves so they don't have to admit how sexual it actually can be."

"Trust me, it's not. I really have never sexualized Jiu Jitsu."

"Oh yeah?" she asked, kicking him softly with her leg. She was completely naked now, though he was still fully dressed. She could feel him taking in every inch of her and enjoying what he saw. "Then why are you here?"

Matthew smirked. "That's not because of Jiu Jitsu. That's just because of you." He slid over her into a position he often used in class where all his weight was on top of her and she couldn't move.

"Are you serious?" she asked. "You're putting me in side control?"

"I already have you in side control."

He lifted himself up slightly so that his knee was on her belly and she could no longer talk. She tapped on his leg—this was the universal motion in Jiu Jitsu for your partner to let you go so you wouldn't get injured.

"That's not fair," she complained in a strained voice, when he didn't move.

"Don't get there," he joked, a common (although useless) piece of advice upper belts like to give her, when she got stuck in positions that were nearly impossible to get out of as a white belt. Still, he let her go. Then he watched her to see what she would do.

"What are you trying to prove, that you're better than me at Jiu Jitsu?" she said, pushing her way out from under him. "I think everyone in the world knows that already."

"No, I was just trying to get you to stop talking," he said, kissing her and putting his hand back on her hip and sliding downwards.

"I'm talking because…I just don't think I can do it." She pulled away his hand and sat on top of him so he would stop. Which wasn't weird at all, because she was often on top of him in class when they practiced chokes. But this time she was naked. And this time, Matthew used the opportunity to stick his fingers inside her.

He let out a small laugh. "I don't know about that," he said. "Looks like you can to me. Like you really, really want to."

"Okay, well," she stammered. He wasn't wrong. "I think we can agree that my brain and my body are not in agreement here." The longer they stayed there, the more it seemed there was no way out of this mess. It was only a matter of time before they would cross a line they could never uncross. It seemed inevitable. Maybe he was right, that it always had been.

"I can see that," Matthew said with a nod, but he didn't remove his fingers. Instead, he began moving them around, distracting her so thoroughly she couldn't keep talking. It was like his body understood hers better than she did herself.

She closed her eyes and willed her brain to work. To work better, anyway. Her body should not be the one calling the shots, after all. She had a family to think about. She had a life. But then again, she was still, in some very deep, buried ways, that girl who liked to drink and smoke and watch things explode. Despite her newly tamed nature, apparently, she still had a penchant for drama and a very addictive personality. No amount of life could change her into another person, even if she believed that part of herself was in the past, before Dima and before Amelie; clearly, it wasn't. Something told her that Matthew could see that about her. He probably ran into a lot of people with the same character flaw and could sniff it out.

Mina rolled to her side, a pleasurable sigh escaping her lips.

"What, you don't like that?" Matthew asked, rolling to his side too, trying to get back in there.

"No, I do. I really do," she said, squeezing her legs together. "I just feel like an idiot. You probably do this all the time, don't you?" she asked, unable to look at him. She covered her eyes with both hands. She knew he had marriage problems, and she had still invited him over when she was alone in the house. It was practically an invitation to her bed.

"No," he said pointedly. "I don't."

"Really? Never?"

"Never."

She shook her head, her eyes still closed.

"Come here," he demanded, pulling her body closer so she was under him again and kissing her, nibbling on her lower lip. This time, she let him. He had an authority to his voice that was very hard to say no to. He kissed her all the way down her chest and stomach until he got between her legs, and when she felt his tongue there too, she didn't stop him. Part of her still wanted to, but her knees had turned to jelly.

As he was down there, she had to keep telling herself that this wasn't her husband, and she shouldn't be doing what she was doing. She was thinking it so much she accidentally said it aloud.

"This is so bad," she mumbled. "I am so bad."

"Oh, I know," Matthew said, taking his head out from between her legs. "You're a bad girl. You need to be punished." At which point he flipped her around and then spanked her. She liked that too, it turned out. She really liked it. Matthew pulled her waist back so that she was bent over against the bed. Suddenly he was inside her and she was so filled with conflicting feelings that she wasn't sure if she was about to cry or have an orgasm. Turned out a little bit of both.

"I'm going to straight to hell," she said, after her legs had stopped quivering against the bright yellow duvet cover, which had started falling to the floor. She really meant it too, despite being a lapsed Catholic. Some things became so wrapped up in your consciousness from an early age it was nearly impossible to untangle them, and hell was one of them. But she couldn't stop herself from wanting Matthew and in the moment, she didn't want to.

"I'll meet you there, I guess," Matthew said, and that was the end of their talking.

CHAPTER EIGHT

Later, in class, Mina could hardly focus on the move they were learning she was so paranoid about everyone noticing something between Matthew and her. But either they already knew something was going on with them, or they really couldn't tell. She would have partnered with Dylan, but he wasn't there—sometimes he would go missing for weeks on end, then show up randomly out of nowhere—so she chose to partner with Felix instead. He didn't say anything, but he did glance over at Matthew, as if to point out that it was very unusual that they weren't drilling the new move together, before shrugging it off.

It was not a complicated move, a sweep she had already learned a few times, but her mind was so all over the place she could hardly remember that she was supposed to be knocking Felix over. He was getting really annoyed at her for having to repeat himself so much, but this was nothing new. Felix was always annoyed; at her and most people. They were friends, inasmuch as you can be friends with a person who is that unhappy and that consistently drunk, but his demanding, impatient teaching style did not vibe with her learning style, which was why she didn't usually partner with him.

"What?" she asked, once she had successfully gotten him to his back and had mounted him. "Was that wrong?"

"No," he said, but it didn't feel like it. "You're just, like, somehow worse than usual today. I didn't think it was possible. What's up with you?"

Blushing, she sat down on the floor and feigned heat exhaustion. This was easy to do at the gym, as it was always very hot. It was summer and there was no A/C. "Sorry. I'm distracted."

"Yeah no shit. Clear the cobwebs out of there already, Jesus."

Were they really so obvious? Did Felix know something was up? You'd have to be blind not to notice how much Mina and Matthew had talked at the gym the last six months. But she talked to Dylan and Felix a lot too. She had never made any obvious portrayal of attraction there, and neither had he. In fact, he was always so proper she hadn't been certain he was into her until the other night. Still, she couldn't stop thinking about it, about how to act normal. It was hard to act normal when it was an act in general, but it was extra hard that day when a ticking time bomb had been planted in her life, threatening to destroy everything in its way, including the gym.

She was so distracted and guilty the entire class she could hardly pay attention and it wasn't until they were rolling that she stopped to think she was probably only making things worse. Rolling was the term they used for three-minute sparring sessions with a rotating group of partners, which took up most of the class after the intro- ductory lesson. Though it barely looked like you were moving from the outside, in the beginning, rolling was the most intense workout because you were basically just trying to get someone twice your weight off of you, or avoiding chokes, which takes all the energy a person can muster. Because of this, and her hormones changing so drastically after weening Amelie that she no longer had much of an appetite, Mina had lost fifteen pounds since she started.

A few rounds in, Mina went to sit down and take a break, hoping to catch her breath and regain some composure. She was getting Kimura'd and X-choked by white belts whose names she barely knew, which was a bad sign. As a four-stripe white belt, she was usually able to escape these simple submissions by higher ranking members let alone newer people. Clearly, she was too distracted to be rolling; she should have counted her lucky stars she hadn't injured herself from mere carelessness and called it a day. But then Matthew signaled to her to come over.

Maybe she should have skipped class. Or he should have. Surely this had been a bad idea, for them to both go to class right after what they'd done. But no, now she was lying underneath him again and hoping what they had done earlier wasn't a neon sign beaming all around them. Her stomach filled with butterflies, which made the rest of her floppy. Floppy was not a good mode in Jiu Jitsu. Floppy meant you ended up on your back with someone's full weight keeping you pinned to the floor. She focused long enough to shrimp her way out and get her legs around his waist, but then she looked at the sweat dripping off his pale head and onto her Gi and got distracted again, thinking back to how sweaty they'd gotten in bed earlier that day. She hadn't stopped thinking about it since. Three times they'd had sex before Matthew had to go home. She hadn't done that since her college years.

"Well, that was a rookie mistake," Matthew said as she opened her guard but didn't get up to sweep him quick enough. "You're gonna have to pay for that." She let him knee-on-belly her without any resistance. Her heart just wasn't in it. His knee knocked the air out of her, which at least stopped the problem with the butterflies. Then he slid into high mount and trapped her arm in an armbar, which was what they called a series of moves that, taken to their conclusion, would break another person's arm by overextending it. She tapped out again. It was probably the fifth time and the three minutes weren't over yet.

"Jeez, that might be a record." Matthew laughed as he let go of her. "Are you just letting me win?" he asked. He wiped the sweat off his head with her Gi sleeve before sitting up and starting again. He looked annoyed. "That's not like you."

"You always win anyway," she said, bumping and slapping his hand, which signaled the start of a new round. "That's what happens when you're a brown belt, and a man." This time she walked straight in between his legs to try to knee slice her way into side control, but he merely swept her back to the floor with a scissor sweep. It had taken all of two seconds for him to be back on top.

"Sure, but you usually try a little harder," he mumbled, grabbing hold of her wrist so that her arm was trapped around her own neck in what they called a gift wrap, and whistling the beginning of a Christmas song as he did it. Then he took her back, using her Gi collar and his other arm to choke her from behind. She tapped out again. He was just showing off now. It was one of the things that had made her attraction to him worse, because he was so good at Jiu Jitsu. Better than she would ever be, probably, because he had to be for work, whereas she only went for fun. Plus, she was years behind him, and most people at the gym. She was always losing. The only thing that kept her going was that she was losing far less badly than she used to.

"I'm distracted," she said, fist bumping him again, then sitting down so he couldn't sweep her again. "I'm sure you can understand why."

"Not really," he said, undeterred by her starting position. Soon he had her ankle wrapped under his armpit, but he paused for a moment before finishing the leglock and catching her eye. "That was really fun earlier. Can we do it again?"

"Oh my god," she said, tapping out even before she needed to and standing up. She didn't mess around with leglocks or heel hooks; she'd seen several people tear their ACLs that way. Normally she liked that Matthew rolled with her so aggressively, compared to other higher belts who were often too nice, letting her get dominant positions she would never get normally, or going so slowly that it forced her to think too much and freeze under the pressure. But this was a bit much. "No."

The buzzer rang and they shook hands. Matthew let his hand linger while looking her right in the eye. It was the closest thing to a

wink without winking she had ever seen. "Hm. We'll see about that."
It was all she could do to shake her head and walk away. She didn't
even bother staying for the last five minutes of class. She just walked
right out the door and went straight home. Amelie was watching
Coco again with her cousin Maya, and after Mina paid Maya ten
dollars and sent her home in an Uber, she curled up in bed with
Amelie and cried. She told her it was because *Coco* always made her
cry—which was true—except that this time she hadn't been able to
focus on the movie. Instead, she thought about the inevitability of
her life falling apart.

* * *

Except that it didn't. A day went by, then two, then three, and for a
while it felt like everything would just be normal. Like nothing had
ever happened. The only thing that changed was that she stopped
going to Jiu Jitsu, for the first time since she'd been really sick from
one of Amelie's endless daycare colds, back in January. Of course,
she couldn't just avoid the gym. She walked past it several times a
day. There were four Open Guard locations, but the main one was
in Bridgeport, just down the street from her. Usually, it made it so
much easier to keep her workouts a daily habit, when she could
practically see the gym from her house. Now, it made her feel guilty.
Every time she passed it and didn't go inside, she was reminded of
what she'd done, and she didn't like being reminded of that. Well,
her body did—but not her mind. The two seemed to exist on totally
separate planes now.

The problem was that Amelie didn't know what she'd done. And
Amelie loved the gym. Which was why, a few days later, her inner
clock must have told her telepathically that there was a kids' Jiu Jitsu
class to crash, and she ran down the sidewalk to the gym just as the
door had been unlocked. This happened so often Mina really did
wonder if she had somehow memorized the schedule. Mina let her

run inside, stopping to take off her sandals. She didn't see anyone on the mats, but the blue belts who taught the class were used to Amelie coming by while they set things up, and she figured Amelie would get rid of some energy and then get bored so they could walk home. It wasn't until she was trying to show Amelie how to do a cartwheel that she looked up and noticed Matthew was coming out of the men's changing room. And his daughter, Dallas.

"Mellie!" Dallas screamed, running after Amelie, who also ran towards her, giggling all the while. She gave her friend a hug, then took her by the hand to the back room, where there were a bunch of kids' blocks and books. "Hi, Mellie, Mellie!" she repeated.

Mina looked at Matthew, aware that they were once again alone in a room together. She tried not to think about the last time it had happened, but her body reminded her. The butterflies returned, and her knees went a little weak, and she was glad she didn't have to do any Jiu Jitsu. "You teach the kids class now?" she asked, her eyebrows raised.

"No, just opening up for Jonah. He's running late."

"Oh," she mumbled. She pretended to look out the window. He didn't let her get away with it; he never let her get away with anything, really, it was part of what she liked about him. He met his problems head on. He merely walked in front of the window to block her view until she was forced to be face-to-face with him.

"Are you avoiding the gym?" he asked.

She swallowed. She had forgotten how direct he was. He was direct, and he noticed everything. It was very unusual in a person. Usually, people were too wrapped up in their own heads to notice anything until it was right in their face. And even then, they'd likely try to ignore it or tiptoe around it. She'd gotten so used to this type of behavior she hadn't even realized she'd adapted it as her own.

"Yeah, I guess I am," she admitted. Because she liked to be direct too. It was the world that didn't allow for it.

Matthew frowned, crossing his muscular tattooed arms over

each other. She tried not to stare at his biceps. She tried, but she failed. "Why?" he asked.

"That was weird for me the other day," she admitted. "Wasn't it weird for you?"

"No," he said. "How was it weird?"

"Maybe I'm paranoid, but I just felt like people would be able to tell."

"How?"

She shrugged. "Vibes?"

"Vibes," he repeated, skeptical.

"Like I said, maybe I'm being paranoid."

Matthew paused, an inscrutable expression on his face. "It's going to look weird if you just stop coming to class all of a sudden."

"Maybe we shouldn't partner in class, then," she said.

"Again, it would be weird if we didn't," he said. "You have to act normal. And you can't afford to keep missing classes if you ever want to get your blue belt."

She rolled her eyes. "As if I am remotely close to getting my blue belt," she said.

He was right though. She didn't like missing so much Jiu Jitsu, despite the fact that she had only missed two classes so far; she usually went every day, sometimes twice. Her muscles felt wobbly, and she worried she had already forgotten everything she knew. Plus, all her friends went there, and without Dimitry around, she'd been pretty isolated. But that was how her mind worked nowadays; she avoided problems as long as she could. She'd noticed that leaky pipe for months before it broke, for example, and her way of dealing with it was to avoid that part of the basement. But Matthew was not just a leaky pipe problem. Matthew was a your-house-is-falling-down sort of problem.

"You are, though. I can go to the West Loop location, if you want," he said.

"No, no, I can't ask you to do that. It's so out of your way," she argued. "And there is never anywhere to park."

"I'll manage."

"Where would you even fit that obnoxious truck in the West Loop? It takes up half the parking lot."

Matthew let out a small laugh. "Did you just call my truck obnoxious?"

Mina bit back a smile. "It is very ostentatious," she said. "I mean, really. Who needs a truck that big? I'd say you were trying to make up for a lack of something else, but now I know that's not true."

Matthew laughed again, this time shaking his head.

"What?" she asked, smiling now.

"Sorry, I'm just trying to remember how many times I helped you move furniture with my 'obnoxious' truck. Two, three times? And that player piano?" He pushed her playfully in the shoulder, which made her realize how much she'd missed being around him; even a few days felt like an eternity. It wasn't just that she was attracted to him; she liked his personality too. They had fun together. She couldn't remember the last time she had fun with Dimitry. His version of fun was sitting at home and watching Netflix, or looking at his phone. The man was hardly ever home but when he was, he was constantly scrolling through feeds; it was very unattractive. Just another thing she had been ignoring about their relationship, apparently. How she hadn't noticed any of these issues until Matthew was kind of a mystery. Not that it made sense to compare the two. Matthew was probably on his phone a lot at home too; she just didn't have to see him in his normal day-to-day life. If they actually spent a few days together, Mina guessed their attraction to each other would burn out pretty quickly. But that wasn't exactly an option.

"Okay, I guess sometimes a truck can come in handy," Mina admitted.

"Now, let's see how many pianos your bike can move," he started.

Before he could finish, they both heard a loud thump, followed by a scream, coming from the back of the gym. "I better go check that out," she sighed.

She found Dallas and Amelie staring at a five-pound barbell that had fallen over from wherever it had been stored. The place was a complete mess, so it was hard to tell where that was. She put it on a higher shelf, one they couldn't reach, then picked up Amelie and set her back down on the mat, ignoring her protests.

"How many times have I told you to stay away from the weights? Those are for grownups only."

"Why?" Dallas whined, as she tried to pick up another weight, which Mina also moved to a higher shelf.

"Because it's very heavy and you could get hurt," she explained.

"Get over here," Matthew ordered in a stern voice. Dallas ran towards him, and he bent over to slap her on her poor little butt.

"You pull one more stunt like that and we're going home," he said sharply.

"Noo!" Dallas screamed. Then she began crying. Which made Amelie start fake crying in empathy. Mina shook her head. The last thing she needed right now was a tantrum, especially two of them at once. And really, was that necessary? Spanking over an accident? Sometimes she really felt bad for Dallas, and for Ariel. Their home life was probably not easy. For a moment she wondered if she was making it worse, by existing. Surely Matthew would be making similar comparisons.

"Girls, girls," she said. She reached into her backpack and pulled out two bags of cheese crackers. "Who wants a snack?"

Luckily this seemed to placate both Amelie and Dallas. Once they were both sitting down and eating, Mina took a deep breath and looked at Matthew again.

"What?" Matthew asked, watching her. She must have been frowning.

Mina looked down. She shouldn't have said anything, but she couldn't help it. Once someone had been inside you, you were at least allowed to tell them what you thought, Mina figured. "I just don't know why the spanking is necessary."

Matthew let out a mean laugh. "All right, go smoke some more patchouli, and we can wait around for everyone to just magically learn how to behave."

"You don't smoke patchouli," Mina said.

"Oh really," Matthew sneered.

Mina looked to the door, hoping some of the other parents would start filing in, but it was still pretty early and no one else had arrived yet. She knew she shouldn't be alone with Matthew in public, but now that Amelie was sitting and eating so nicely, she couldn't exactly leave. Well, she could, but she would have to listen to her whine unhappily the entire walk back, or, more likely, she would have to carry her home when she refused to walk. Before she could decide what to do next, Matthew decided for her.

"Come here," Matthew ordered Mina, putting a hand on her back and pushing her forward. He crossed the room and led her through a curtain to the women's changing room. Then he pushed her against the wall and started kissing her. Right there at the gym, with their kids in the other room. She could still hear one of them squealing.

"Matthew," she said, pulling away to take a breath. "Seriously? We can't."

Instead of answering her, he pushed her even harder against the wall, his hands reaching under her thin tank top, which was damp with sweat from the hot afternoon. "I can't stop thinking about you. It's driving me crazy."

She had the same problem, but she didn't want to admit that and make things harder. "Well, stop. We're married."

"I know that," Matthew said.

"If we keep doing this, we'll get caught. Everybody always does," she said, still pressed up against him, his hands searching beneath her pants. The problem was that her body was still not in agreement with her morals or her paranoia. Always her body, which seemed to have its own mind lately. Her body was melting into him like it belonged there. It didn't want to go anywhere else. What if she was enjoying the wrongness of it all? Maybe she really was going to hell.

"We can be careful," he muttered.

"How is this careful? Jonah has cameras."

"Not in here," Matthew said, as if he had been thinking of this when he directed her there. He kissed her, holding her neck with one hand, so hard she could barely breathe. "Open your eyes," he demanded.

She opened them, looked into his light blue gaze; the wolf was back. Her pulse bounced against his fingers. "The kids…" she mumbled. Her stomach was filling with butterflies and she could practically feel her underwear getting damp. But she kept her eyes on his.

"The kids are fine."

She tried to turn away to check, but he didn't let go.

"I'm not done with you yet," he said in a voice so deep she wondered where it came from. It made her nerves flutter, half in fear and half in desire. He kissed her again, still squeezing her throat. For a moment she wondered if part of him wanted to keep squeezing until she passed out; did he have that much darkness in him? Or was it just a game? And why did it turn her on so much? There was clearly more wrong with her than she even realized.

Suddenly, the door slammed closed, and she heard a jovial, familiar voice saying,

"Oh, hey, Dallas. Hey, Amelie."

It was Jonah, the owner of the gym. Matthew let go of her neck, and Mina's heart began pounding so loudly she wondered if the girls could hear it all the way in the other room. Matthew raised a finger to his lips. His other hand was still down her pants.

"Hey, Jonah!" Matthew yelled.

"Hey, Matthew! Thanks for opening up, man."

"Where did you put that new box of bleach?" Matthew asked Jonah. This was usually kept in the girls' room, so it would explain him being there, but it still made her nervous. Matthew watched Mina with the strangest expression on his face, eyes lit up and mouth curled into a smile. Almost as if he was enjoying this sneaking around stuff a little too much. Which, now that she thought about it, he probably was. The guy was probably an adrenaline junkie. Whenever he used to tell them stories about car chases and arrests gone wrong, his eyes would light up, like it was the coolest thing that ever happened. She had enjoyed the stories at the time—who wouldn't? But what did it say about him, really, that chasing cars and murderers made him so damn excited? She may have been a little turned on by the wrongness of what they were doing, but there was no part of her that wanted to get caught or enjoyed how close they were getting to it right then. She'd been obsessing over it for days, all the ways they could have messed up, the ways they could get caught. How much Dima would hate her. She didn't want to get divorced. She didn't see herself as a divorced mother. That's not what she wanted for Amelie, or for herself. Half her time now she spent hating herself; the other half, she spent pining.

"Oh, thanks for reminding me!" Jonah called back. "I think it's still in the car, let me go grab it."

They heard the door close again. Matthew took his other hand out of her. Still watching her, he licked his fingers, which just made her wet all over again.

She shook her head at him and zipped up her pants. Then she rushed out of the dressing room, across the hall, and into the back room. Flushed, she began cleaning up some of the mess the girls had made, while Matthew returned to the mat with the nearly empty bleach sprayer like he was about to clean it, so that when Jonah came back in carrying the cleaning supplies, nothing looked at all out of the ordinary. Or so she hoped.

"Hey, Mina," Jonah said, dropping the heavy box by the back door. "I didn't see ya there."

"Amelie was just trying to destroy your gym again, sorry," she explained, hoping he didn't notice her cheeks were bright red. Hoping, too, that his sense of smell wasn't quite as good as hers. Matthew had started spraying the mats, which helped. The cleaning solution they used for the gym had a pretty strong odor, which made sense, considering the amount of sweat it acquired on a daily basis.

"Everything okay at home?" Jonah asked, cutting the box open with a sharp knife. "Haven't seen you much this week."

Mina felt guilty suddenly. Jonah was extremely muscular and tattooed up to his neck, with a rotating door of strange haircuts and facial hair combinations; if you didn't know him you might be terrified to talk to him, but he was too nice for his own good. Half the members had their own set of keys, and she had been going a full two months before he remembered to charge her for her membership. She didn't know what to tell him, so she figured she would go with some semblance of truth. "Well, it's just been hard to get out, you know, with Dima gone so much. It's just me and Amelie at home."

"Oh, that's right, where is he again?"

"Texas, I think. Hard to keep track."

He nodded. "Right, right." He put a hand on her shoulder. "Well, hope you'll come by soon. I've got that rashguard you ordered." He stopped and looked around the mess of the gym. Jonah was a fourth-degree black belt in Jiu Jitsu and could destroy anyone who tried to mess with him in less than two seconds, but he could not keep house. Mina was constantly replacing full garbage bags with empty ones, and piling all the empty beer and wine bottles in boxes by the back door when he wasn't around. She had no idea if he even knew who was cleaning it, or if he noticed it had been cleaned at all. But he had made such a home there for his members—like Matthew and her, many were friends outside of the gym—it was easy to overlook. And he was so likable she was not the only member pitching in to help him with various gym maintenance. "Hm. Well, it's here somewhere…"

"That's okay, I'll be back soon. Probably tomorrow," she said.

Which meant, of course, that she would actually have to come tomorrow. Jonah leaned over and started taking out the remainder of the large bottles of the bleach, placing them in the girl's room. While he was busy with that, Mina darted through the hall and towards the front door, where Amelie was blocking the entrance and spilling out the remainder of her crackers on the floor.

"All right, time to go," she told her daughter. She looked at Dallas, whose cute little face and blonde hair was covered in crumbs, her striped dress wet with water or juice. "Bye, Dallas, see you soon!"

"More crackers?" Dallas asked.

"You had enough crackers," Matthew yelled from the far end of the room. "Go get dressed for class."

"Help?"

"You don't need help. You're not a baby. Get dressed," Matthew ordered. "Now."

Mina reached into her backpack and found another cracker bag to give Dallas, if only to annoy Matthew. She didn't like the way he spoke to her sometimes, in this angry tone, with barely a hint of love. Maybe it was the hippie in her, but she only disciplined Amelie when she tried to do something dangerous like run into the road. Dallas's missteps were totally harmless. So that she wouldn't have to make her distaste so obvious, Mina lowered her gaze to the floor, where she began picking up the crumbs Amelie had spilled there. Then she threw them in the overflowing wastebasket while Dallas took the bag Mina had given to her and ran joyfully across the mats to the women's changing room, where Matthew was waiting with her Gi.

"Don't make me tell you again," he ordered. Dallas took the tiny pink Gi and disappeared behind the curtain just as Jonah was leaving through it. The girl was barely older than Amelie, just over three; it was perfectly okay for her to ask for help getting dressed, she thought. She couldn't understand sometimes how his tone differed so much between his daughter, his wife, and his friends in Jiu Jitsu. With her, he could be sort of aggressive and he definitely liked to give orders, but there wasn't this anger he had with Dallas or Ariel. Like he was mad at them for having to be something he cared about, something he had to protect. Would he rather be alone? But she couldn't see that either. She really had no idea what went on his head. It was probably part of why she found him so enticing. He constantly surprised her.

Dimitry, on the other hand, always said everything he thought and felt the second he thought and felt them, and none of it was ever surprising. Which was probably a good thing for a marriage, but sometimes it made her feel like they were too much like roommates. A person needed some mystery, right? Not to mention romance. They had neither.

Mina took the opportunity to get Amelie's sandals back on, then her own. They were just leaving the gym when she felt an arm on her shoulder, pulling her back with force. She turned to see Matthew.

"What are you doing now?" he was asking her. Had he really followed her out? And left Dallas alone inside? Jonah was a nice guy, but he owned a gym; he wasn't a babysitter. He had his own gaggle of kids at home.

"Movie time, movie time," Amelie repeated in singsong, jumping up and down. It was indeed movie time. According to the clock at the gym, it was nearly five. She never understood how Amelie knew this. It was like she had learned to read the sun. When it came to movies and snacks and the three-to-five-year-old kids' class at Jiu Jitsu, her child was a damn genius.

"I'd like to come check on that pipe in the basement," he said. Amelie continued to chant, "Movie time" and pull Mina by the arm, so they started walking towards her house.

"I think the pipe is fine," she mumbled. It was bad enough that they'd slept together. Repeating the mistake just made the whole thing seem ten times worse. Still, Matthew followed her down the block for a moment, then stopped when he reached his truck. "Amelie and I are about to watch a movie," she said.

"I'd still like to check. I'll be by in ten minutes." Then he opened the door to his truck, took out a water bottle, and returned to the gym. Ten minutes later, he showed up at her door.

She couldn't exactly tell him to leave, could she?

Well, she could. But she didn't.

CHAPTER NINE

That was how things had started. For so long, she just harbored this tiny crush, and then suddenly, her entire life had flipped upside down. Now all she could think about was how to see Matthew again, and how to keep anyone else from seeing them. They had nosy neighbors, and in Chicago, houses were basically sandwiched together side by side to the point where she could see into many of their windows. She knew several minutes before the mailman was coming because she could hear her neighbors' dogs barking house by house. The same would go for Matthew if he came in the front door, because they could see him from the window. If he parked by the gym, someone might go there and notice he wasn't inside. If he parked by the house, someone might notice that, too. One of the other couples they socialized with lived only two houses down from her, and at least a handful lived close enough that they could walk by. It would be better if he could come by without the giant eyesore of a truck, but he seemed to be glued to the thing.

So, for the next few days, he parked by a coffee shop a few blocks away while Amelie was in daycare and she drove him over. Even that stressed her out, because they still had to walk from her car to the back door, which was barely hidden from view by their gate.

That was the main problem of having an affair; it was only adding more stress to her life. But it was also her escape from the stress of her life; she couldn't stop thinking about him, and she didn't want to stop seeing him either. The sex was just too damn good. It was like he knew exactly what she would like before she understood it herself. When she wasn't sleeping with him, she was thinking and thinking and thinking about it in her head. She knew it was terrible, but she was an addict. And she was now addicted to Matthew; his knowing gaze and his gruff, vulgar way of speaking to her. The choking and spanking and all the other stuff too; she was addicted to it all.

She also understood things couldn't continue this way. Dima would be back soon. Her plan, so far as she had a plan now, had been to stop once he returned. She'd done it before with momentary smoking relapses. Dima was gone often, and there had been several times over the years where it made Mina get a little antsy to have that much solitude, but usually she didn't mind the extra time to think and read. It was different after they had Amelie, though, especially the older she got. She was a little terror during his absences now, fighting her about everything, spending half her days having tantrums. Because of her cognitive delays, Mina couldn't tell if she understood that her dad would be back, that he hadn't left for good. By the time she'd get used to him being gone, he would return, and the whole cycle would start all over again.

On top of that, she was rarely sleeping more than a few hours at a time, and was going a little bit crazy. She had never actually realized when they made the decision to have a child that she would basically be forced into single motherhood. But it wasn't like she could tell Dima to stay home; they needed the money. They always needed the money. But was it worth her sanity? She was no longer sure if she had any left.

Unlike cigarettes, which she had always been able to curb before getting addicted again, Matthew was impossible to curb; and he didn't want to stop. He didn't seem to ever get enough of her. She really didn't understand why sometimes. His wife was pretty, if a little overweight. It must have only been interesting because it was something new. Or he enjoyed the power dynamics of the situation.

He got more and more rough in the bedroom, and she had been really enjoying it; the handcuffs, the rope, his Open Guard brown belt.

Agreeing to every demand allowed her to get lost in the moment instead of spending the entire time working her way through her to-do list in her mind. It was kind of like Jiu Jitsu, that way; something about the violence cleared her mind of distractions. It was almost meditative. Mina wasn't sure how she could stop herself from sleeping with him now that she knew how compatible they were in the bedroom, far more compatible than she and Dima had ever been. She hadn't even realized until Matthew how much she had shut down and stuffed away her sex drive while she was married. Dima was her best friend, and until recently, he had made a great life partner.

But after her experience with Matthew, she understood more clearly than she ever had before that she had never really been satisfied with Dima sexually. Part of her had always known this, of course, but it had been in a deep-down sort of way that she never really brought to the surface or addressed. She had told herself it didn't really matter in the end, that people throughout history who had been put into arranged marriages managed to make it work, so how big of a deal could it have been? But it was a big deal, apparently. Apparently, if you put your needs on hold for ten years, you just snap and sleep with the first guy who sends you vibes at your gym.

It was stupid, she knew. It was so stupid to keep seeing him that part of her wondered if she might be trying to blow up her life. Was she really so unhappy? Was he? There was also the other matter of his wife. Even while she still texted with Ariel occasionally, she worried all the time about her finding out. So far, there hadn't been any strange questions or suspicions voiced, but somehow that made it seem worse. Like there was a bomb waiting to go off.

"Where does your wife think you are right now?" Mina couldn't help but ask him on the third afternoon in a row that he came by before class. Because the advanced class was an hour and a half before the beginner's one, it was early enough that Amelie was still in daycare. "She must know class doesn't start yet."

"I just tell her I'm rolling early with a couple of the guys."

"Which guys? Most of them don't get off work this early," Mina said.

"How would she know that?" he asked, shaking his head.

"If it were me, that would be the first question I'd ask."

"That's only because you know everyone."

"No, it's because to tell a good lie you have to be specific."

He eyed her warily. "You really chose the wrong career path."

"I don't like lying. I just happen to be good at it."

"And why's that?" he asked, his eyes narrowing. "Something I need to know about?"

"My parents were a bit overbearing," she explained. "Very strict Catholics. I had a nine p.m. curfew and wasn't allowed to date. I had to lie about everything when I was younger. I hated it. I made a promise to myself in college not to do that again, which now I have to break, thanks to you."

To her surprise, Matthew squeezed her shoulder tight. "I get it. I hate liars."

"You told me once that you lie all the time," Mina argued.

"I lie at *work*," he said. "Do you know the kind of people I have to deal with on a daily basis? It would make you sick."

"Well, then, I should make you sick. And you should make yourself sick too."

He shrugged. "Nah. It's not really the same thing." Unlike Dimitry, who could go on about the details of a specific type of building he liked for hours, or ruminate endlessly on a dream or passing feeling he'd had the night before, Matthew was not the most talkative man, especially when it came to anything personal. She had probably talked to him about personal stuff more in the last week than the whole time she had known him, and even that sometimes felt almost painful, like Matthew was so attached to his words he didn't want to part with them.

"You're still deleting your messages with me, right?" she asked.

"Yes. Thank you for continuing to be paranoid."

"It's really not that paranoid. Dimitry knows all my passwords."

Matthew's eyebrows raised. "Why?"

"Because we actually have—had—a pretty honest and open relationship before all this. I had nothing to hide."

"Sounds like you need to change your passwords," he said.

"That would basically be like telling him I'm having an affair." She stood to get dressed, but Matthew only watched her from the bed and didn't move.

"Fair point."

"He's coming back tomorrow," she said. "So we need to stop with all the texting and sneaking around stuff."

"I mean, we could."

"Is there another option I'm not aware of?"

"We can work around it."

"I don't want to work around it," she said. "I feel bad enough as it is."

"You keep saying that," he said. "But do you?"

She did. She really did. Like all addicts, she didn't know how she could stop. In some ways, with Dimitry being gone, it almost didn't feel real. It was kind of like when she hadn't told her family she was a smoker, so it almost felt like maybe she wasn't one, until the day they caught her. She was twenty-four by then, but it was the most embarrassed she had ever felt. Not that she was smoking—half the women in her extended family did too, at least when they drank— but that she had been caught in a lie. The weight of what they had done—now nearly a dozen times—hadn't hit her yet. But surely it would the second she saw Dimitry. Bad behavior was easier to hide when it lived in the shadows. Once you turned a light on, it was a different story entirely. And, eventually, this would happen.

Or it would need to happen anyway. It was like that children's book, *There's No Such Thing as a Dragon*. When the kid's parents refused to look at the dragon, insisting it didn't exist, it only kept growing and growing. Once they finally looked at it, the thing shrunk and disappeared.

"What are you suggesting exactly?"

He shrugged. "That you don't feel as bad as you say you do. That your marriage is just as fucked as mine."

Mina flushed red. "My marriage is fine. You're the problem." Even as she said it, though, she started to realize it wasn't true. That was what happened when you started lying. First you lied to everyone else, then you started lying to yourself. It was just inevitable. It was a very slippery slope once you started messing around with the truth. Words were powerful.

"Sure," Matthew said, rolling his eyes. But he stood up from the bed, as if to leave. "You keep telling yourself that." He sounded angry. She thought he was going to storm off, but instead, he lifted her and flipped her back on the bed and lay on top of her. His hand started reaching into her pants, which she had just put back on. She didn't stop him. Instead, she let him take her clothes off again and then they were going at it again. Maybe if she just got it out of her system, she kept thinking.

But she couldn't seem to get this out of her system. Maybe this was just a part of her system now. And how on earth would she manage it? She didn't think she could even hide a newfound smoking habit from Dimitry, let alone an affair. Their lives were too intertwined. They knew each other's Facebook passwords and email accounts. There was nowhere to hide. No, it was just not manageable. Most of the time, her life *without* the added stress of meeting up with Matthew was barely manageable. She didn't think it could take any more weight. How could it be that her escape from her overwhelming life was also the thing making it the most overwhelming? Obviously, the best solution was to stop it. And yet, here she was, letting him slap her and choke her and enjoying it, even asking for it sometimes.

Afterward, Mina sat down and put her head on her knees, the

conversation they'd just had instantly returning to mind. She closed her eyes, then felt a clammy hand on her shoulder and opened them.

"Hey. Look at me," Matthew said.

She looked at him.

"It's gonna be okay," he said. Matthew put his hand on her thigh and squeezed it.

"How?"

"Just think of it this way: this is our thing. No one has to know about it."

"But it's not," she said. "It's a mess."

"Only if you start talking about it. Just...don't do that."

Mina rested her head on his shoulder, inhaling his scent. She wanted to remember it in case anything happened. "So we just, like, continue in our lives like it's any other day?"

"Yeah. That's exactly what we do."

"I don't know how I can do that."

"You don't have a choice," Matthew said. "That's the situation we are in."

"Do you feel bad when you see Ariel?" she asked. She kept wondering how she would be able to look Dimitry in the eye when he came home. How she would be able to sleep with him again after someone else had been inside her. It all felt impossible. She wanted to just get into bed and never leave.

"A little," he said.

"How do you deal with that?"

"I just don't think about it."

"I can't do that," she said. "I think a lot, about everything. That's what happens when you're a writer."

"Yeah, I know. It's troublesome."

It was becoming clear to her that she was unable to stop things from happening with Matthew, so the only way to end it was to convince him to end it. This was proving to be a difficult task. For now, she needed to focus on getting through the next few days without having a complete mental breakdown.

"Okay," she said, trying to change the subject. "What are you going to say to Dimitry if you see him?"

Matthew sighed and stood, getting dressed quickly.

"What will I say? I'll say, 'Hey man. How was your trip?'" he said. "People aren't psychic. They don't just know things from looking at you. My job would be a lot damn easier if that was the case."

His job. She kept forgetting about his job. Him being a cop felt like a looming problem for some reason that she couldn't explain. But that was because she did indeed think people could know things from looking at you. Mina was the kind of girl who had learned to read tarot cards and checked her horoscope in the paper. She sought meaning in the smallest of things. What was the meaning of this affair? The word alone made her shiver uncontrollably. She still loved her husband. She really did. Sure, he didn't make much money, and sure, he got distracted by his phone too easily. He left his clothes all over the house and talked too much when they socialized with other people, not noticing when their eyes began to drift away from him. And there was the sex stuff. But no one was perfect.

Matthew was probably a far more difficult person to live with; she knew from being at his house when he had just woken up from an overnight shift that he could be very moody and hostile. He had a drinking problem and all sorts of other problems, surely. She didn't want to be the woman at his side at a dinner party. She didn't want him to be a father to her kid. Those things she only wanted with Dimitry. He was the nicest person she'd ever met. The problem was, at least in the bedroom, that he was maybe too nice. As she had been learning recently, that wasn't what she wanted at all.

"What?" Matthew asked, watching her expression in the dark room. He was dressed now in his white Gi, his brown belt with two stripes on it tied in the front that he had just used to tie her up. It was jarring, to see him in his gym clothes there. Like mixing up their worlds.

She shook her head. "Nothing."

"No, not nothing."

She stood up, looking around for her pants, and felt so many emotions bubbling up she thought she might start crying. And she was really not the crying type, *Coco* aside. You'd have to be heartless not to get sad at the end of that movie. Once she had her tank top back on, she turned back to him, pulling her jeans up as she spoke. "I like you. I can't keep liking you and also be someone's wife."

Matthew came over and sat down next to her on the bed. To her surprise, he put his head in his hands. "I like you too."

This surprised her, and somehow made everything worse. "So? Should we...stop?"

Matthew wiped his forehead with his sleeve, another movement she was entirely all too familiar with from the gym. It was doubly weird to see it there at her house. In her bedroom. Where they had just been so intimate. "It's also the only thing getting me through the day right now," he said softly. "Thinking about seeing you."

"Oh," she said in almost a whisper. That wasn't at all what she had expected him to say. She believed him too, because it had been that way for her even before they had ever kissed. It felt like a punch to the gut, this minor glimpse into his interior life. He had always kept that so protected from her she wasn't sure he ever thought about her at all. She thought he might be one of those rare beasts who just went through life without giving much thought to anything. One of those people who only acted and never learned from their actions. It fit with her idea of what a cop was; of course, she had never really known any cops before, so her understanding of them came entirely from TV shows she watched and books she read.

"Why?" she found herself asking. Maybe his home life or work life was worse than she knew. He was the kind of man to go looking for a fight in some bar rather than face whatever was wrong. She could just tell that about him. But Matthew was closing back up again, a turtle crawling into its shell. Sadness enveloped the room, like they'd just stepped into an Elliott Smith song. It felt like an ending. And still, still she couldn't imagine never seeing him again. So maybe it was a beginning.

"We'll figure something out. Play it by ear," he said. As always, his voice had so much authority that she actually believed him, before remembering that they shouldn't be figuring anything out, they should be stopping. How was she the only one who could see that?

Despite what he said, Matthew really seemed unconcerned that they were breaking their marriage vows. He merely squeezed her knee with his hand and then snuck out the back door. After he left, Mina felt an almost disabling combination of sorrow and fear. It truly was dizzying. For a moment she had such an urge to go buy a pack of cigarettes she almost put on her shoes to walk to the store. But she didn't. Instead, she gathered all the bedsheets, blankets, and pillowcases, and threw them in the laundry machine.

When she got out of the shower, it was already time to pick up Amelie and meet Dimitry.

MARCH

CHAPTER TEN

Surprisingly, Matthew didn't follow Ariel to her car, or seek her out at home. He seemed to be accepting his lot in life, that he was once a man with too many women in his life, too many beds, and now he was a man without a home, without a wife. He ran a hand over his shiny pale skin, then shook his head, as if trying to wake himself up. She still kept half expecting him to leave, so she continued to stand in her office, watching as he sat down on the couch, looking defeated.

"Where's your stash?" he asked.

"My what?"

"Your secret cigarettes," he said. "Where are you keeping them these days?"

Mina, also feeling tired, sat down on the opposite end, stretching across the couch. To her surprise, Matthew took hold of her bare foot and began absently massaging it. "There's no stash. I quit," she said.

Matthew frowned at her, disbelief covering his face. He didn't stop massaging her foot, so she leaned back into the cushions, enjoying the sensation as much as she could, considering all the distractions of the moment. A police siren in the distance sent her heart back into panic mode until she could hear it tapering off instead of getting closer. She let out a relieved sigh.

"I did," she said. "No cigarettes. I barely drink anymore. Gets me into too much trouble."

"Hm," he grunted, leaning back into the couch and letting go of her foot, as if he had just realized what he was doing.

"If you want to go get some, though, I would not say no."

Matthew narrowed his eyes at her. "Is that a good idea?"

"No. But that's sort of the side effect of hanging out with you," she said. "Bad ideas all around." Flashes of memories burst through her mind then—straddling him in the back of his truck right next to his daughter's car seat, a blow job in a dive bar's dirty bathroom— before she shook her head, trying to shake it all away. Exciting as it had been at times, she didn't like remembering that summer if she could help it. Too many bad things swallowing up the good.

Matthew chuckled, then stood. "I'll be right back," he said.

He returned ten minutes later with a pack of Marlboros and a fifth of vodka, which he immediately poured into a glass and drank straight. He smelled like smoke, as if he couldn't wait to get back there before lighting up. She understood the impulse, one that she had been fighting all evening. Mina had sobered up in the meantime, and made herself another Old Fashioned. It was dumb to try to keep up with him, so she didn't even try. She just sipped slowly as they sat outside and smoked, sharing a cigarette between the two of them.

"You should go find Dylan," Matthew said after they'd sat in silence for several minutes. They'd always been able to do that, be comfortable in each other's silences. It was one of the things she had liked most about him, that he also needed a lot of time to think and be alone. Sometimes she had gone days or even weeks without texting him, and he had never once inquired why. Compared to Dimitry, who could never stomach any silence on her part and would constantly be checking in on her, assuming she must have been thinking horrible thoughts about him if she didn't respond right away, it was a breath of fresh air.

"Find Dylan? You just basically kicked him out of my house and now you want me to find him?" she asked.

"I'm having second thoughts now. Maybe I should have gotten him to tell me where the car is first."

Mina shook her head, annoyed. That had been exactly what she was trying to do before he ruined everything. "I can try calling him," she said, taking out her phone. But the call only provided an error message, like the number had been disconnected, which she was basically expecting. As long as he'd had the phone, she had never been able to reach him with it. He was always out of minutes. "No luck."

"You could really get into trouble, depending on what CPD's angle is. I can't tell you how many times I've been called to a scene with a burned-up car, and there's a body in the back. It's a real mess."

"It's actually a van, not a car," she said.

"What? That's even worse."

"Why is it worse?"

"Unless I missed something while I was gone, Dylan doesn't have kids. What the fuck would he need a van for, if not to transport large items that he probably shouldn't be transporting?"

"Maybe he's in a band," she suggested. "Or he likes to help people move."

Matthew laughed, the not-amused version. "I really hope you're joking. Or you're dumber than you look."

"It's not about intelligence," she said. "It's about trust."

"Well, I trust this guy about as far as I can throw him," Matthew said. "Go find him. Or at least find the van."

"I don't think I can find him. I don't know where he lives."

Matthew shook his head again, about to mumble some more expletives, then decided against it. Instead, he took out his phone. "What's his last name? I can check his last recorded residence. If he is still on parole, he would have needed to provide one to the state."

"Really?" she said. The problem was that she had been telling the truth; she didn't know his last name. She knew Dylan's ex-wife enough to be friends with her on Facebook, but she used her maiden name. Still, maybe she could reach out and ask her about it. It was already eleven, but she sent her a message anyway. She probably wouldn't hear back until the next day, but at least she felt like she was being proactive.

"How do you not know his last name?" Matthew asked, after she'd explained this to him.

"He never told me," she said.

"Didn't that seem odd to you?"

She shrugged. "No. Not everyone knows my last name," she said. "The cops asked me the same thing."

"Well, it is a tad weird. You've been friends with the guy for how long?"

She shrugged again. "I don't know. Since I started rolling, I guess. He was more Dimitry's friend, really, until we separated."

Matthew laughed. "Some friend."

"What does that mean?"

"I saw the way he looked at you," he said, squeezing her thigh.

Mina rolled her eyes. "If I held that look against everyone, I'd have no friends."

"Maybe you should find yourself some female friends," he said with a chuckle.

"You know I don't get along with other women," she said, shaking her head.

Even at the gym, the small group of women who had frequented the place seemed to all instinctively dislike her, and she had never understood why, or cared to find out. This was another pattern in her life, not fitting in, and she preferred to spend all her time with Matthew anyway, or a few of the other guys she got along with because they were fun and not so easily offended. She was not a fan of groups of women anyway. One-on-one, she could relate to a few women at a time, and she usually had a revolving door of girl friends to go out and drink with; they never seemed to last more than a few years, with the exception of Lila, who she'd known since they were kids.

Ariel had been one of those friends for a while, albeit a peripheral one, someone she could have playdates with but never really felt like she knew all that well. But because of their distance, at least they'd never had any drama. Until the Matthew debacle. And even that, Mina didn't take all that personally. Yeah, they'd been friendly, and no, it wasn't okay what she had done. But Ariel and her were not exactly BFFs. There was a deep connection between Matthew and Mina that Mina didn't feel with Ariel, or most people, really, one that could not be explained with words. It merely existed, even now. It would probably continue to exist as long as they continued to bump into each other's orbits. She felt so comfortable with him right away, like they'd known each other their entire lives.

"Yeah, I don't blame you. Women are difficult," he said.

She laughed, taking the cigarette back from him and inhaling. "I don't know, I think you've had it pretty good with women."

"Uh, have you met my wife?"

She shrugged. "I mean, she's not the most interesting person, or the best listener," Mina said. "But you must have liked her at some point. Why did you even marry her if that's how you feel?"

Matthew was about to give her that look again, the don't-go-there look, when she preempted it with a punch in the shoulder. "Just tell me," she said. "I want to know."

Matthew took the cigarette back, inhaling the remainder of it before answering. "I don't know. She's a good person. It wasn't always like this."

"What changed?" she asked, ignoring the impulse to argue that she was not so sure this was true. The vitriolic, horrible things Ariel had said to Mina during the weeks and months that followed the blowup had changed her mind on that front. They were a hundred times worse than anything Dima had said, and he was the one she'd cheated on.

Matthew shrugged, throwing the cigarette butt over her porch and standing up. "Fifteen years is a long time to be with someone."

She stood too, opening the door to let him back inside, then following him to the couch. Her phone buzzed in her pocket, but before she took it out to respond, she sat down beside Matthew again.

"It was Dallas, right?" she said. "What changed things?"

He shook his head. "Don't go there," he said. "I can't even think like—"

She rubbed his shoulder. "I get it. It changes you. Sometimes it destroys you. I think if we never had Amelie, I'd probably still be with Dimitry too," she said. "But I would rather have Amelie, so I guess it was all worth it in the end."

Matthew nodded in agreement, though he didn't reply. He didn't need to. She had been there, after all. She saw their marriage crumbling the older Dallas got; she saw it because the same thing was happening at her house. It wasn't the child's fault, of course, in either case. It was the strain and stress of balancing parenthood with work and all the various other needs an adult has. If there are major problems between a couple, or if there is any kind of imbalance—and in both their cases, they had both—it could eat away at the entire relationship, bit by bit. A life could only take on so much weight before it began to collapse, after all.

Her phone buzzed again. She reached into her pocket to check what notification she would be getting so late at night, and was surprised to see Meghan's name. She had completely forgotten about messaging her.

Dylan's last name is Elliott, said the first message. It was followed by, *If you see that fucker, tell him he's lucky I didn't call the fucking cops.*

Mina blinked. She hadn't expected her response to be so angry. Last she had talked to Dylan about it, things had been okay between the former couple; they had broken up years back, before she had met either of them. They'd seemed so much in love in their old photos, and she wasn't entirely sure what had broken them apart, as it all happened before he was in prison. But then again, she knew now a lot of what people shared with the world was mostly for show. A Facebook feed full of nothing but smiling faces or long affirmations about love now concerned her more than made her jealous. People who were really that happy didn't feel the need to prove it to everyone they'd ever known.

What happened? she typed to Meghan. While she waited for a reply, she glanced up at Matthew, whose eyes were closed and seemed to be near dozing off. Was he really intending to sleep over? How would that look to Amelie when she got up in the morning? For once, she was glad she still wasn't talking much.

"Dylan Elliott," Mina said, jarring him awake with the edge of her foot. "Can you look him up? Maybe we can find out his address."

Matthew jumped a little, blinking, then reached for his phone, and Mina looked back down at hers. Meghan had sent a new message.

You tell him if he pays me back, I won't call the police on him, okay? Meghan's message said. *I just want my shit back.*

He's stealing again? Mina wrote.

That's really the least of it, girl. I know you're friends, but take my advice and stay far away from that guy, okay? Or you'll also have a bunch of Russians knocking on your door soon.

Russians? Mina wrote.

What was she talking about? It made her think of Dima, for some reason, not that he was that kind of Russian. He was far too anxiety-prone and nice to be involved in any criminal activity, but he had mentioned some rich cousins with less-than-discernible jobs. Mina thought he was just saying that to make her think he was cooler than he was, though. She'd met his whole family, including those cousins, and they did not seem like criminals to her; if anything, they were a tad on the nerdy side. Most of his relatives were engineers and lawyers and doctors, not mobsters. She shook her head; she didn't like to think about Dima too much these days; it filled her with too much guilt and sadness. And anyway, it wasn't like he had anything to do with this, or with Dylan. He lived in Jefferson Park now and had joined a different gym; they only saw each other when they were dropping Amelie off at each other's houses.

You mean like the mob or something? Mina asked Meghan. *Or just Russians generally speaking?*

Never mind, I already said too much. Just tell him what I said. I gotta go, Meghan wrote. Then she logged off, and Mina was left staring at her phone, more confused than before. She would have sat there for minutes if Matthew didn't push her foot with his to get her attention.

"Three pending felony charges," Matthew said, shaking his head. "What a shock."

Mina looked up, as she pocketed her phone. "What are the charges?" she asked.

Matthew whistled, then read aloud from his screen. "Theft-movable property, Felony I. Theft-movable property, Felony I."

"Is that cars?" she asked.

"Not necessarily," Matthew said. "Just something worth a lot of money."

Without thinking, she grabbed his phone and looked at the list. "What's that last one?" she asked, trying to decipher a string of long, vague text, followed by another felony classification with a different description that she was too tired to follow.

Matthew took his phone back, then looked at her and yawned. "That is definitely drugs or guns," he said. "You really should call and report your car stolen now."

"But that will just add to his charges!" she said.

"Not your problem," he said.

"Well, was there an address on there?" she asked.

Matthew glanced down again and nodded. "Yeah. Jackson Boulevard. The Salvation Army building."

"I'll go there in the morning and talk to him. Then I'll report the van stolen. Okay?"

Matthew yawned again. "Whatever. You do you," he said, spreading out across her couch.

"So, you're sleeping here then?"

His eyes had already closed, but he nodded. "Got any better ideas?"

She bit her lip. They'd never had one sleepover during their affair.

They'd fucked in his truck, in various Airbnbs, in her own bed, in his, and several hotel rooms—but they'd never slept in the same bed together, or even the same roof. How could they? They both had families to get home to. Plus, he slept during the day like a vampire and she slept at night, when she could sleep, anyway.

In any case, it was weird having him there. But she couldn't exactly kick him out since it was partly her fault he had nowhere else to go. Maybe it wasn't the worst thing in the world, having him around, at least on such a strange night; he had always made her feel so safe. And since her dog had died and she lived alone, she didn't exactly feel as comfortable alone at night as she used to. So she went to the closet and found some extra pillows and blankets, laying the pillow under his head and the blankets over his resting body. From the looks of it, he had already fallen asleep. She was jealous. She wished she could fall asleep that easily.

She spent half the night tossing and turning, and then Amelie barged into her room at six in the morning, demanding cereal. Once she was done eating, and noticed the mound of blankets with pale feet sticking out from the edge of the couch, Mina explained that her friend had nowhere else to go so she had let him stay over. Amelie turned back to the task at hand, flipping through a Disney princess coloring book, without as much as a confused look.

At least one thing about her day was going to be easy. Mina got dressed, and after a quick struggle with Amelie's shoes, which she had suddenly decided she hated, they were all ready to go.

"You need a ride?" Matthew grumbled from the couch as they were about to leave. She hadn't realized he was even awake, and was so surprised to hear his voice she dropped her phone.

"Don't you have work or something?" she asked him, bending over to grab it.

"No. They haven't reinstated me yet. I'm gonna go to District 1 and check on my status, and then I'm free for the rest of the day."

"Oh," she said. "Well, I guess if you're on your way out anyway,

I'll take the ride."

Matthew sat up with a groan, wiping sleep from his eyes. He found his Vans on the other side of the couch and placed them on his feet. A minute later, they were all in his truck. She tried not to think about all the various things they had done in that truck, but it was hard not to. Too many memories. She could tell he was avoiding a trip down memory lane too, judging from the smile he shook from his face once they had started driving. Once Amelie was inside her daycare, the same one Dallas used to go to, so he knew exactly where to pull up, Mina got back in the car, assuming he would take her home. But he drove her straight to the Salvation Army building on Jackson Boulevard.

"Call me if you need help," he said, pulling up to a fire hydrant and double parking there. He wouldn't look at her, and she felt even more confused than ever. "Do you want me to come in with you?"

She shook her head. If she did manage to find Dylan in there, she knew he wouldn't talk to her in Matthew's presence. No, she needed to find him alone.

"Why are you being so nice to me?" she asked, suspicious.

He shook his head and groaned. "Fine. Get the fuck out of my truck," he said, annoyed.

She rolled her eyes. "Gladly," she said. Immediately, she regretted not taking him up on his offer to come inside. The building where Dylan lived was dank and dirty and filled with bedraggled men of various sizes and ages. Testosterone poured in from every crevice and piece of skin in sight. She could practically feel every eye in the building directed right at her, and was grateful she was at least wearing a large red puffer coat over her tight ripped jeans and tank top.

"Can I help you?" asked a tattooed giant of a man. He was sitting at the front desk, his hand cradling a phone receiver to his massive shoulder, glaring at her like she had interrupted him in the middle of the best meal of his life. It was more than a tad off-putting.

She cleared her throat, her heart pounding with adrenaline. It was hot in there, so hot she had to unzip her coat, and suddenly she felt like she'd come into a war zone without any armor.

"Sorry, I'm looking for a friend of mine. Dylan Elliott?" she said, trying to keep her voice steady.

"We don't allow visitors here," growled the large man, before putting the phone back to his ear.

"Oh okay," she said, turning around to go. But before she could, she heard a voice calling out to her from behind.

"Hey!" the voice said. She turned around. It was a different man, older and heavyset, carrying a cup of coffee down the hallway as he walked. His shoes, oversized Nikes, squeaked against the linoleum floor. "You asking about Dylan?"

Mina nodded, swallowing the lump in her throat.

"Dylan didn't come back last night," he said. "Dude's MIA."

"Oh," she said. "Do you know where he could have gone?"

The man shook his head, and she caught him staring at her chest. She blushed, pulling the sides of her open coat closed. "Well wherever he is, he ain't coming back here."

"What do you mean?"

"You break curfew, you're out. They gotta pretty strict policy here."

She nodded. She was pretty sure Dylan had mentioned this to her before, which was why she was surprised not to find him there. "Okay. Thanks for letting me know."

The man took another long, creepy glance at her before turning around. "Good luck to ya."

"Thanks," she said. She had no idea then how much she would need it.

CHAPTER ELEVEN

After Mina made a quick beeline out of the Salvation Army lobby, she turned the corner and leaned against the cold brick of the building to try to catch her breath. So many things cycled through her mind in that moment. How did she end up here? What had she done in her life to lead her to this exact moment? Oh, right. Dimitry. Jiu Jitsu. Sex. And she couldn't forget Matthew. Matthew had been the start of all her unraveling. Not that she could blame him entirely, considering the state of her hormones and her overactive sex drive at the time.

Even there, under the frigid cold air, the pungent rotting smell of the nearby dumpster fresh in her nose, she was still reminded of that first conversation with January, about what had gone wrong with her marriage, her body, her life. It was seared into her memory, insight she could never seem to escape. And even then, she understood Matthew was just the symptom, not the problem.

"Mina," January said, gingerly, just as they had been about to wrap up. Mina had already grabbed her purse from the floor and stood, but when she heard the tone in January's voice she sat back down. "Why did you marry your husband, if you didn't enjoy sleeping with him?"

Mina swallowed. She had been considering this question herself a lot during that time, and it was getting harder and harder to understand it, let alone explain it. "I'm not really sure. I guess I thought maybe it would get better?" she said, then shook her head. "No, that's not the only reason. I think I was just sick of dating assholes, and Dima was just so nice. No drama. His family loved me. It just felt like what I should do. Like it was time to grow up, and he was the person I could do that with."

"Would you say you were promiscuous before you met Dimitry?"

"Oh yeah. I would sleep with anyone I was attracted to, basically. Sometimes, I barely liked them." She blushed. "I just really enjoyed sex. I know that isn't a very healthy behavior. That's why I stopped."

"You say it's an unhealthy behavior, that's interesting." January wrote something else down in her notebook, then looked up at her again. "Is it possible you married Dimitry as a punishment to yourself?"

Mina raised her eyebrows. She hadn't ever considered that. "A punishment? Why would it be a punishment?"

"For your uninhibited sex drive. Your attraction to 'assholes,' as you say," she said.

"I always thought of it as a mature decision," she answered. "Marry the nice guy who sticks around. Isn't that what we're supposed to do?"

"I only ask because of how you've described your sexual relationship with Matthew. The sado-masochism. That can also be seen as a punishment, of sorts."

She blinked. "Yeah, I guess." She looked down at her hands, which were clutched together in her lap. The gravity of it made her dizzy. If it was true, it would be difficult to unravel, let alone fix. "But I like that stuff."

"I understand that."

"What would I be punishing myself for, exactly?"

"That's hard to say. It could be all sorts of things. Maybe shame, or something from your upbringing. It's okay to want sex, and enjoy it. But when you need something, you are giving that thing your power. That's where it becomes unhealthy." January closed her notebook, then glanced at the clock. "Well. Just something to think about for next time."

And she had thought about it. She still thought about it now, all these months later, as she wondered if her celibacy was only another subconscious way of punishing herself, this time for cheating. Maybe it was, maybe it was just timing. Maybe she was doing what January suggested, taking back her power. She wasn't sure. Everything in her life last year had been so tightly controlled, every minute spent doing the things she needed to do, and hardly any doing what she wanted to do. January had eventually explained that might be where her interest in masochism had come from; as a momentary release from the burden of responsibilities and hardship. But why did she still find it attractive when men were mean to her outside of the bedroom? That part she didn't quite understand.

In any case, things had leveled out during these months she'd been alone, which felt like proof that her sex drive really was the problem. And now that she had thrown her celibacy out the window, surely she would have to pay for that somehow.

And that was when she turned her head and saw what was making that extra-pungent smell by the dumpsters. She was no longer sure it was just regular city garbage. It looked like a body. A body on top of…a bicycle?

Mina swallowed the scream boiling up in her throat and forced herself further into the alley, a hand over her nose and mouth. No reason to panic before she had reason to. She'd always had an over-active imagination, after all; an overly sensitive sense of smell. She was probably seeing a garbage bag filled at an odd angle, a dummy from a nearby clothing display. There were dozens of them up on State Street, just blocks away. And the smell was rotten, more so than usual, but Chicago was the rat capital of the country for a reason. Inching closer slowly, her eyes darted from wall to wall, looking for signs of the critters. But she saw none. Only piles of snow etched onto rivers of ice, and random debris that had been blown around to the ground. It was so slippery back there she had to hold on to the side of the building so she didn't accidentally slip. Finally, she reached the heavy dark shape she'd thought she'd seen from the corner of her eye just outside the door of the halfway house. She leaned over, the smell getting stronger, so putrid she had to hold her breath to keep herself from gagging. It appeared to be something clothed, something heavy, though she didn't see anything to tell her right away if it was a person. For that, she had to turn it over. She wrote mysteries, however, and had seen enough detective shows to know never to touch a body. Standing up again, she used the edge of her snow boot to push it a little. It hardly budged. She pushed again, this time harder. And this time, there was no question about it: what she was looking at was a body.

Dylan's body.

CHAPTER TWELVE

Mina stumbled backwards, slipping on the ice and falling down on the ground beside Dylan's cold, frozen human shape. A sharp burst of pain zigzagged across the bottom half of her body, but she could hardly register it. She guzzled down a breath of air before plugging her nose again, the smell of it too much to bear. She must have been in shock, because she felt stuck in place, the snow and ice slowly melting into her clothes. Pushing herself forward on her hands and knees, it was all she could do to angle her head far enough away from the corpse to puke out everything she'd digested recently on the white snow next to it.

She scrambled to her feet, wiping her mouth and nose, looking to see if anyone had stopped walking down Jackson to notice her there, puking on the icy ground. But it looked like business as usual. Only then did it occur to her what she needed to do. She had to call the cops. Or an ambulance, at the very least. She took her phone out of her pocket, her hands shaking so hard she was glad she had finally installed facial recognition so she wouldn't have to attempt typing in the number code.

When it opened, she asked Siri to call 911. As it began ringing, however, she changed her mind. As a resident of the south side, even if it wasn't the really bad part, she had called 911 on more than one occasion. It took forever to get through, and even longer for police to respond, being that there was so much rampant crime in Chicago. Reaching again into her pocket she fished out the business card she'd received the previous night. Then she ended the call and, holding down the home button, spoke out the number written on it.

"Detective Conner," a rough voice growled on the other end.

"Hi," she said, surprised how high-pitched her voice sounded suddenly. Shrill, even. She cleared her throat. "Uh, this is Mina Banksy? We spoke last night?"

"Yes, of course. What can I do for you, Ms. Banksy?" the man said, sounding more relaxed now. "You think of something that can help us?"

"Um, yeah," she said, and suddenly her eyes filled with tears and she started crying so hard she could hardly speak.

"Ms. Banksy? You all right? You sound distressed. You need an officer to come help you? I can be there in ten, just find a safe place to—"

Mina swallowed, forcing herself to breathe, then speak. "Sorry—I'm okay. It's just that… I found Dylan."

"Oh," he said, startled. "When we spoke yesterday, Ms. Banksy, I didn't mean for you to go—"

"I mean—I found…his body."

There was silence on the other end of the line, followed by some static, something being jostled or moved. "Where are you?"

"In the alley behind the Salvation Army building. 324 Jackson Blvd."

"I'll send some uniforms over there immediately, and I'll be right behind them, ma'am. Just stay put." She heard some talking in the distance, then his voice returned. "And don't touch anything."

She swallowed, still able to taste the vomit in her mouth. She had to pull her scarf up over her mouth keep from puking again. "I won't."

Ten long minutes later, as a team of uniformed cops and an EMT poured into the narrow alley, Mina hadn't moved from the cold circle of ground she'd been sitting on when she called the detective. She was probably still in shock. She couldn't stop staring at Dylan's body, at his worn, chiseled face, now blue and disfigured.

His blank eyes surrounded by little red dots. At the slivers of skin between his sneakers and pant legs, pale and covered in little hairs. They hadn't been as close as she and Matthew, or even Felix, but she considered him a good friend, someone she was always happy to see either at the gym or when he showed up at her house unannounced and she'd make him a cup of tea, because he didn't drink now that he was done using.

She'd seen dead bodies before, of course; in the last ten years, the cascade of deaths in her family had left her feeling more alone than ever before. First her mom, then both sets of grandparents. Even an uncle had passed, and her only close cousin. So many that if she wanted to be among family she was better off going to the cemetery where they were all buried next to each other. This loneliness had been a large part of why she couldn't give up her relationship with Matthew; she had so few close people in her life, and without him, she had even less. Still, this was different. Dylan was her age. They had grown up a few suburbs apart, probably knew some of the same people. And judging by the crime scene analysis thus far, and the amount of little yellow flags being placed around his body, she didn't think Dylan had died of natural causes. Or an overdose, for that matter.

"Ms. Banksy?" a voice said.

She looked up to find Detective Conner standing over her, reaching out a hand for her to shake. But she was still frozen in place. Beside him was a uniformed cop holding a blanket. Only then did she realize she was shaking. The cop took the liberty of placing it around her.

"You up to answering some questions?" he asked. "Officer Menlo would like to take a statement."

She swallowed, then nodded. "That's fine. Can I just… get some water?" Mina looked towards the 7-11 across the street, and managed to force her legs into a standing position. She was about to start walking in that direction when someone put a warm plastic bottle in her hand. She turned around to see Matthew standing there. Where had he come from? However he had managed to find her, she was suddenly relieved, like she could let out a breath. Just his mere presence leveled her. Which she knew made no sense, considering all that inner violence he had inside him, but for some reason he still made her feel safe despite it.

"Matthew?" Detective Conner asked, also noticing his arrival. "I didn't realize you were back. Why aren't you in uniform?"

"Uh, I'm not, officially." He moved closer to Mina and put a hand on her shoulder, squeezing it tight. He watched her and waited until her gaze met his. "You okay?"

She shrugged, breaking eye contact. She didn't want to lie. Okay was not exactly how she would describe her feelings at that moment.

Detective Conner looked between the two of them, his brows furrowing. "Friend of yours?" he asked, but she wasn't sure if he was addressing her or Matthew, and apparently neither did Matthew, because they both answered at the same time.

"Yeah," she said, right as Matthew said, "Something like that."

She gave him an annoyed, quizzical look, which the detective must have interpreted accurately because the next thing she knew he was shaking his head. A cold wind swept in around them, and she shivered.

"I see," he said, averting his eyes. He cleared his threat. "Officer Stone, we were just about to take a statement from Ms. Banksy, so…"

Matthew crossed his arms over his chest. "I'd like to be there for that."

The detective's brows furrowed even further. "I'm not sure that's—"

Mina swallowed the water she'd guzzled from the bottle and began nodding. "I'd like that too. Please."

"She's not under arrest, right?" Matthew asked.

"Under arrest? No, of course not—"

"Okay. Then I'll bring her to the station," Matthew said, grabbing her shoulder again, this time pushing her forward, past the detectives. He turned around to face them. "Unless there's a reason you want this young lady to freeze to death out here?"

Detective Conner sighed. "Fine. I'll just finish up here and we will meet you down there in fifteen minutes or so. That work for you, officer?" At the word officer, she detected more than a hint of annoyance. But Matthew ignored it.

"See you there," he said, pushing her through the narrow, crowded passage and into his truck, double parked in the exact same spot as where he had dropped her off.

"What was that about?" she asked him as she grabbed the handle of the passenger-side door.

"Not now," he hissed. Once they were in the truck, Matthew put his pale hand over his face and ran it up and down several times.

"What?" she asked, rubbing her hands together for warmth, and curling her knees up under her coat. "You're acting like you're the one that just found a dead body."

Matthew exhaled, then reached into his pocket to extract a set of keys, starting the truck. He pulled a cigarette from behind his ear and lit it, handing it over to her after only one drag. "Figured you'd be needing that." She did need that, more than anything. She took a long delicious drag as he started driving, opening the window a crack. He handed her a piece of gum. "And that."

She took the gum and popped it into her mouth. It reminded her for a moment that this was the sort of thing he dealt with for work on a daily basis. No wonder he was so messed up. "Matthew. What are you doing here?"

"I heard it come up on the radio when I was at the district, and I thought, hell, I know that address. And I know someone who might be looking through an alley there too," he said, shaking his head. "Still hoped I was wrong."

"It's Dylan," she said, her voice choked.

He nodded. "I saw."

Mina blinked back the rush of tears that were once again threatening to exit her face in an overwhelming river of emotion. "I…" She swallowed, and took another drag of the cigarette, before speaking again. "I feel like it's my fault somehow."

Matthew began shaking his head. "No, Mina. Get that out of your head right now. He knew the game."

"But if I had let him stay last night…"

"Then you would have found him in that alley tomorrow instead. That's all."

She closed her eyes, leaning her head into the seat. She felt the heat of Matthew's hand on her leg and let herself relax a little.

"This is why I came straight over. You can't blame yourself when you talk to the cops, okay? And you cannot—I repeat—you cannot tell them you saw Dylan last night. You don't know anything, and you only went there this morning to ask about your van. That's it."

She nodded, her eyes still closed, and listened to the humming of the engine for several minutes before speaking again. "You know, sometimes I still can't believe they let you be a cop."

Matthew laughed. "Yeah, I was kind of surprised too."

Mina curbed a smile off her face. She could guess how he had passed the psych exam; he was capable of acting normal sometimes, nice even. It was just that his true self, the darker, not nice side, was always battling his good side, and it was a universal truth for a reason that bad was stronger than good. It seemed pretty clear which would win out.

The only reason he hadn't cheated on Ariel for fifteen years beforehand could have been more a matter of trust, of not finding the right person to do it with, someone with just as much to lose if the secret got out. And then he found her. Or they'd found each other, maybe. Not that either of them had intended for it to become such a long, drawn-out affair; it was practically an entire relationship by the end. Once feelings got involved, they should have stopped it, but they only got more confused, more entangled. And the sex only got better and better, which certainly didn't help. At several points they had even considered leaving their spouses for each other, but either he or she always ended up deciding against it. She was no longer sure why; probably they were both just scared. It wasn't like they lacked chemistry or things to talk about.

She shook her head and sighed. She wanted to kick herself for letting her mind go there again. How many times in the last year had she tortured herself with these thoughts? Her eyes were still closed, and she could feel Matthew's hand moving lower to her knee, caressing it gently. She knew that would be the closest she would ever get to some kind of empathetic display for what she'd been through, but it was fine, because it was more than she had ever expected from him already. It was still hard to wrap her head around the fact that he was back in Chicago, that he was next to her at all. For a moment she even forgot about Dylan's bloodshot eyes, his waxen frozen head.

But then just as quickly she was thinking about it again. Suddenly, she remembered something else, something she had been unable to focus on at the time due to all the adrenaline and disgust coursing through her body. She opened her eyes and sat up.

"Do you think he was strangled?" she asked, squeezing Matthew's hand tight.

"Huh?"

"His eyes. There were all those little red spots around them, you know, like burst blood vessels?" she said.

"I didn't get a good look at him," he said. "But if you say they're there, possibly."

She leaned back in the truck seat again. "They're gonna think someone from the gym did it," she said in a near whisper.

"What? No, they won't. Do you know how many people get murdered around here on a daily basis? You don't need to know Jiu Jitsu."

She shook her head. "I don't know," she said. "No marks on his neck."

"That you could see."

"Seemed like someone who knew their way around some arteries."

Matthew looked at her for a moment, then back at the road.

"Not saying it's impossible," Matthew said. "But why would anyone from the gym want to kill Dylan?"

"That I don't know," Mina said. The truck began to slow down, the CPD building looming ahead. Matthew put his blinker on and then turned slowly into the parking lot. "But I had the same looking dots that time you…you know."

"Oh, I remember," he said, parking the car and turning it off. He smiled, eyes flicking over her face. "Hard thing to forget."

"Yeah, I'm sure it is. Don't get to choke out a lot of females and not get arrested for it, I imagine."

"You imagine correct," he said, with a laugh. "Lots of things I did to you I could get arrested for."

"Oh, I know," she said. "That time I gave you head while you were driving? And you had that open beer in there too?"

Matthew laughed again. "I actually forgot about that," he said. "Yeah, that was probably the worst one."

"Definitely."

"As I recall, you had a pretty great time," he said, turning to wink at her.

She shook her head again. He was right. She always had a good time with him. "It was the uniform," she explained. "It's always that damn uniform."

"Oh, I know."

"I can't believe we're talking about this right now. I have to go give my statement about finding Dylan's body, and we're rehashing our fucked up sexual past?"

Matthew turned off the truck and placed his keys in his lap. "Well, it took your mind off seeing a corpse, right?"

"I guess…"

He pointed at her. "You stopped shaking," he said. She looked down and realized he was right. "You ready?"

"No," she said. "But is anyone ever ready? For anything?" She thought about Jiu Jitsu, and her divorce, and Amelie. All of it she had felt unprepared for in a deep, disturbing way, but she had managed to get through it eventually. Maybe it would be the same with this.

Matthew took the cigarette from her and inhaled, finishing it in one drag. He opened the door and tossed the butt to the ground. "It's like anything else, Mina. Just take it one step at a time."

They didn't talk again until Matthew had walked her through the building, winding his way through various hallways and swarms of people, both criminal and police. Something was said about Officer Menlo, how he wasn't going to be taking her statement after all, and they were redirected down another hallway. It smelled like burnt coffee and bleach in equal parts, the lights so bright they hurt her eyes. Finally, they were at an office door, one that said Senior Detective Andrew Conner. He'd beaten them there, somehow, and was already at his desk writing furiously into a notepad when Matthew began knocking on the door.

She watched as he stood up and walked over to them, opening the door expectantly.

"Good to see you again, officer," he said. Then he turned to Mina. "Thank you for coming down, Ms. Banksy. Now, you mind if we speak in private?"

She turned to Matthew, who was looking at him with confusion. "Officer Stone, as I understand it from your lieutenant, you're not officially back on duty yet. Therefore, I don't see how this conversation will be relevant to you. And besides that, it's not really—"

"Fine. I'll wait in the hall," Matthew said, leaving the room without as much as a glance in her direction. Mina sat down, feeling herself get nervous again. She was lightheaded and the bright fluorescent lights above them were starting to give her a headache. Or maybe it was the fact that she had expunged everything she'd eaten that day, barely drank any water, and then smoked a cigarette on top of it.

"Now, Ms. Banksy—"

"Please. Call me Mina," she said. "Ms. Banksy makes me sound like an old lady."

He chuckled. "As you wish," he said, reaching for his pen and paper. "Mina. Take me through what happened this morning."

"Sure. I went to Dylan's rehab to see if he was there. I wanted to find out what he's been up to with his—my—van."

Detective Conner looked up. "Last night you said you didn't know where he lived. Was that a lie?"

"No. I didn't know then," she said. "I only found out later."

"And how did you come upon this information?" he asked.

Mina stared at his desk, the cluttered collection of papers, pens, and fast-food wrappers distracting her from her racing heart. "Um. Matthew looked it up."

"I see," he said, taking down more notes. "So this morning, you called and asked Matthew to look up Dylan's address."

"No. It was last night."

Detective Conner looked through his notes and then raised his head. "We left your house at… nine thirty p.m. So, this would have been what, after ten? A little late for a house call, no?"

Mina tried to keep her face neutral, glancing up for a moment and then continuing to stare at his desk. "I'm sorry, I don't see how that's relevant."

"Just trying to get a picture of the timeline of events, Ms. Banksy. I mean, Mina."

Mina forced her gaze to meet his. "I didn't call him with the intention of getting Dylan's whereabouts. It's just that when I told him about your visit, he offered to help. I didn't even know he was back in Chicago."

"Huh," the detective said. His eyes bored into hers, trying to register something she couldn't quite place.

"What?" she asked. "We're friends."

"Nothing. Keep going," he said.

"So by then it was late, and I couldn't really go anywhere with Amelie asleep in her bed. That's why I waited until the morning to go look for Dylan, once she was in school," she said. "That's what we call daycare. Anyway, I went inside to see if I could talk to him, and someone told me he hadn't come back last night, so I left."

Detective Conner wrote all this down, then paused, waiting for her to continue.

"That place sort of frazzled me, I guess," she started.

"How so?"

"It was just…I don't know, creepy," she said. "I kind of ran out of there as quickly as I could, and turned the corner just to catch my breath. And that's when I noticed the smell."

Detective Conner's eyebrows raised. "The smell?"

"Yeah. That's what I noticed first. I have a very sensitive nose," she explained. "I thought maybe it was just that the city hasn't been around in a while to empty out the dumpsters, but when I looked down the alley, I thought I saw a body. That's how I found Dylan."

"So you smelled something odd, and went down an alley by yourself? That didn't seem dangerous to you?"

"Why would it be dangerous? It was, like, nine in the morning."

"Still. It's not the safest area for a young lady to be poking around alleys."

She stopped herself from rolling her eyes. "I'll keep that in mind next time I find a dead body next to a dumpster. Thanks."

Detective Conner smiled wearily, his thick gray mustache twitching. "I just mean it seemed like maybe you knew something bad had happened with Dylan. Or you know something about that vehicle you lent him. Is that what made you spend your day chasing after him?"

She shook her head. "No. It was just a coincidence."

"In my line of work, there are not a lot of coincidences."

"What exactly are you implying? That I'm involved in all this somehow, because I let Dylan use my van?"

"No, not at all," he said, leaning back in his chair, which made a loud squeaky noise on its descent. "I don't think you're involved. I just think you're not telling me everything."

"I told you exactly how I found Dylan. What else do you need to know?"

Detective Conner reached for his notes, shuffling through the pages before finding one that appeared to be covered with a long list of names. "Now, this gym you mentioned, the Jiu Jitsu gym. I took the liberty of checking the membership listing, and I noticed that not only was Dylan a member, but so were you. And Matthew. Until six months ago, that is, when you both canceled your memberships."

An aching began in her stomach again. She took the bottle of water and forced herself to drink it. "Again, I don't see how that's relevant."

"Forget the van for a moment. It's since gone missing anyway. This is now a murder investigation, Ms. Banksy," he said. "Everything is relevant."

She blinked, trying once more to ignore the bright lights, but she felt a deep headache coming on. "Do I need a lawyer?" she asked.

"Well, that depends on you. Do you think you need a lawyer?"

She shrunk into her chair. She had no idea how to talk to the police. Why had she thought her writing would prepare her for any of this? The fact that she wrote about the police sometimes didn't make her any more well-equipped to handle their questioning than her characters, nor did the fact that she had slept with a police officer countless times. When he handcuffed her in bed, it was not the same as being handcuffed in a police station, which felt more and more possible the longer she sat there. She wanted to get out of there. She needed a drink. A strong, alcoholic one. Or at least a nap. Anything would be preferable to sitting under Detective Conner's wary gaze for another moment.

"One last question and you can go," Detective Conner said, piling the pages on top of each other into a neat stack. "I know you've had a rough day. I can see you're still in shock."

"It's definitely been a day," she mumbled, crossing her arms over her chest.

"Dimitry Polyakov," he said. "That's your husband, correct?"

"Ex," she corrected, her brows narrowing. What did he have to do with this? "We're separated."

"He's also listed as a member at the gym," he said. "Until six months ago."

She nodded, trying not to react. Mina didn't think it was any of his business what had happened six months ago, but she knew if he didn't already suspect, he would probably be asking her about it any second now. Or maybe he already assumed.

"I'm sorry to have to bring this up, but like I said, since this is now a murder investigation, I need to get some clarity here," he said. "You, Officer Stone, and your husband were all members of Open Guard until you up and quit within the same month. Perhaps it is a bit forward of me, but I have to ask: what happened six months ago?"

Her heart began thumping loudly in her chest, and she was so damp with sweat she felt it dripping through her clothes. He clearly had an idea of what had happened, and if he could see the color of her face, which she could feel turning pink, she was only confirming his suspicions. But this was not something she felt compelled to have on public record.

"I think I'd like to call a lawyer now," she mumbled, squeezing the bottle in her hand so hard water began pouring out of it onto her lap.

Detective Conner leaned back into his chair, a thick, judgmental smirk on his face. "That won't be necessary. I think I have all the information I need."

JULY

CHAPTER THIRTEEN

When Mina returned from class the night Dima came home, he met her by the front door with his arms crossed and a frown on his face. For a moment, she began to panic. Had she left some sort of evidence of Matthew somewhere? Had she not cleaned the bed well enough? Could he just feel that another man had spread his seed all over their bedroom? Mina really wasn't sure. She stopped in the doorway, her Gi drenched in sweat, the edges of her hair wet and curling, shoulders tight and sore. She had really gotten her ass kicked today. But she at least felt better after she'd had some exercise. Well, until now. Now her nerves began fraying all at once.

"What, Dima?" she finally forced herself to ask, making her way quickly across the living room towards the bathroom.

"What happened in the basement?" Dima asked, following her.

"Huh?" she asked. In order to avoid eye contact, she stepped into the bathroom and turned on the shower, slowly taking off her Gi pants and top, her back turned.

"It's really wet down there. Did it get flooded? And who's sump pump is that?" he asked.

Mina was glad she was already so red from rolling, because she would have surely given herself away. She stepped into the shower and stood directly under the water, pushing the shower curtain closed between them. "Oh, right. There was something wrong with the pipe by the water heater. It just started leaking everywhere. Matthew

124

came by and helped me with it."

"Oh. That's nice of him," Dima said. Was that suspicion in his voice? But no, he was looking more concerned than anything. Would everything that had to do with the gym or Matthew now make her sweat with panic? Did he somehow realize something was off with her? She held her breath, waiting for his response.

"You should give him back his sump pump," he said. "Did you call a plumber to see what was wrong?"

She swallowed. From the bedroom, she could hear Winnie the Pooh singing about honey. "Not yet," she mumbled. She had completely forgotten about it, in fact. "I will."

Dima wouldn't leave the bathroom, though. He was really a stickler about home maintenance. "When did that happen?" Dima asked.

"Like maybe a week ago?" she said.

"The pipe broke a week ago and you didn't call a plumber?" he asked.

"I said I will."

"Mina—"

"I was a little busy?" she said, which was true. "I work and have a toddler?" She really had forgotten about it entirely. Furthermore, she had no space left in her brain to add another problem to her life. Even before the thing with Matthew, she always went to bed feeling like she was barely treading water, never able to get to the surface. There was always something just out of reach, some thing she had to do that she forgot or didn't have time to get to. There were deadlines and doctor's appointments and playdates and groceries to buy, and never enough hours in the day. That's just what it was like to have a child. She thought it would be easier once Amelie had gotten a bit older, but while some things became easier, like naptime and eating, other things became harder, like keeping Amelie entertained, so that the scales never really tipped too far in any direction. Plus, now there were tantrums. So many tantrums. She actually missed the newborn stage at times.

Mina turned the water up even hotter, steam engulfing the room. Considering the other things she had done while he was away, she shouldn't have been annoyed, and yet she was. That was what happened in a marriage. The same petty grievances circled themselves around, keeping you constantly ready to fly off the handle, like clay that's already been scored. In this case, at least, it would direct the attention away from her wrongdoings. He was so busy being frustrated at her for not maintaining order in the house that he could barely notice what was really going on.

"You said Maya helped you a lot," Dima said, concerned.

"She did, but just for Jiu Jitsu. She's twelve, she can't really manage watching Amelie for more than an hour. Plus, your sister has her entire schedule packed to the brim with activities. The girl barely has a second to breathe."

For a moment, it was quiet, and all she could hear was the hot water running over her bruised body. She stuck her head out to see if Dima had stormed out, but he was still standing there, rubbing his temples. Now she began to feel guilty. Part of her had expected him to take one look at her and accuse her of adultery. But maybe Matthew was right. People couldn't read your mind. She would have to go on acting as if nothing at all had changed. Like they were just the same old married couple they always had been.

"What is it?" she asked.

He sighed. "Mina, we barely covered our bills this month. We can't afford to get mold in the basement."

"We're not getting mold in the basement! There was a sump pump, remember?"

He took in a deep breath. "Matthew is a cop, not a plumber. Whatever he did to stop the water from leaking is probably not a permanent solution. For all you know, it's leaking again right now."

"But it's not. You were just down there," she said, her voice starting to tremble a little at the sound of Matthew's name. She hadn't seen him at the gym earlier and had felt a little disappointed. He must have already been at work, or he was sleeping after a late shift. It was probably for the best, she figured, and yet, it only fed her desires that much more to keep herself away from him longer. Hearing his name made her entire body flutter with nerves, her desire now entirely tangled up in dishonesty and stress and panic. Was this how life was going to be now?

"I'll call a plumber tomorrow," Mina added, clearing her throat.

"And please stop asking our friends to do you favors," Dima added. "You know I hate that."

Normally, this sort of statement would result in some level of dispute, but this time, she knew better than to argue. She was just relieved that he hadn't pressed the issue with Matthew coming over. A feeling in her gut of utter panic combined with guilt began to grow.

"Okay," she mumbled, hearing him leave the bathroom. It took her five minutes to stop panicking and another five to stop feeling guilty. When she got out of the shower, dripping water all over their hardwood floors, she passed Amelie's room, where Dima was reading a story to Amelie in the rocking chair that Mina once used to feed her in the middle of the night. She was dressed in her *Little Mermaid* PJs and sitting so patiently in his lap, in a way she would never do for her. This was the first moment it really hit her what she had done. For a moment, an aching sorrow, which started in the pit of her stomach and then bloomed across her body, nearly took her breath away. Then she blinked, and it was gone.

CHAPTER FOURTEEN

Now that Dima was back, Mina became determined to end things with Matthew. Even if that meant sacrificing the gym temporarily, and even if that meant she had to spend every single day thinking about Matthew, thinking about what they had done and how much she wanted to do more of it. There were moments she was thinking about him so hard she worried his name might come right out of her lips. And yet, for a week, she exaggerated her menstrual cramps and let Dima go to all the night classes, and she went to a couple of the noon classes in the West Loop instead.

In some ways, it helped that she was so busy. And the fact that Matthew worked nights so the only way it was truly safe to message him was when he was at work, and she was usually already asleep by then; she couldn't risk it when he could be at home with Ariel, or when she was at home with Dima, so she just didn't text him. He didn't text her either, so she figured he either understood or had come to the same conclusion.

Her days began to feel lackluster and uninteresting, but at least they were quiet. Time dragged on this way, slowly, bogged down with immense heat, heat so suffocating she was kind of glad to miss Jiu Jitsu. Instead of going to the gym, she spent a lot of her days chasing Amelie around the parks of Chicago, lost in thought. She was there so often that it caught her entirely by surprise when a CPD car pulled up beside her at the entrance to McGuane Park, its lights swirling.

Was she getting pulled over? Could they do that to a pedestrian? She broke out in a cold sweat and looked down at the ground, hoping the lights were directed at a car ahead. But then a voice called out to her from the driver's seat.

"Hey," the voice said. Her heart began racing. She wasn't doing anything wrong walking Amelie to a playground, but she had a very healthy fear of authority.

The car pulled forward until it was right beside her. Amelie waved at the car, a big smile on her face, and only then did she realize who was in the driver's seat.

"Hi!" Amelie screamed.

Mina turned to find Matthew in the driver's seat, alone.

Amelie loved cars, and she could see even from her stroller that his car had a lot of extra screens and buttons to mess with compared to a regular car, so she began trying to jump out of the stroller to get in there. But Mina, who had never seen Matthew on duty before, felt strangely uncomfortable suddenly. It turned her on as much as it unnerved her. She held Amelie by the hand and told her to wait.

"What are you doing here?" Mina asked, in a near-whisper. "This isn't your district." She didn't know that much about what he did at work, but she had known fairly early on that he had chosen a station outside of Bridgeport specifically to avoid running into people he might know—if she remembered correctly, it was somewhere downtown, or possibly River North.

She wasn't sure what made her more nervous: the fact that he had come out here to look for her, or the fact that even if he wasn't in his own district, he was a cop, and she had chosen to forget this several times over the course of the last few weeks. Of course he could find her anytime he wished. He certainly had the resources. Also, she was a mom of an antsy toddler; there weren't that many places where she might be at any given time.

Matthew stuck his arm out the window and squinted in her direction. He was chewing gum and looking far too nonchalant, all things considered. She noticed a young group of teenagers look their way and cross the street to the nature preserve that was also a park and hiking trail. Cigarettes or maybe joints trailed behind them. Matthew was undeterred. "Come get dinner with me," he suggested.

Mina paused, frowning. Amelie was still pulling on her arm, and Mina stuck her back in the stroller, handing her a packet of fruit snacks that she kept in her pockets for emergencies. "Dinner?" She glanced down at her watch. "It's eleven a.m."

"Yeah, I was supposed to get off a few hours ago," he said, as casually as if they were just acquaintances running into each other. "But I got stuck at work."

Curiosity got the best of her. Part of why they'd gotten so close at the gym was because she loved hearing about Matthew's job. She spent an inordinate amount of time talking to all the cops at the gym, actually, the ones who enjoyed sharing that information with her. Some of them really did not. "Why's that?" she asked.

Matthew waved his hand absently. "We had to arrest this guy, arrests take forever. So much paperwork."

"What did you arrest him for?"

He let out a long breath. "It was a domestic thing. Guy's wife has a restraining order out on him, which he chose to ignore," he said. "Almost had to tackle him."

"Well, you're pretty good at that," she said, trying to make light of the situation. Amelie began squirming in the stroller again and whining to go in the car. "Just get him in that rear-naked choke."

"We're actually not allowed to do chokes," he said. "Anyway, hop in."

She looked at him skeptically, then looked at Amelie, who was about halfway into his window by now. Mina grabbed her and sat her back down. "You want me to go in your police car? With Amelie?"

He leaned back into the seat, thinking on it for a moment. "I can meet you there," he said. He slid on a pair of aviator sunglasses, which made him look all the more authoritative for whatever reason.

She didn't feel like she had the choice to say no.

"Where?" she asked.

"What's that coffee shop you like so much?"

"Bridgeport Coffee?"

"Yeah. I'll meet you there," he said. "Coffee with soy, right?"

"How do you even know that?" she asked. She had hardly finished the question, however, before he had sped off.

She watched him drive down Halsted towards 31st Street, going at least ten miles over the speed limit, and began sweating profusely. She wasn't sure if it was because she did want to see him, or because the whole situation had suddenly become fairly stressful. She had Amelie with her and they were in public. Yet Mina really felt as if she had no choice in the matter, so she walked the four blocks over to Bridgeport Coffee, ignoring Amelie's meltdown as they passed Cermak, one of the local supermarkets. Dima didn't leave the house much between deliveries, and Bridgeport Coffee was busy enough that it wouldn't be too noticeable, them having coffee. Or so she hoped.

When she got there, she found Matthew sitting at a wobbly table near the front. He had a mug and a donut in front of him, the sun from the large windows drowning his head in bright yellow light.

"I thought you said cops don't eat donuts because it's too cliché now," Mina said.

"Definitely not in public." Matthew laughed.

She sat down, pulling Amelie's stroller beside them. Amelie practically jumped out of her seat trying to reach for Matthew's donut. She was about to stop her when Matthew handed it to her.

"I actually got it for Amelie," he explained.

"Oh," she said, watching Amelie immediately smear chocolate all over her cheeks. It was the happiest (and quietest) she'd seen her all day, which wasn't too surprising. She loved sweets. They usually didn't let her eat a lot of sugar, because when she did, she became a monster about getting more. It was kind of like Mina and cigarettes. Or Mina and Matthew. Whatever that feeling was that was so encompassing and pleasurable that you wanted to repeat it endlessly no matter how bad it was for you, it was clearly derived from your id, or whatever it was that two-year-olds were controlled by. Being an adult only meant you had to learn to process it and ignore it better. She and Matthew were doing a pretty bad job of this, so how would she really be able to tell Amelie she wasn't allowed to have chocolate? Of all the bad behaviors going on, a donut was by far the least offensive.

"The coffee is yours," he said, pointing at the mug. "I'm waiting on a sandwich. They any good here?"

"No, not really," she said. She took the mug, and started drinking it. Her sweat output doubled immediately. It was boiling hot in there, the A/C dripping over the front door barely making a dent in the heat of the old, small space, but she had never liked iced coffee so she was used to it. At least she didn't recognize anyone. Bridgeport Coffee wasn't like the gym, where she knew everyone and talked to them all the time because she went there daily. She had never talked to the baristas in any of the local Chicago coffee shops, and only knew them by face. There seemed to be a rule in Chicago about being a barista, which was that you had to be as short-tempered and unfriendly as possible to your customers.

"So, what is this? A date?" she asked.

"No, it's not a date. I wanted to see you." He shrugged. "Is that so wrong?"

"Yeah, kinda," she said. She looked towards Amelie, who was generally not able to last sitting at a café for more than two minutes but was so happy to eat her donut she wasn't making a peep. Having his own toddler, Matthew probably knew this would happen.

"You've been avoiding the gym again," he said.

She looked up at him and nodded.

"Stop doing that," he said. Matthew continued chewing his gum, watching her with a deadpan stare she could see even with his aviators on.

"I have to," she said. "It's just too…"

"What?"

"It's too hard to see you right now. I don't trust myself around you."

Matthew smirked, raising his brows slightly over the tops of his sunglasses. "Okay," he said, nodding.

"What?" she asked.

"Remember what I taught you about getting your leg unstuck from half guard?"

"Yeah. *Turn and Face Your Problems.*" This was meant to be taken literally; she had to sit down and turn towards the person in order to get the right angle for leg removal. It had been very helpful to learn. Many of the moves they learned in Jiu Jitsu involved turning and "facing your problem," actually, which generally meant facing the person instead of turning your back to them. It was against your nature to do this, and it had taken many months for her to untrain her brain so that when someone tried to trap her from the side, she had to turn to face them to get out.

"Is that what you're doing by avoiding the gym?" he asked.

She shook her head, pleased as she was at the metaphor. Not that he had invented it. Jonah had often sung its praises as a lifestyle, yet she saw generally the inverse of this off the mats. As much as she loved the gym, she wasn't blind to its faults. It attracted a lot of people with problems, ones they ignored or didn't even notice, the flagrant alcoholism being only the start of it. Marriages in freefall, depression, and complete social ineptitude were as common as not. Black belts in particular seemed to have full reign on inappropriate behavior towards women that was all kept very hush hush, like priests in the catholic church.

Then there were people like Dylan, who could hardly stay out of prison long enough to be allowed to live in an unsupervised apartment. "That is not the same. That's not my leg getting trapped by your legs. If I go to the gym and see you, I want you. And that's not fair to Dima."

"Is that the real reason?" he asked, frowning.

"It also stresses me out too much. People aren't idiots. They notice things, and then they talk about it when you're not around. They notice us talking so much."

"Nothing wrong with talking, Mina," he said. "You start changing your behavior drastically, that's really when you start to look suspicious. Just act normal."

She thought about it. Was he right? With him in uniform, talking to her in this critical voice, she couldn't shake the feeling that she was in trouble for something. But not with Dima—with Matthew. Which made no sense. If anything, it should have been the opposite. "Normal? Like making out in the girls' changing room?"

Matthew folded a napkin on the table, then unfolded it. "Sorry," he said with a shrug. "We shouldn't have done that."

Mina put her fingers on her temples. Talking to him was one of the most frustrating things she'd had to do in a long time. Every time they had a conversation, she only felt more confused after. It was the exact opposite of her conversations with Dima, which usually helped her make sense of things. "Don't you feel...?" She paused as someone began grinding espresso beans behind them, then started again when the grinding ended. "Bad? About what we did?"

"I do. You know that," he said. "But I also like seeing you. This thing between us."

She forced herself to take a deep breath. Even though it was packed, and people were constantly coming and going and bumping her shoulder as they did it, she couldn't help but feel like everyone was staring at them. Cops had a gravity to them that made you want to look. She used to do it all the time.

"You feel differently?" he asked her.

She shook her head. "I don't know. I'm confused. Some days I feel so guilty I think it's going to pop right out of my mouth."

Matthew swallowed, his face turning tense. "Well, don't do that."

"I'm trying my best here. It's not like I want to tell him. He might kill me, seriously."

"Well, I might kill you if you tell him," he said.

A tightness began to grow around her chest. She narrowed her eyes and looked at him. "Do you really mean that? Because I can't tell."

Matthew shook his head, but it wasn't clear if it was from annoyance or denial. "We're turning into a broken record," he said, letting out a frustrated breath of air. "No one gets killed. No one gets divorced. I don't want that for Dallas."

Amelie took a break from her donut to look at them and ask: "Dalleh?" She started looking around the café, as if just noticing her friend wasn't there. She still had trouble pronouncing full words and certain letters; it had been a rather large source of conflict at their house as of late, the speech delays. Dima and Mina were of two different minds on what to do; she thought Amelie would grow out of it and that they shouldn't push her. Dima thought they should spend every spare second of the day going over flashcards and sending her to speech therapists and doctors, but then he was never in town long enough to take her himself, so it would fall on her. She had been taking her, but so far it hadn't helped much.

"Amelie, honey, Dallas isn't here, she's at school."

"Dalleh, schoo," Amelie said in return.

"That's right." Mina nodded. "You don't have school today. But Dallas does."

Amelie didn't respond and went back to her donut.

A garbled voice began speaking from the radio on Matthew's shoulder, but he ignored it. She couldn't get past seeing him in uniform. It was extremely sexy, and it made it very hard for her to keep her hands off him. She was supposed to be in control here, putting a stop to things. That was why she had been avoiding the gym, after all. Wasn't it? But in that moment, all she wanted to do was put her hand on the crotch of his uniform pants and start unzipping them. The couple of times they'd had sex with him in uniform were etched permanently into her memory.

"You need to go?" she asked, looking at the radio.

"No," he said. "That's not for me."

For a while, they didn't say anything. She didn't know what to say, because she didn't really understand why they were having coffee in the first place. Unless he was trying to tell the entire world that they were having an affair. Correction: that they had had an affair. Technically, it was not currently still happening, not that they had made that official by saying it out loud. Technically they were just two friends having coffee in a loud coffee shop playing Tegan and Sara, as if she needed more ways to feel nineteen again.

Someone called out Matthew's name, and for a moment she began panicking, worrying it was someone they knew. But it was just the barista with his sandwich. Matthew stood up to grab it, then sat back down to eat it in silence. Mina put her head in her hands and tried to calm down. But she really couldn't. Not with Tegan and Sara playing, not with all this strong coffee in her system. Not with this intense energy coursing between them even as they didn't speak. It was there, and it wasn't nothing. She would have killed for a cigarette.

Amelie turned to Mina. "Mama okay?" Amelie asked, though the way she said it, it sounded more like yoo-kay. This was a new phrase of Amelie's that she'd been repeating all week, but it was the first time she used it in context. Usually it was a bit random, unless she was asking it of her dolls.

She blinked, surprised. "Yes, baby. I'm okay."

Matthew finished his sandwich and looked at her. "Huh. I don't know. She doesn't seem so okay. Why is mommy so sad?" he asked.

"Matthew," she groaned.

"I think it's because she needs a vacation," Matthew told her, wiping the edge of his mouth with a napkin. "Have you ever been on vacation?"

"Vac-ayshoh?" she repeated, pinching another piece of donut off with her tiny fingers and shoving it in her mouth.

"Yeah. Like you go on an airplane, then find a beach to sit on, have some snacks at the hotel. Have you been to a hotel, Amelie?"

Amelie shook her head no, looking very serious, despite the brown chocolate icing smeared across her chubby cheeks.

"It's a place where mommies and daddies go to sleep sometimes, when they need a break," he explained. His radio garbled again, but he ignored it.

"Like nap time," he added, still watching Mina, who was shaking her head at him.

Amelie looked at her, her brows furrowed. "Mama, nap!" she said, reaching out to pat Mina on the head.

"I know of a real good one in Chinatown," Matthew said. Mina glared at him. Was he seriously implying they go to a hotel? Like she was some sort of mistress? In front of Amelie, no less? There was no chance she might repeat any of this, or know what he was implying, but it was still uncomfortable.

"I don't need a nap, honey," she told Amelie, which was actually a lie. She was pretty tired and could use a nap at any given moment of any given day, but when you were a mom, naps were pretty impossible to attain, even when she tried to coordinate it with Amelie's. By the time she could get her brain to stop turning, Amelie would be up from her own nap, wanting something; either that, or once she had finally managed to fall asleep or get close to it, the dog would see someone parking in front of the house and start hollering. Someone always wanted something from her, that was the problem. Too much wanting. Her own, and other people's. She cleared her throat. "And if I did, I could sleep at my own house."

"Is that right?" Matthew said. "Because you've told me several times now that you can't."

Mina couldn't argue with that. She had told him about her trouble sleeping, not that she had needed to, considering how often she'd texted him during his overnight shift while Dima had been away. He stood up, and pushed a napkin in her direction with some writing on it. *The Oasis, tomorrow at 12*, it said. He crumpled up the paper his sandwich had come in and threw it into the wastebasket behind them. "Kobe!" he said nonchalantly.

Mina didn't get it. How could he be so cool and collected when their lives were falling apart? Did he really think they weren't in any danger? His confidence was truly startling. She had the obvious realization again that Matthew was nothing like her husband, and that she had no idea where this ordeal would lead them. That, by kissing him, she had walked herself into a lion's den. As he sauntered out the door like he had no cares at all in the world, Amelie, oblivious to it all, looked up at her, blinking.

"Kobe?" she asked.

CHAPTER FIFTEEN

The next morning, she couldn't even stomach having breakfast she was so nervous. She had no idea why; obviously, she wouldn't be meeting Matthew at a hotel. In Chinatown, of all places. The thought of checking in made her feel dirty. Was she supposed to use her own name? And what about money? Was she supposed to pay for that?

She would meet him, she decided, after mulling it over all morning. But just to talk to him. Yes, that was the best option. There was a good chance if she didn't meet him, he would find her anyway, so it was better to not let it come to that. It was another boiling hot day, and she couldn't concentrate at all on work, so she went for a long bike ride for the first time since summer had started to clear her head. That her bike ride happened to end at The Oasis was merely a coincidence—or, it would look that way to an outside observer, she hoped.

Only once she had locked up her bike and headed indoors, did she realize there was a problem. She had no idea how to go about checking in. Was Matthew already there with a set of keys? Was she supposed to ask what room he was in? Surely, he wouldn't be using his actual name. Would he?

She took out her phone and was about to message him, when she felt someone watching her. She glanced up to see Matthew at the end of the hall, his head ducking out from an open elevator. He waved at her to go over there, which she did.

Once the doors closed, they both instinctively pressed their bodies against each other, kissing as passionately as if they hadn't seen each other in months. So much for ending things. When the doors opened again, Matthew took her by the belt loop and pulled her into a room marked 417. Her original plan of just talking was clearly going by the wayside. She was undressed before the door had even closed all the way, and then, still standing, he was inside her. The talking would have to come later, she told herself. Everything felt too good to think straight. Only after she had washed the semen off her face and chest and was starting to get dressed did she remember she had meant to never do that again.

Then Mina's phone started buzzing in her pocket. Worried it was Dima or Amelie's school, she took it out. It was Ariel. *Are you around? Could sure use a glass of,* followed by an emoji of a wine glass.

"What's going on?" she asked, not looking up. She could hear Matthew coming out of the bathroom. Ariel had never asked her to hang out, not once. It was always Mina making plans for them, usually for the four of them.

She showed the text from Ariel to Matthew. Matthew shook his head, and started rubbing his beard. He didn't answer.

"So what should I say to that?" Mina asked. "No, I'm in a hotel room with your husband?"

"Fuck, Mina," Matthew said. He stood by the windows with his back turned, his clothes already back on. "That shit isn't funny."

"I'm not trying to be funny. I really don't know what to say."

"Say you're busy," he said, looking out the window. "Say anything, other than that."

"You seem to forget that I hate lying," she said.

"You're really damn good at it for someone who hates it," he said. His face had turned pale, ghostly. She put the phone away without replying.

"I'm sorry," she said. "I would never actually write that, you know."

"Do I?"

She stood and crossed the room, hugging him from, behind. "Hey. What's wrong?" she asked.

Matthew just inhaled loudly, squeezing her arms and turning around to face her.

"I'm just…glad to see you," he said into her hair.

"Me too. But, something's wrong, right? Why did you want to meet me here?"

"You know why," he mumbled into her ear.

"But didn't we decide," she started, then cleared her throat. "I thought something happened."

"Maybe what happened is that I'm done letting you order me around."

"Me? Order you around? That's, like, literally all you do to me when we're together," she said.

"Yeah, but you like that," he said quickly.

"I do…in bed. But this is not sustainable. Mentally, I mean," she said. "And it's not sustainable in other ways either. We're going to get caught."

"Not necessarily."

"Not necessarily? We just keep sneaking around forever and no one will be the wiser? That sounds realistic to you?"

Matthew didn't answer.

"And, I mean, it's just sex, right? We should just stop before it gets any messier," she added.

They were quiet for a moment, the hissing of the A/C unit and car horns from the street below the only sounds she could hear. It was cool and comfortable in that room, and it strangely did feel like a sort of vacation. It also felt like an important moment. Another line they were crossing. But she wasn't quite sure what line it was. She wanted to talk more, really, she did, but he smelled so good and his hands knew all the right places to go and exactly how to press into them, and in less than a minute they were naked and had barely made it under the sheets before they were having sex again. Every time it happened, she wished he would start being terrible in bed. But it only seemed to get better and better. She barely lasted two minutes.

"That was really fun," she said, after.

"Yeah. Really fun."

"This is probably the best sex I've ever had in my life," she said. "It's really making things difficult."

"Me too," he said, standing up to get dressed.

"Seriously?" she asked, surprised.

"Yeah, seriously. Really hard for the whole submissiveness thing."

"Well, then how are we ever going to stop?" Even as she said it, she didn't want to consider that option, of them not being able to stop; nor did she want to think more deeply about why they couldn't stop. What if it meant something? What if it wasn't just sex? That would make everything so much more confusing than it already was.

"It's a problem," he admitted.

"Doesn't every problem have a solution?" she asked.

"Not this one."

"But we have to do something, Matthew. We can't just do this forever."

She sat up in bed, feeling naked suddenly, and covering herself with the many layered white sheets. The rumble of the red line as the train passed through the nearby Chinatown station made the building vibrate. She was suddenly frightened, and she wasn't sure why. She could practically see her life unraveling on her like a loose spool of thread. "I was kind of hoping we would just get this out of our system and move on."

"Is that what's happening for you?"

She blinked, thinking about it. "No," she said. She pinched her fingers over her forehead, where she felt a throbbing pain starting to emanate. Panic. That's what she was feeling. Total, dizzying panic. The idea of continuing this made her head swim, but the idea of stopping did too. She was conflicted, stuck. Her breathing quickened, and then became erratic, so much so that it was physically noticeable. Finally, Matthew sat up, watching her.

"Are you okay?" he asked her, concern shadowing his face. "Is it your rib again?" She shook her head, though it really did feel similar to when she had sprained her rib in class. Like she couldn't take a full breath. She tried to slow it down, but this only made it worse. If she wasn't careful, she might have a full-on panic attack. She hadn't had one of those since her mom died. And yet, how could she feel anything else? If they couldn't stop, there was only one solution. They would need to tell their spouses.

"Do you have a cigarette?" she asked. She suddenly needed one, badly. Matthew had been chewing Nicorette gum and sucking on Zyn pouches for as long as she'd known him, but she figured he must have a secret stash somewhere.

He cleared his throat, his brows now furrowing into worry. Turned out he was pretty serious about his gum. "I can buy some. I saw a shop across the street." She was so dizzy and lightheaded she let him go. It took her several minutes of slow, mediative breathing to calm herself down enough to leave the bed and get dressed. Then she remembered she hadn't texted Ariel back. Shit. She grabbed her phone and typed, *I'm sorry, I can't! I've been totally swamped with work today. Maybe tonight? Everything OK?*

They sometimes went hours without responding to each other, but it was rare, so she felt like it had been an epic failure to wait so long when she happened to be with Matthew. What if she started to feel suspicious? Thankfully, she texted right back: *Oh, no worries, just having a bad day.*

So sorry! Let's get everyone together soon, though, okay? Mina wrote back. She was being paranoid again, clearly. Could she really have a playdate with her ever again without being incredibly stressed out? Maybe she could if Matthew wasn't there. She was thinking about texting her about meeting on a day Matthew was sure to be at work just as the door slammed shut. Matthew was back. Her panic had subsided, but only slightly.

He threw the pack at her, and she caught them. Then he opened the door of the balcony. He surprised her by taking one of the cigarettes, and lighting both of theirs. Then they stood there in silence, not looking at each other.

It was hard, not being who you really were. They were both smokers who were trying not to be smokers, lovers who were trying not to be lovers. But they would always remain people who desperately wanted something they couldn't—shouldn't—have. She felt certain there was some deep knowledge that this fact should illuminate, but she couldn't quite grasp what. Certainly, it had something to do with their innate badness. Ariel had never smoked; Dima had never smoked. He barely drank. He seemed perfectly content with being sober and lucid at all times, with being married to her and never kissing anyone else again.

But Mina and Matthew, they shrunk away from the world, wanted things that were bad for them. This was just another way of doing it, this affair. She had spent so many years focusing on her career, and then her baby, that when Amelie was suddenly not a baby anymore and she had actually published not one but three books, there was suddenly a huge black hole that burst open inside her, like a vacancy of attention. No one ever talked about what happened when you got the things you worked so hard for. How, in some ways, it only made it worse, to not have a goal. How it put you into total freefall.

Whatever it was—her long-ignored marriage problems, her wacky hormones, or Matthew himself—she was certainly not feeling like herself. Or maybe this was her true self and the well-behaving semi-happy person she'd been before was some version of a coma she was waking up from. It didn't matter in the end what it was. This was where it had brought her.

All of this was in the air between them as they smoked on the patio of the Chinatown hotel, watching the busy Chicago traffic move and beep and curse below them on Archer Avenue. There

was a lot she wanted to say, a lot she could say. But the only thing
she did end up saying was,

"I think maybe we should tell them."

CHAPTER SIXTEEN

Matthew turned quiet. He had retreated into himself again, like a turtle. His expression was odd, like he was looking out into the ocean just as he was about to fall in. It was panic, she realized.

"What?" she said.

He rubbed a hand over his face, then settled it over his forehead, without turning to face her. "How can I impart to you what a terrible idea that is?"

"I'm not saying it will be easy. It's gonna be a shitshow. But what else can we possibly do at this point if we aren't able to stop?"

He took in a deep breath and finally turned his head to look her in the eye. "You're talking about destroying lives," he said.

"We already did that, though," she said. "The second we got together, we ruined our marriages."

He took another breath. "I'm not even talking about our marriages. I'm talking about Dallas. And Open Guard," he said. "I can never go back there if this gets out."

"Well, maybe you should have thought about that before you started kissing me right outside the fucking gym," she said. Until it came out, she didn't even understand she was annoyed at him, but she was. He was the one who had said he couldn't stop. What did he mean by it then? That they would just keep messing around in secret until the secret ate her alive? The stress of it alone kept her up at night, not to mention the guilt that would follow. "And anyway, it's just a gym. Won't they eventually get over it? It's none of their business anyway."

"No, it's not just a gym, and you know that. They'll make it their business."

"They will get over it. What are they going to do, stop us at the door?"

"If that's where you're at, then okay, I'll go to West Loop. I will never talk to you again," he said.

"I didn't say that was where I'm at. I just think we need to figure out what we're going to do. That's one solution we haven't considered yet."

"That's not a solution," he muttered. "That's the fucking end."

"You're being dramatic," she said, turning away from him. She lit another cigarette. "Don't make me out to be the emotional attached girl. That's not me. You're the one who wanted to get coffee."

"Because I like spending time with you," he said.

"Well, so do I," she said. "But isn't that also a *problem*?"

Matthew watched her for a moment. "So, what are you suggesting? That we run off together like some Disney fairytale?"

"No," she said with a frown. She wasn't sure what she meant when she said they should tell them, other than the feeling of relief it brought her thinking about it. She didn't know if they were compatible outside of exactly what they were, just a superficial sexual relationship. Sometimes she wasn't sure they were friends. He hardly knew anything about her. It was probably one reason the sex was so good. That and the fact that they didn't share too much about their lives, all the petty grievances and daily tasks that got in the way of attraction once you were together for so long.

"I mean, can you imagine us together?" she asked. "We'd probably hate each other after three months. You seem like a nightmare to live with."

"So do you," he said with a snort.

"I'm fine," she said, rolling her eyes. "I'm just saying…I guess what I'm saying is that this probably only works so well because we only see the best sides of each other. Daily life isn't the same as whatever this is."

"Then why on earth would you want to tell them?"

She looked out into the busy street and really tried hard to think about what her future could look like; one with Matthew and one without him. As nice it sounded to have a bed of their own, a life where they didn't have to lie and sneak around, she couldn't imagine truly being with him; living in his cluttered dark house, married to a cop with a drinking problem and an inability to access his own emotions. But she also felt so drawn to him despite all that, in a way she never had before. Whenever they weren't together, she thought about him constantly, waiting for their next chance to meet. It was a small torture, wanting something so badly that you couldn't have. She couldn't imagine doing that for much longer, sneaking around to hotels, lying to everyone. The reality of Dima and Ariel finding out about them hung over her like a heavy cloud on a good day, and now it was like a storm was brewing and there was no way to stop it. The more they saw each other, the harder it got for her to keep her lives separate, and the more likely they were to get caught.

"I don't know. If we don't at least try to be together, or whatever, we're always going to wonder," she said. "I don't think we can have very healthy marriages if we're always wondering about that."

"I've thought of that too," he admitted. "But I just can't. I can't do that to Dallas. And I can't afford it either—neither can you."

"If we're not going to be together, then we should stop," she said.

A decision needed to be made. On top of the sneaking around, the ambivalence was driving her a little crazy, like she was constantly being torn between two places. One of them was bound to slip up. Someone would see something they shouldn't see, and if that happened enough times, Dima would hear about it. Maybe if they were different people, or didn't go to the same gym, they could go on longer. But they were who they were. And this wasn't going to fix their problems, in the long run. It was only making things worse. She understood all this in a singular moment of clarity, and once she did, she couldn't unsee it. Sure, she and Dima had some issues to work through. That was tough enough on its own. But this tipped the scales to such a degree there was no way to ever balance them again, not if it continued, or got any more serious.

"We stop for real."

She thought he might argue with her, but it seemed like the idea of people finding out had made him do another one eighty.

"Okay. Fine," he said. "Let's try that."

"Really?"

"Yeah. If it's that or tell them, then yeah." He threw his cigarette onto the street below, then turned around to exit the balcony. She did the same and followed him inside. Already she could feel herself missing him, but she knew it was the best solution.

"Okay, then," she said, trying not to look as surprised as she felt.

Matthew was picking up his keys and phone, sliding them into his jean pockets. His silence unnerved her a bit.

"I'll see you at the gym, then?" she said.

"Yeah," he said.

She walked forward, closing the space between them. "Why are you being so weird right now?"

He sighed, like she was a toddler throwing a tantrum, rather than a person asking a simple question. It annoyed her tremendously. She thought she had been acting fairly maturely, unemotional to the point of coldness. She wasn't the one asking him to get coffee, or telling him that she couldn't live without him. She was just the one who couldn't say no.

"I'm doing what you want, right?" Matthew said. "If we're done, then let's be done. I shouldn't be here."

"Okay, but what, we're not going to even be friends anymore? We can't finish this conversation?"

He paused, taking in a long breath, trying to settle his face into an expression of patience, but all she saw was the opposite. "Is there more you wanted to say?"

She blinked, feeling embarrassed, not that she understood why. "No. I guess not."

"Listen, I'll leave first. Wait ten minutes before you go, okay?" Matthew asked, tying his shoes.

Mina nodded. It was the right decision, in the end. She was going to buck up and move on. That was the only thing she could do. Plus, she should be glad he had agreed. Her life could go back to normal if she wanted it to.

She just had to see if there was a life for her to return to.

Later that night, after having a few drinks on her own and slipping away into her office after Amelie was asleep, she could already feel her resolve slipping away. She opened Instagram and hovered over Matthew's name for a long time before finally clicking on it, opening a new conversation.

Do you think the guilt will eat us alive? she wrote. Her cigarette had gone out and she lit another one, blowing the smoke out the window. A siren began wailing down the street from her house. *Sometimes I really think it will.*

Don't let it, he wrote back right away.

How can I do that?

Just put it in a box, he said.

I don't know how to do that, she wrote.

Just try. Try for me, he wrote.

She didn't hear from him the rest of the night. Even though it made her sad, it was the most relaxed she had felt in a really long time. Now she just had to sit in her sadness until it turned into something else, something more manageable, like sadness generally tended to do. Like he said, she would need to put it in a box; the wings and the anchor. The magnet and the wind. The shape it came in. She would build a room for it, with walls so bright they blinded and a roof so high you couldn't see the top. Then she would burn it all down.

CHAPTER SEVENTEEN

Over the following few days, and then a few more, it did really seem like things were over between them; the messages and secret meetings came to a halt. She didn't see Matthew again until next week's class, and even that was a surprise because he was so late. Part of her had gone in hoping Matthew wouldn't be there, but he often showed up late, so she was never entirely sure. She kept trying not to look at the door, but then found herself looking at the door anyway. Ten minutes in, he wasn't there yet, so she partnered with someone else, one of the only other women who came to Thursday classes, Violet.

Violet was only twenty-two and already had her purple belt; she always smelled like clean laundry mixed with the CBD joints she purchased from next door. She taught a couple of the women's-only classes at Open Guard, and when she wasn't doing Jiu Jitsu, she did aerial yoga or walked dogs. The girl was in great shape, never taking any rounds off, and nice, if not a bit aloof. The other females were *not* nice and aloof. The men, on the other hand, were some of the kindest she had met. She'd gone to the same Pilates studio for more than a year and not one person ever talked to her. They came in staring at their phones and left staring at their phones.

No one had phones out at Jiu Jitsu. It seemed to be a part of some unspoken etiquette. There were several of these rules she had picked up on over the months. Another one was that no one ever talked about what they did for work, not right away anyway. Sometimes

she didn't find that out until she had already talked to a person a
hundred times, and it was usually because they would add her on
Facebook and she saw it on there. She took this to mean that in Jiu
Jitsu, you were only judged based on how you performed Jiu Jitsu,
and how you behaved in class. In Jiu Jitsu, jobs didn't matter. And
phones were a reminder of your regular life, which was not a part
of Jiu Jitsu. In some ways, it really was a cult. But it was the kind of
cult she was happy to join.

"Good morning, Matthew," she heard Violet say suddenly. He
must have come in the back door, but she couldn't see, because Violet was blocking her vision with her body. They were working on a
sweep. Mina was very bad at sweeps, generally speaking, but it was
much easier with a woman. They weighed less. There were only a
dozen or so women at her gym, and rarely there at the same time,
so she almost never rolled with them and the lack of extra weight
threw her off entirely when she'd ended up partnered with Violet.
Eventually, she clumsily got Violet to the floor, then turned to see
Matthew, who had sat down against the wall. There was an even
number of people in class so he would either have to join another
group or skip the drill altogether.

"Morning," Matthew said, barely looking at them. Everyone
knew Matthew worked night shifts, so even though it was nearly 7
p.m., it was technically his morning. Mina could tell he'd been up
later than usual and had just woken up. He became ghostly when
he was up late, which meant eleven or noon or sometimes even two
p.m., because CPD was so understaffed. It would take him the entire
class to wake up enough to say more than a word or two.

"You need a home?" Violet asked, implying he could join them.

"I'm good," he said, still staring into space. The gym was starting
to warm up, and even without joining in he was sweating already.
He continued to sit by the wall as they finished the drill. She tried to
ignore him, but she always found herself acutely aware of his presence,
so this was hard to do. Today it was even harder. His energy was

darker than dark. Perhaps because she had so much of her own, she was very sensitive to darkness in all its shapes and sizes. This energy from Matthew was not only from tiredness, but something else too.

Once they finished practicing the new move, the buzzer rang, which meant it was time to roll. After her initial roll with Violet, he came straight for her. He actually knocked her over with a double leg takedown because she was still standing. This was a very aggressive beginning to their session. She had seen him do the same takedown to other men, but with her he usually sat down and let her attempt the first move, like everyone else did with beginners, or women. Not today. It was a little off-putting, especially as she was already out of breath.

"Wow, you're in a mood," she said, from her position on the floor. He was on top of her already, trapping her arm into such a tight Kimura she would not be able to get it out or roll through it like usual. She had to tap out, and it had only been ten or twenty seconds. Even for him it was a bit over the top.

"I'm not," he said. They returned to a seated neutral position to start over. She was not dumb enough to stand up again.

"Yes, you are," she said, when she was stuck under him again moments later. He put so much pressure on her body with his signature "knee on belly" she could hardly move. This happened to her a lot in class. Most of what she had learned in the time she'd been rolling was how to get out from underneath men heavier and stronger than her. She hardly even knew how to do any submissions. He got her arm again and Americana'd her until she tapped out. Her arm even began to ache afterward, he had done it so quickly, which annoyed her. The last thing she needed was to sit out for a week because of another strained rotator cuff. "Are you mad about something?"

"I'm just doing Jiu Jitsu," Matthew snapped.

She frowned. "No, you're being mean."

"Go to a yoga class if you think this is mean," he said, getting her in side control again, then reaching for her Gi collar, aiming for a baseball choke she was not going to let him get.

"I hate yoga," she said, shrimping her way out from under him, only to be swept under him yet again. "You know that."

The rest of the rolling session went in a similar fashion, and then, to her relief, it was over. It was the first time she was glad they were done. They bumped fists and his eyes caught hers, and they were burning. Burning with what, she didn't know. Rage? Lust? It was hard to tell the difference with Matthew. Maybe they were part of the same thing to him; it could certainly feel that way sometimes when they were having sex. She liked that in bed. Here, not so much. She narrowed her brows, questioning him without words. Sure, they were in Jiu Jitsu, and sure, there was nothing technically wrong with anything he had just done. But they both knew it was out of character. It was also not especially productive for her to roll like that since she couldn't work on anything and had to spend the entire time avoiding injuries.

"Good roll," he said, catching his breath.

"Uh, no. It was not," she said, still frowning. People were already switching partners, but they remained sitting across from one another.

"Sorry," he said finally. "Rough morning."

"So glad you could take it out on my ribcage," she said, massaging the side of her rib to make sure he hadn't re-sprained it. She'd been so concerned about her rotator cuff she had barely noticed he had crushed that too. Before she could ask him about what had made his morning so bad, someone else had come over to roll with him, and then a different friend of hers came by to roll with her, and the buzzer was going off. It was crowded, and she ended up rolling every round until it was over. After class, she went to sit and catch her breath on one of the chairs by the window. She watched Matthew head towards the men's changing room when a new white belt stopped to ask him a question; soon he was demonstrating a move, something from side control. Mina took her time leaving. He was so patient and serious about Jiu Jitsu it was sometimes jarring, compared to his other behaviors. The girl was pretty, and Mina stupidly found herself feeling jealous for a second. She'd never even been jealous with Dima, and now here she was feeling that way about a man who was already married to someone else. She was so zoned out watching them she didn't even notice Felix had sat down next to her with a beer in his hand.

"Hey," she said. "Drinking already, huh?"

"What do you mean already?" he said, not looking at her. "It's 7:30."

Felix was one of the most regular attendees at the gym. She had yet to go to a class where he hadn't been there. After months of seeing him every day, and getting drunk with him at gym parties on more than one occasion, all she knew about his personal life was that he worked in computers, IT or something, but had recently been laid off. He didn't seem to have a wife or kids or even a girlfriend, which was a bit strange for his age, especially since he was so good at Jiu Jitsu, she imagined there had to be at least one woman out there who would find that attractive, but then again, he was a bit strange in general. He got hyper-focused on the most boring topics. Various types of Gi's and companies that made them, the history of martial arts; he also knew way too much about guns for not actually owning one. He seemed to have a good heart, but it felt like talking to a Wikipedia article sometimes.

Currently, he was delivering a monologue about how the mats at the gym should be redone with a better construction, and exactly how to do this. She stopped listening. She got her sandals on slowly, still trying to decide if she should wait on Matthew, who had just finished explaining whatever it was he had been explaining to the girl. Even with him ten feet away she found herself missing him. Just as she had decided to leave it alone and stood to leave, he came over and told her to take her sandals off. By then it was just him and Felix and her in the front room; everyone else had left or they were in the process of changing and leaving.

"You're barely sweating," Matthew said. "Did you sit out the rest of class?"

"No, I didn't. That's just because I don't sweat," she argued.

"Everyone sweats," he argued.

"I do, but barely. I am definitely not sweaty enough to drip it on your face, like you have done to me several times."

"That's because I don't have hair," he said. "You have hair."

"You men just sweat like crazy. Dima's hair is always drenched after class."

Matthew blinked at the mention of her husband's name, or maybe the fact that he had hair. Because the gym was geared more towards older students, there weren't all that many men with hair left. Or maybe the men of Jiu Jitsu preferred to shave their heads, she didn't know. If you looked around the gym on any given day, you'd see far more tattoos than hair.

"I feel bad about earlier. Let's roll again," Matthew ordered, waving a hand in her direction.

She didn't move, but still, he sat down on the mat in one of the most common starting positions, with his knees up and both feet flat on the floor.

After the last time, she really didn't want to roll with him. Her shoulder was sore and she was winded as it was. Plus hardly anyone was there, and she knew Felix would be watching them the entire time. Felix was a bit off socially, but he seemed to notice random things. He also liked to narrate and criticize her rolls as she was rolling, and it always made her so flustered she would be ten times worse.

"Come on, I'll be nice," he said.

She shook her head. "Your nice is like most people's mean."

Felix laughed at this; she hadn't even realized he'd been following their conversation, as he had turned his focus to his phone after she started talking to Matthew.

"All right," Matthew said with a shrug. He stood and disappeared to the locker room.

"You should see him with everyone else if you think he's being mean," Felix told her, taking a sip of his drink.

"Yeah, says the guy who is even meaner."

"Well, I'm not flirting with you, so I don't have to be nice," Felix said nonchalantly, taking another sip of his beer.

Mina couldn't rearrange her face quick enough to hide her surprise, even though it wasn't all that surprising; she had been expecting someone to notice it for months. The air was suddenly hot and heavy, like a blanket.

She swallowed. "He's not flirting with me," she said.

Felix rolled his eyes. "Right. And you're not flirting back either," he said.

"I'm married," she said. "So is he. That would be pretty dumb."

"Well, I don't disagree with you there," he said with a shrug. "It's really fucking dumb, and you two should quit it."

Adrenaline began pouring through her body like she'd drank an entire carafe of coffee. Her heart was racing again, guilt and stress and lust all rolled into one. Of course Felix had noticed. The whole gym probably had. For months they were always off chatting in various corners of the gym before and after class, not to mention all the times they chose to partner up for drills, and that was all before they'd hooked up. Mina didn't know what to say, and her silence was probably the biggest giveaway she could have given Felix. He looked at her for a moment, and she thought she saw some flicker of emotion there, but maybe it was just judgment. Then he blinked and it was gone.

Matthew, in the meantime, had returned in his street clothes with a beer in his hand. It had often been the case recently that the three of them ended up here drinking after class, but now it felt sordid and messy. How was she supposed to just sit there like Felix hadn't called them out on something that was so obviously true? She couldn't. It was too awkward. She stood and grabbed her bag.

"You sticking around?" Matthew asked, nodding in her direction.

"I gotta get back," she said, trying not to show him how scared she was. Once one person knew, it was only a matter of time before others did. The place was as gossipy as any high school. Even if Felix never told another soul, if he had noticed, others would too. The gym was full of people with professions that required them to be attentive to details: lawyers, cops, security guards. She was glad that at least only the flirting had come up, and nothing else. Flirting you could still explain away. Nothing illegal about flirting.

It was sloppy, talking so much at the gym still. She would need to put a stop to that too. But even if she could manage to stop, she worried that she was already on a train that could only ever go off the tracks and crash. It was only a matter of time.

"See ya," Matthew told her as nonchalantly as a person could, though his eyes caught hers for a moment too long. It was all she could do, to extricate herself from the situation. The words rang through her head the entire walk back home, but she felt proud of herself for the first time in a while.

Leaving was the right thing to do. Of course it was. If she didn't do it now, then she'd be forced out eventually. Maybe Matthew was right about the gym. People wouldn't like it if their relationship ever became public. That was clear now. She had read enough to know these things never turned out well for the woman, historically. Technology had progressed, but society was still far behind. Better to stop now, before she destroyed her entire life over some body parts that happened to fit together perfectly.

MARCH

CHAPTER EIGHTEEN

Matthew was waiting for her in the hallway, and she figured he would drive her back soon, but then Detective Conner called him inside and they were in there for so long that Mina decided to just get on the Orange Line back home. No one stopped her on the way out, so she figured they must be done with her statement for now. By the time she got to her house, she only had a couple hours left before she would have to pick up Amelie. She had so much she was supposed to do that day, but once she'd arrived, sweaty and bedraggled from the overheated train and still dehydrated, all she could manage to do was take a shower and have a glass of wine. She took a second glass to her bedroom, sipping on it while curled up in her bed, trying to forget everything that had happened in the last day. Not that she could. But it was worth a shot.

The one upside to not owning a car was day drinking. Because she hadn't eaten since throwing up her breakfast, after two glasses of wine she was feeling a little buzzed, and had managed to settle down enough to be able to eat a piece of bread, after which her stomach stopped rumbling at her to feed it something. She was about to close her eyes and see if she might be able to take a quick nap before pickup, but then her phone rang.

"Jesus Christ, Mina, are you okay?" said a voice on the other end of the line.

Mina tried to clear the grogginess from her head. She cleared her throat. "Huh?"

"Dylan is dead? And you found his body?" said the voice.

She sat up abruptly, finally registering who it belonged to. "Dima?"

"Do you need me to get Amelie from school?" he asked, sounding concerned for her for the first time since their separation.

"Um, you don't need to…but that would be nice," she said. "I have a splitting headache."

"Yeah, I've heard that happens when you go around looking for corpses."

"Excuse me?" she asked, straightening up on the bed. "What makes you think I was looking for anything?"

"Never mind," he said. "I'm just a little freaked out. I just saw Dylan."

"You did? When?"

Dima paused. "I don't know. Yesterday? Maybe the day before."

"Was he driving a white van when you saw him?"

"What?" Dima asked, sounding annoyed. "I don't know. Why?"

"Forget it," she said.

"Do you want me to come over?" he asked, his voice softening.

"No," she said. All she wanted to do was close her eyes and sleep; she wanted to forget any of this had ever happened, at least for a little while.

"Well, let me get Amelie from school, then. I'll bring her here and give you the day off. You can pick her up tomorrow from school."

"That sounds fine," she said, closing her eyes again. "Thanks."

She thought he had hung up, but then she could hear him breathing on the other end of the line. "I know you would never tell me if you need any help, but I'm here if you do, okay?" he said.

She nodded, surprised, blinking back another wave of nausea. It made her feel guilty, whenever she was reminded how nice her ex-husband could be. Far nicer than Matthew, that was for sure. Not that it mattered to her body, but it did matter a little to her heart. "Thanks," she managed to say before hanging up the phone and collapsing into a fitful sleep.

When she woke up again, it was night, and someone was banging on her door. She was so tired it took her several minutes to finally make herself get up and answer the knocking. Even then, she was a tad out of it, like she was still mid-dream. This was when she remembered why she really didn't like to day-drink.

"Jesus, I was starting to think you were dead," said the voice behind the door. She had to squint in the darkness to make out who it was. Only when a tiny little body that looked remarkably like her squirmed out of the person's hands and began smiling at her through the glass of the door did she finally figure out it was Dima and Amelie. "Can you open up? It's like a frozen hellscape out here."

She shook her head. "Sorry," she said, letting the two of them inside. Dima didn't usually come inside the house anymore, so he must really have been cold, or distracted. Watching Amelie zoom off towards the kitchen, her shoes leaving a wet gray trail behind her, she waited for an explanation.

"Can't even say hello, huh?" he asked, bitterly.

"Hello," she said, rubbing sleep from her eyes. "I was asleep. I'm a little out of it."

He nodded, not looking at her. She was wearing only a thin pair of leggings and an oversized CPD shirt that she still sometimes slept in. She put her arms over her chest and asked him what was going on.

"I have to go to work tonight," he said, looking around the house as if to see if anything had changed. Or maybe to see if she had a visitor over. "I know I said I would take Amelie...but we really need the money."

"It's fine," she said. "It's almost bedtime anyway. We'll manage."

"Sorry," he said. "I'll be back in a couple days, I can take her then."

"I said it's fine," she said. "It's not like how it used to be, she's older now. We do okay."

As if to contradict her, as Amelie was wont to do, she came storming back into the living room then, shaking a box of Lucky Charms and demanding, "Cereal! Cereal!"

"Okay, honey, go get a bowl." Mina said.

Dima finally turned to look at her. "So you're okay?" he asked.

"I will be," she said. "Just a disturbing image to shake. And the smell. That might have been worse, actually." She shook her head. "I don't think I've really accepted that he's dead, you know? Not like we were best friends or something, but…" Her voice trailed off. Dima was focusing on her too intently and it made her nervous. She was talking too much, probably. "What?"

Dima's gaze fell to the floor, then to Amelie, who had returned with a bowl and began placing it on the table. "Nothing." He continued staring at the floor, like he had more to say. Dima was not a man who could keep much in. It was, at first, what drew her to him, and then what pushed her away. Knowing a person's every thought could feel suffocating.

"Dima," she said, trying to prompt him, give him silent permission to say what he needed to say.

"I know it's none of my business, but what were you doing there?" he asked, still not able to make any direct eye contact.

"You're right, it's not your business," she agreed.

"You two weren't…" he started, then sighed.

"No, of course not," she said, even though that, too, was not his business. He finally lifted his tired gaze to look at her.

"I don't know why I even ask. Not like I can believe anything you say," he said, shaking his head.

She was about to argue that it really didn't matter if he believed her or not, as that was yet another thing that was not his business, not anymore, when he interrupted her with another question. "Can I ask you something else?"

Mina wanted to say no, because she knew whatever it was

wouldn't be good, but she also felt guilty and didn't want to make things worse, so she said yes.

Dima looked at her, his arms at his sides. "Is it because he's so good at Jiu Jitsu?"

Mina's face flushed. He wasn't talking about Dylan anymore. He was asking her about Matthew. They'd never really discussed it at the time, because he'd been in such a hurry to get out of the house and have nothing to do with her anymore. "No."

"Then what?"

Mina looked around the room. She swallowed the lump in her throat and tried to think about a good answer. She wasn't sure she had one that would make sense to him. She wasn't sure she even knew what the answer was. "It was...I don't know, Dima. I think something is wrong with me."

"Well, that's for sure."

"I mean, like, with the wiring in my brain," she said.

"Yeah, I know that. I thought you were getting better."

"I was! I am. I'm talking about before. Back in summer."

"So, what, Matthew's dick was the cure to your hormonal imbalance?"

She shook her head. "See, this is the problem. I can't talk to you when I'm sad. You can't deal with it," she said. "You only have happiness and, like, whatever buried rage comes out in Jiu Jitsu, and nothing else in between."

"But you could talk to Matthew?"

"Yeah. I could. I mean...I don't even have to, he just gets it."

Dima let out a bitter laugh, crossing his arms over his narrow chest. The neighbor's two Yorkies started barking from next door, followed by the Shepherds from across the street. Probably a FedEx delivery was making its way down their block.

"So, because he's got mental problems, you decided to throw away ten years of marriage?"

"That's not really how it works. I wasn't thinking—"

"About me? About consequences?"

She shook her head. "No, that's not what I mean." She sighed.

The dogs stopped barking and it became deathly silent in the house. She felt so overwhelmed with sadness it almost knocked her over. She sat down on the couch and tried to steady herself. As much as she had craved some change, she now regretted forcing so much of it upon them. Once you broke something that badly, she understood you could never fix it again. That's why she hadn't even attempted to convince Dima to stay with her. She knew he wouldn't; and even if he tried to, he would never trust her again. And maybe he shouldn't. She didn't trust herself, certainly. Maybe she wasn't meant to have a normal life, and it had been stupid to think she could.

"It felt like I was someone else, when I was with him," she continued.

"Why did you need to be someone else? I liked the person you were just fine. I love—loved that person."

"I don't know. Maybe I didn't love that person. I can't explain it."

"I don't understand what that means," he said. "Try harder."

But she couldn't. What could she possibly say? That she had fallen for someone because of their smell? That it was the best sex of her life? That in some ways sleeping with Matthew felt like what she was meant to be doing? This would not make him feel better, to know all that. And it all felt like so long ago. She could hardly remember how she had let it happen, let alone how she had been able to continue it for so long.

"I am trying, Dima," she said. Behind them, Amelie began screaming for more cereal. "I know it was stupid. Sometimes…I mean, this used to happen to me when I was younger, when I was in a really bad place. I would just want to, like, drink and smoke and sleep with everyone and just blow up my life. I don't know where the urge comes from. I really don't."

She could see Dima was trying to process what she was saying; it was the first time she had ever admitted something like that to him.

But she figured why not? It couldn't possibly make things worse. The worst had already happened, was happening now.

Dima cleared his throat, his voice a little hoarse. "You can't let yourself be happy, obviously," he said. "Maybe you feel like you don't deserve it."

"I don't know if that's true, Dima," Mina said.

"Well, you were happy. With me. I don't know what changed."

"You know that song Johnny Cash sings? *I See a Darkness?*"

"That's a Bonnie Prince Billie cover but yeah."

"I feel like that's what happened with me and Matthew."

"He saw a darkness?" Dima asked, unconvinced.

"Yes. And I did too," she said.

He paused, staring at her for what felt like a long time. Like he was trying to see it too.

"Okay, then," Dima said.

"I know that doesn't excuse it."

"No, it doesn't."

"But I hope it sort of explains where my head was at."

They stood in silence for a while, and she really felt like maybe they were getting somewhere—not to reconciliation, but maybe some type of understanding. Until, that is, her door opened again. In came Matthew, without so much as knocking. He didn't even notice Dima standing there until he had nearly knocked him over to get to the couch.

Dima noticed him, however, and his face went tight. "Are you fucking kidding me?" he started.

Matthew finally turned his way. "Can we just all be adults for once?" he said, kicking off his shoes and sitting down on the couch like he owned the place. He ran a hand over his tired eyes and left it there. "I don't have the energy for this today, man."

"Sure," Dima huffed, his hands had balled into fists; he looked like a tea kettle ready to pop. "You two were the ones sneaking off and fucking in a truck like teenagers, but I need to be the adult."

"Can we not...?" Mina started, meekly. If she wasn't so uncomfortable, she might have asked where on earth he had received that bit of information. She surely had never told him about the truck, or any details at all about where or when they'd slept together.

Matthew didn't seem to notice. He leaned back further into the couch. "Maybe if you had been able to make your wife come, then..."

He didn't get to finish his sentence, because Dima had his hand around his throat before he could. Matthew's eyes popped open, and within seconds he had Dima underneath him, his knee pinning him down against the hardwood floor. How many times had Mina imagined a scenario like this playing out in her head over the months she and Matthew had been seeing each other? Thousands, probably. Now that it was happening in front of her, she felt just as paralyzed as she had been in her mind.

Then she turned and saw Amelie standing in the doorway, blinking, and found her voice. "Matthew, stop," she managed to say. Matthew followed her gaze, and released his knee from Dima's chest. Dima sat up, catching his breath, as Amelie ran to him, nuzzling against his body like a shield. She was confused more than anything; she certainly knew Jiu Jitsu when she saw it, and even she seemed to understand it didn't belong here, in the house, when they were all dressed in street clothes, a glass table just feet away. She kept watching the two of them, as if waiting for an explanation, but it never came. The men just glared at each other in silence.

"Dima, you can go home," Mina said. "It's fine. Matthew's just here because of the thing with Dylan."

"I don't give a fuck why Matthew is here," Dima said. "I wasn't married to Matthew, last I checked. What he does with his dick isn't my business."

Mina lowered her head. She felt like she could puke or cry, or maybe both, but having Amelie in the room kept her together, at least enough to get through the odd scene unfolding in front of them. So many terrible combinations of people kept ending up in her house the last few days; she didn't know how much more she could take.

"It wasn't all my fault, Dimitry," she said, softly. "You were…" She waved a hand in the air absently. "Gone."

"I was at work. Making money for this family," he argued.

"Sure. Because we had so much money." She continued to shake her head, thinking of how little they talked that last year of their marriage, how he was so distracted all the time, always on his phone. Sometimes she had felt closer to him when he was on the road, because at least they would text each other every so often. "Even when you were home, you weren't really home."

"What does that even mean?" he asked, so angry his accent began sneaking out into his voice. He'd worked so hard to get rid of it when he moved to Chicago, that most of the time she forgot he was Russian.

"Forget it," she sighed. "It's late. Amelie needs to go to bed."

Dima looked at her for a long time, waiting for an answer. But what was she supposed to say? Sometimes things just didn't work out. And while she hadn't gone about it the right way, by escaping into another relationship while she was still married to him, she understood in retrospect that they'd both had one foot out the door of their marriage long before Matthew came along. "Fuck it," Dima said, turning to leave. She could hear him swearing in Russian as he stepped into the cold winter air and stormed off to his car.

Mina turned to grab Amelie off the floor, squeezing her tight. "I'm sorry, baby," she told her, not that she was entirely sure what she was sorry for. That Mina couldn't keep their family together? That she'd had to witness such an adult exchange, something she wouldn't be able to understand in her head but might linger somewhere in her heart? Kids were sponges, this she knew.

"It's a real revolving door over at your house these days," Matthew said, his lips curling into a smirk. He was back on the couch, his hands crossed over his stomach, his eyes pointed to the ceiling, as if nothing odd had just occurred. "Do I need to take a number or something?"

"Very funny. What are you doing here?" she asked. Amelie squirmed out of her hands and ran back to the kitchen, returning a moment later with the same box of Lucky Charms. And because Mina was so frazzled, she sat her down at the dining room table with yet another bowl of the sugary substance.

Matthew shrugged. "Didn't know where else to go."

"You really know how to make a lady feel special," she said, rolling her eyes as she sat down beside him. He reached out and grabbed the inside of her thigh.

"Oh, I can make you feel special all right," he said with a wink. His fingers meandered farther up her leg, towards the crotch of her pants, where they stopped and began circling. It felt like summer all over again; Matthew had always said he didn't like lying, and yet, he was always so turned on after they'd been in some group setting with both their spouses there. He was one of those men who always wanted to win; in Jiu Jitsu and everything else too. He told her once he'd liked rolling with Dima and thinking about how he was going to have sex with her later.

"That's not what I meant and you know it," she said, grabbing his hand and moving it just as Amelie ran into the room screaming, "Movie? Movie?"

"Sorry, baby, it's too late," she said, wiping the blue chalky substance from the corners of her mouth. "Let's brush your teeth and go to bed," she told her.

Once she'd put her down in her toddler crib, Amelie relaxed right away. The door barely had time to close before Matthew was behind her, his hands meandering down her body, then slapping her butt, hard.

"All that murder and Jiu Jitsu got you turned on, huh," she said into his ear, pushing him into the bedroom.

"Uh, look who's talking," he said, putting his hand into her pants and then out again.

"That's just my natural state around you," she said.

"Fuck, that's hot," Matthew said. He lifted her up and threw her on the bed, stripping her of all her clothes. "Come sit on my face right fucking now."

"Okay, officer," she said, smiling. "Anything you say."

"You keep talking like that, I'm gonna have to get my cuffs," he said, pulling her down the bed by her legs and getting on his knees. She closed her eyes, allowing herself to get caught up in the moment. "Then you'll really get what's coming to you."

"Sounds like a good time," she said. It had always been so easy, being in the moment with Matthew; so easy to get into character, to be the girl he wanted her to be—because that was the girl she wanted to be too. And suddenly she remembered why she had destroyed her life over sex to begin with. Because it was just too good. Because it was fun. It was the world that saw female sexuality as some tawdry but precious thing, something to put in a jar and protect. But it was her body, after all. Dima didn't own it, and neither did any other man. She was a woman, and a mother, and she wasn't dead yet.

Wasn't she allowed to have a little fun?

CHAPTER NINETEEN

The van showed up the following day, abandoned in a Walmart parking lot somewhere south of Bronzeville. CPD had it towed to the station as evidence, and it was unclear when she might be getting it back. Which was fine with her, since she didn't really want it. If she ever got it back, she would probably just sell the thing; she could use the money, and it wasn't like Dylan needed it anymore. She needed to move on with her life; she had a draft due to her editor in a week, and was about forty thousand words behind, and she could really use the advance money yesterday. She intended to go straight from Amelie's daycare to Bridgeport Coffee and spend all day there on her laptop and knock out at least half of her required word count. Well, maybe not half. But a few thousand words at least.

The problem was that as much as she wanted to forget what had happened with Dylan, the world didn't let her forget. Dylan's murder, the strangeness of it, had made headline news, and everywhere she looked in the café, she saw his face: on the front page of the *Chicago Tribune*, on someone's iPhone screen, in her Facebook feed, which was mostly still people from Open Guard. She couldn't get away from it. For hours, she kept stopping every other page to think about what his body had looked like. Then she would stop and wonder what might have happened to him. None of it was conducive to writing, which really required her full attention.

Eventually, she packed up her things and made her way back to her house; at least there, she didn't have so many distractions. Her TV wasn't connected to any channels anymore, just Netflix. But as she neared her house, she saw a line of cop cars camped out in front of the gym, blocking the parking lot, which was full of motorcycles and trucks. She checked her phone—it was Friday, just past one, which meant the Friday noon class was ending. She hadn't been to the gym in months, and had no desire to step foot in there again, but as she tried to walk past, she got stopped by Detective Conner, who was exiting an unmarked SUV on the other side of the street. He ran across to catch up with her when he saw she wasn't slowing down.

"I just came from your house. We're gonna need another statement from you," he said, stopping in front of her and blocking her way.

"I told you everything I know already," she said. She tried to walk past him before anyone else noticed her hovering in front of the gym. Friday noon classes were always packed to the brim, and almost everyone she knew would probably be there. It wasn't exactly the energy she needed to deal with that day. Or ever.

"Certain things have come to light," Detective Conner said.

She frowned. "What things?"

"We'll need to talk to your husband too," was his response. By this point, she should have expected all her questions would go unanswered. It was not a two-way street, dealing with detectives in real life.

"Ex-husband," she corrected. "And you can't. He got called into work today, so he's gone."

Detective Conner blinked, giving nothing away. "I just checked with his employer this morning," he said. "I was told that Dima Polyakov hasn't been working there since December of last year."

"What?" she asked. He was just trying to unsettle her, right? There was no way that could be true. Just as she was about to ask him what he meant, someone grabbed her shoulder and pulled her into a violent hug. Because her head was buried into this person's chest, only by smell did she understand who it was. Weed and patchouli mixed with sweat and the faintest hint of massage oil; the one girl from the gym she had ever gotten along with, Violet.

"Mina, oh my God," she said, pulling away from her, but leaving her muscular, tattooed hands on her shoulders. She was only wearing her Gi pants and a thin sports bra, her face and arms exposed to the chilly air, her blonde hair stuck to her damp forehead with sweat. "You poor thing. How are you?"

She swallowed, suddenly nervous. Once Violet noticed her there, everyone else was bound to, even though she was still outside in the parking lot. "I'm okay. How are you?"

"Oh my god, who even cares how I am? Forget me. I heard you found Dylan," she said, and once more, Mina couldn't help but wonder how everything got around so quickly at the gym. It was like a high school cafeteria sometimes.

"Yeah, I did," she said, turning back to face Detective Conner, but he had disappeared. He must have gone inside. She really needed to talk to him. Was he lying about Dima? Were they allowed to just make stuff up during a murder investigation? She couldn't remember from any TV show she had watched. She would need to ask Matthew. He must have been lying. How had Dima been paying for anything if he wasn't going to work? He didn't have his citizenship and he'd never gone to college; he wasn't qualified for almost any job above minimum wage, other than his current one. "Sorry, did you see where that detective went?"

Violet shook her head. "Probably inside. They're talking to everyone from Open Guard today after class, at least that's what Jonah just told me. Almost like...I don't know, like they think one of us did it?" She shook her head, appalled. "It's crazy."

"Well, he was strangled," Mina said with a shrug.

"Really?"

"Yeah. I think so. I'm not a doctor or anything, but..." she trailed off, looking towards the gym again, her stomach filling with anxiety, but also nostalgia, hearing the buzzer going off between rounds and the sound of camaraderie echoing out into the air. Someone had opened the doors to get fresh air in there, so the noise was traveling downwind and it almost felt like she was inside the gym. "That's what it looked like to me."

"Are you thinking about coming back?" Violet asked, watching her gaze. "To the gym?"

She shook her head vehemently, turning her head away from the view of whoever was behind that open door. "No. No way. I can't!"

"You can if you want to. But if you don't want to, that's totally different."

"I mean, I really miss Open Guard," she said, her voice wavering a little. "But everyone hates me."

Violet bent over slightly to look her in the eye. "Girl," Violet said. "I won't deny that it gets complicated when you get involved romantically with anyone in Jiu Jitsu. You know I went through the same thing with Max. People like to gossip. Then some other thing happens, and they move on. And if they don't…well, that's on them, not you."

Mina just shook her head. She didn't know what to say to that. Maybe she was right, but it certainly didn't feel that way. Every time she walked past the gym, which was often since it was right down the block, she felt reminded of the whole mess all over again. She felt unwelcome. Not that anyone had told her anything directly. But she had just assumed.

"You're not together now, are you?" Violet asked, the most personal she had ever gotten with her to date. "Or was it just a sex thing?"

Mina blushed. "No, we're not together," she admitted. "But, yeah, it was something more. I'm still not sure entirely what." She inhaled a deep breath. "The chemistry was just, like, insane." She paused, not sure how much she should say. She'd gotten so used to keeping it a secret. "I know that doesn't excuse what I did, but…"

Violet watched her, wide-eyed, and Mina realized she was right, it really was high school all over again, but with children and mortgages and alimony payments instead of keggers and algebra.

The only difference was that she had hated high school, and she loved the gym.

"People make mistakes," Violet said. "That's how we grow. You have to forgive yourself. I learned that the hard way."

"Are you sure you're only twenty-two?" Mina asked. She probably shouldn't have been talking about this right outside the gym, let alone listening to a child about life lessons, but Violet had always seemed much older than she was, while at the same time appearing constantly on the verge of a breakdown. Her Instagram posts were always about self-care and energy bubbles and the stars, which was just generally not a sign of good mental health. It may have just been her age, though. It was hard to be young, and it probably didn't make things easier to be constantly surrounded by so much alpha male energy; not to mention the older women, who often made the gym feel like a cliquey middle school. There was a reason Violet was the only female at the gym she'd ever really talked to.

Violet smiled. "Actually, twenty-three now. But I've done a lot of therapy."

"Oh, right. Isn't your mom a therapist?"

Violet nodded, raising her brows. "Hence why I have to do so much therapy."

Mina couldn't help but laugh a little. "Yeah, I've heard that about psychologists and their children."

Violet squeezed her shoulder. "Anyway. Those people in there judging you, well, most of them really don't have a leg to stand on. Trust me, I've been around for a while. Only Jonah makes the decision of who can or can't go to Open Guard."

Violet probably had more to say on the subject, but Mina felt anxious again. The truth was that she did care what people thought. It was because she often thought the same thing. Not that it was her fault, exactly, because she knew that wasn't true. But that maybe it made her a bad person for wanting someone she couldn't have and trying to have him anyway.

"I gotta go find that detective," she told Violet, and without another glance back in her direction, she forced herself through the doors of the gym she used to love so much it felt like a second home.

The windows were all fogged up, and she was instantly hit with the familiar smell of sweat and bleach, which made her sad and happy all at once. But then she looked around and saw all the faces of the people she was once friends with, some still rolling, some standing around drinking various liquids out of cups and bottles, and all her emotions were replaced with a stony, terrifying panic. Before she could track down the detective, someone lifted her up into the air and threw her down on the mat.

"What the—?" She looked up to see Felix hovering over her. It had been so long since she'd been to class, she had actually forgotten how he used to just throw her around at random because she was light and he found it entertaining. At the time she had found it both annoying and comforting, like having an older brother tease her. She had always wanted brothers. Instead, she had one sister, a narcissist in the true definition of the word, who lived in California and who she hadn't spoken to in years.

"Where the fuck have you been, Mina?" Felix asked her. She hobbled up to her feet, rubbing her back where she had landed on it rather harshly. "Not training, that's for sure."

"You know where I've been, Felix," she said.

"Yeah, I heard you go to Pilsen MMA now? Fuck that place," he said, crossing his arms over his bare hairy chest. He was still in his sweaty Gi, his hair damp.

"Like I can show my face here again," she said, shaking her head.

"Well, you're here now, and no one is setting you on fire or anything, stupid," he said, flicking her in the shoulder.

"That's because of the cops," she said, pointing in their direction. "They made me come. It wasn't by choice or anything."

Felix just shook his head. "Stop taking yourself so seriously," he said. "Everyone is too busy with their own shit to care what you put in your vagina."

Mina narrowed her eyes at him. "Excuse me? You cared quite a bit, as I recall."

"Is that Mina Banksy in my fucking dojo?" said a jolly voice behind her. She turned to see Jonah, the owner of Open Guard, walking her way, or rather, limping her way, his foot in a black cast. A smile formed on her face before she could help it. She'd always adored Jonah. It was rare that she met someone so genuine and positive and fully invested in their work.

"Jonah, what happened to your foot?" she asked once he had put an arm around her shoulder in a half hug.

He looked down angrily at the boot. "I fucking broke it, can you believe that? Forty-nine years old and I never broke a bone in my life, then I'm rolling with this killer over here the other day and I just hear it snap."

Mina looked at Felix and frowned. "You broke his foot?"

"Nah, it's not his fault. Total random accident. My foot broke itself against his knee, is more like it." Jonah laughed. "It fucking sucks, though, I won't lie. Being off the mat is rough."

She nodded, knowing there was no truer statement. And while she had officially switched gyms, she went so rarely that it was almost like she had stopped Jiu Jitsu completely, so she understood how he felt. The new gym was far enough away that it never seemed worth the time or CTA fare to go, especially since Pilsen MMA only had night classes, and she usually had Amelie at night. At best she would make it twice a week.

"Yeah," she agreed, nodding sadly. "It is rough."

Jonah looked at her and sighed. "You're welcome back here anytime, Mina, you know that, right?"

"Jonah," she started, then sighed. "I know you think that, but what about everyone else?" She gestured to the rest of the gym.

"These fucking idiots? They can barely put one foot in front of the other." Jonah laughed. "Who cares what they think?"

"They all hate me."

"No one hates you," he said. "And if anyone says shit to you, bring them to me, okay? I'll talk sense into them. You know what I always say, Mina. It takes a village," he said, wiping the sweat off his shiny bald forehead.

"I don't have a village," she said, shaking her head.

"Yes, you do," Jonah said, making sure to catch her eye. Then the buzzer went off again, and Jonah limped to the front of the class. "All right, guys, let's circle up and bow out! Then these nice young policemen have a few questions for everyone, and you're all going to be happy to help them with their investigation, okay?"

Jonah clapped once, and the circle of about forty people bowed to each other, then to the giant photos of the Jiu Jitsu greats that hung up on the wall, and everyone began high-fiving each other until they ran out of hands. Once they had dispersed again, she headed straight for Detective Conner, who she finally spotted in the back corner near the men's locker room, huddled in a conversation with a black belt named Jake, who she also knew to be a Chicago police officer, though she wasn't sure which district.

When she reached him, Jake saw her and silently wandered off to the mats. They'd never had a conversation before, even when she was at the gym every day. He was quiet and standoffish, much older than everyone else, maybe retired, if she recalled correctly.

"Detective," she said, but was stopped by his finger, which he lifted to his lips before turning away from her. Conner was on the phone. A moment later, he turned back to her, pocketing it.

"Sorry," he said. "Had to take that."

"What did you mean earlier when you said Dima hasn't been at work?"

Detective Conner sighed. His light brown skin had started to perspire in the hot room, his cheeks flushed. "I'm not sure there's another way to rephrase what I already said, Ms. Banksy. He hasn't been employed there in at least two months."

"But then where the hell is he?" she asked.

The detective looked at her with furrowed brows. "Have you tried calling him, ma'am?"

She shook her head. "No. Listen, can I go? I'll call him when I get home."

"If you go, we're just gonna show up at your house in an hour. We're gonna need an alibi for the night of Dylan's murder. And Detective Miller has a few more questions for you."

"An alibi? Why?"

"We're asking everyone here for an alibi, Ms. Banksy. No need to get your panties in a bunch," he said.

"But you know who my alibi is," she huffed. "He's on your payroll."

Detective Conner's chapped lips thinned. "Just don't go any-where. Detective Miller will take your official statement shortly."

"Okay, can I at least go outside, then?" she asked, pointing to the open back door, which led to the parking lot. "Or will you arrest me?"

"No one is arresting you, Ms. Banksy," he said. "Not yet anyway." Then the man turned and headed off towards the mat, leaving her standing there alone.

She couldn't turn to face the rest of the gym, so she went out the back door, the cold air a refreshing force against her red-hot face. She took her phone out of her pocket and tried calling Dima. It rang and rang, but he didn't answer. It may have been on do not disturb mode. She tried again, because she knew a number that called twice in a row could get through on the second try, but he still didn't pick up. She left him a voicemail and was about to return to the gym, wondering if she might still have his phone set up in her "Find My iPhone" app, when Detective Miller spotted her as he was getting out of his car.

"Ms. Banksy," he said. "Just the lady I wanted to see."

"Yeah, Detective Conner said you wanted to take my statement, or something?"

"Well, yes, but there's something else. It's about your van," he said.

She pulled her arm out of his grasp and stood against the outside wall. The same wall she had once made out with Matthew against. "What about it?" she said. "Can someone just tell me what is going on? So much secrecy, I feel like I'm in the Soviet Union or something."

"We're still gathering information, but—"

"Just tell me."

"It looks like Dylan was using the truck to move furniture from Chicago to Ohio, Indiana, and Wisconsin."

"Okay. So?"

"Well, we have suspicion to believe that it might not be just furniture he was moving, and now that our techs have had a chance to inspect the vehicle, we are pretty certain."

"What does that mean?" she asked.

"Drugs, ma'am. Lots and lots of drugs," he explained. "It took a while to figure out because it was inside the furniture. Dylan and his associates would make small tears in the cushions and take out all the stuffing, replacing it with cocaine and marijuana. Maybe even guns."

"I see." This did not surprise her in the slightest. In fact, she vaguely remembered Dylan mentioning some similar scheme he'd done in the past. She did not share this info with the detective, however. Her face remained blank.

"Look, we don't think you were involved, but the van is registered in your name," he said. "So don't leave the country anytime soon."

"I wasn't planning on it," she said meekly. She couldn't even remember the last time she'd left Chicago. It wasn't like she could afford to go anywhere, and it was hardly worth the effort with a toddler.

"And if you see Officer Stone, we'll need him to corroborate your alibi, so tell him to give me a call."

"Okay," she said. She wanted to ask him why they were interrogating everyone at the gym when clearly his death had to do with dealing drugs, but she knew even if she asked, she wouldn't get a clear answer. She was surprised she had gotten this much information out of the man. "Can I go now?"

"For now. We have a lot of statements to get through. I'll let you know if we need more from you."

"I'm sure you will," she said, and, completely exhausted, finally made her way back home, where she immediately passed out.

CHAPTER TWENTY

When she woke up, Mina checked the clock to find she had barely written five thousand words all day and now only had a few hours before she would have to go pick Amelie up from daycare. She used the first twenty minutes to look for and find her iPad, where she vaguely remembered having installed the Find My iPhone app. She wasn't sure if both their phones were registered on there or just hers, or if it was even the most current phone she owned, but she figured it wouldn't hurt to look.

Unfortunately, it had been so long since she'd used that iPad, neither of the phones were coming up. Even the email account set up with the gadget was an old one of Dimitry's she knew he never used anymore. So much for that. She tried calling Dima again, but only reached his voicemail. This time she left one asking him where he was and demanding he call her back as soon as possible. The second she hung up her phone began ringing. Her heart jumped, thinking it was him, that he would have some sort of explanation for her; that the men in her life wouldn't just keep disappearing like this, one by one. But it wasn't Dima. It was Matthew.

"What are you doing right now?" he asked her.

"Why?"

"We should talk," he said. "I'm about to pull up in front of the house."

"What?"

"Just come outside."

Maybe Matthew knew something about Dima, she realized in a panic, rushing around to find her keys. She put on her boots and ran out the door without even checking to see if she had everything else she needed. Not that she was ever that high-maintenance; mostly what she brought with her could fit in her coat. An ID, a credit card, a CTA pass, and her phone.

The speakers in the truck were blasting a Bad Religion song when she got inside, so cold from the wind chill that she was actually shaking a little. Matthew turned down the volume as she closed the door. The heat from the vents poured out like a fountain, warming her up instantly. She had always liked that about his truck, even if she did often make fun of him for it. It was a pretty nice vehicle.

"You like Bad Religion?" she asked, rubbing her hands together for warmth. "How did I not know that about you?"

"There are plenty of things you don't know about me," he said with a shrug.

"Yeah, that's the understatement of the year," she said. She looked out the window as he pulled out onto the road, heading north. She had no idea where he was going and didn't ask, because she wasn't sure she wanted to know. He was quiet for a while, focusing on driving, until Mina finally asked, "What's up?"

"How come you never told me Dimitry was related to the Milkoviches?"

"Am I supposed to know who that is?"

Matthew pulled the car to an abrupt stop, a traffic light turning from yellow to red in what seemed like a second. He turned to look at her. "Big Russian mob family in Chicago. Lots of drugs and guns, very hard to arrest."

"It doesn't sound familiar," she said with a shrug. "Anyway, Dima isn't that kind of Russian. They're Jews. They're all, like, doctors and lawyers. Nerdy stuff."

"You sure about that?"

"Yeah, I'm sure," she said. "We were together for ten years. I would have heard something about that, I think."

"The names Victor and Igor Bokotey don't ring a bell?"

She thought about it for a moment. "No, those names I do know. They're, like, I dunno, third cousins or something. Do something with computers."

Matthew laughed. "No. They don't."

Mina frowned. She really had thought Dima was joking about his cousins possibly being criminals. Still, she knew her husband; he was not the type to get involved in any of that, especially with his citizenship still up in the air. "What does this have to do with anything? He can't help who he's related to."

"Where is he right now?" Matthew asked.

"I don't know," she sighed. "But I'm guessing you heard that already."

"So, it's relevant," Matthew said.

"Are you saying he had something to do with Dylan's death? Because that's crazy."

"I'm not saying anything," Matthew said. "Just—"

"Just what?"

"You should be careful," he said.

"I never leave my house after eight p.m. How much more careful can I be?" she asked. "Not to mention I can't go half a day without running into a cop."

"Yeah. I heard about the gym," he said, putting the car in park and resting his hands on his lap. "How was that?"

She shrugged. "It was fine, actually," she said. "I'm starting to think we overreacted about that whole thing."

"Oh yeah?"

"Yeah. Have you been back since…?"

He shook his head. "No. Gave my statement at the station," he said, turning to look at her. "They really put me through the fucking ringer. Asked me a lot of questions about you."

"The police seem very invested in hearing about our fucked up lives," she said. "I don't see why."

He grunted. "Well, it's a murder. People generally only get killed over two things. Money or sex."

"But I wasn't having sex with Dylan."

He shrugged again. "They gotta follow the money and sex, either way. I don't blame them."

"So they think I was fucking Dylan. Great," she said, sighing. "I'm just the gym bicycle to them."

"Well, you were friends."

"So?"

"So, most people don't really think men and women can be just friends."

Mina let out an exasperated groan. "That's so not true," she said. He looked at her with narrowed brows.

"You and I, okay, we can't just be friends. But not everyone makes me wet just from being in the same room. That's just you."

Matthew's mouth turned up into a half smile. "You gotta stop saying shit like that when we're sitting in cars." The way he looked at her reminded her of that first night they'd hooked up, so many months ago; like he was a wolf and she was his prey. It made a flutter go through her chest, then travel down to her nether regions. Matthew's gaze followed it there, and then he licked his lips.

"What, the truth?"

He shook his head and laughed. "Now I want to check and see if it is," he said, glancing down at her crotch. "God, you know how to drive a man insane."

"I'm a writer," she said with a shrug, like it explained everything. In a way, though, it did. A lot of the buildup and continuation of their affair she could directly blame on their steamy exchanges online. Words were where she felt the most comfortable; they were like what a police uniform was for him, they gave her power and confidence. They made her who she was. Even if she wasn't quite sure who exactly that was anymore.

His phone rang then, interrupting the moment.

"Yeah?" he asked. He remained mostly silent for the duration of the call, only answering in monosyllables. He clearly didn't want her to know what he was talking about, or who he was talking to. It wasn't the first time he had put her in that kind of position. So she busied herself with her phone too, which was rather unexciting. Not even a missed text, and still no calls from Dimitry. Finally, Matthew hung up and turned to her, a serious pall falling over his already pale face.

"What?" she asked. She knew when he put a hand on her thigh, whatever he was about to tell her was not going to be good.

"Mina, I need you to stay calm."

"What, Matthew? Just tell me." Her heart rate began soaring, and she couldn't take her eyes off his. He squeezed her thigh and inhaled.

"It's Dimitry," he said.

She swallowed a lump in her throat that was growing by the second. "What about Dimitry?" she asked. When he didn't respond right away, she asked again, punching him in the shoulder. "What about him?"

Matthew swallowed, then licked his lips. "They found his car."

AUGUST / SEPTEMBER

CHAPTER TWENTY-ONE

The following Saturday, Mina and Ariel had plans to attend a birthday party for one of Jonah's kids at a nearby park. It was the first time she'd met with Ariel in person since she'd starting sleeping with Matthew, and even though they were on hiatus, she still came armed with an oversized water bottle of whiskey and LaCroix. Mina worried it would be awkward, or that Ariel would notice something was off, but she was, as always, lost in her own world of craft projects and house upgrades.

Plus, they had to spend so much of their time chasing the kids in opposite directions that they hardly had a chance to speak. It wasn't until they had settled the girls into their strollers with some leftover cake that they got to finally sit down and relax. By then, Mina was pretty drunk. She generally tried to avoid drinking heavily when the sun was still out, but it was summer, so the sun was out until she went to bed; plus, she had been so nervous. Only after she felt properly buzzed was she able to contort her face into a neutral position and talk to Ariel like nothing at all was amiss.

"Why is sugar the only thing in the world that makes a toddler quiet for more than two minutes?" Mina asked, shaking her head. She tried her best to avoid sugar with Amelie, but it was impossible at a birthday party, when it was right there in everyone's faces, taunting the kids with its bright blue icing.

"Right?" Ariel asked, looking off into the distance. She certainly wasn't making it easy for her to maintain a conversation that after-noon, not that this was unusual. The amount of effort Mina had to put in keeping a conversation going with most adults these days often drained her so much she would wonder what was the point after. Between smartphones and children and all the everyday distractions of modern life, conversational skills between adults had really gone by the wayside. She often had better conversations with the students in the Open Guard kids' class; at least they asked questions, usually odd ones too. This was partly why she enjoyed being with Matthew. He was easy to talk to, but they could also not talk.

Mina took another sip of her drink, feeling the heat of it in her stomach as she watched Ariel's face, which was pretty but would be prettier if she could find a way to relax once in a while. Her life seemed relatively peaceful; she had a stable income, family nearby, and a daughter who was perfectly healthy and had not been tested six times already for autism, yet she was always looking for problems and then exaggerating their weight, or so it seemed to Mina. It seemed like a way to avoid her real problems, which was her marriage. Even before she'd become so close to Matthew, this was fairly obvious, but now it was more so.

"And it always has to be the most sugary sugar too," Mina said, on conversational auto-pilot now. "Can't be raisins or roasted wal-nuts. Has to have frosting on it."

"I mean, if I could eat that much cake and not ever gain weight like Dallas, I would do it too probably," Ariel said.

"Not me," Mina said absently. "I don't even like cake. I would eat a whole loaf of fresh bread over cake any day."

"Bread?" Dallas said, her mouth full of melting blue icing. "I want bread."

"No," Ariel said. "You've eaten enough."

"I want bread!" Dallas whined. Ariel shook her head, annoyed. Both Dallas and Amelie were starting to try to climb out of their strollers, presumably to go find this loaf of bread. Served her right for mentioning it.

"Let's take them back to the house," Mina suggested, taking Amelie's stroller and starting to push it forward so that she wouldn't jump out. Ariel did the same with Dallas.

"Okay." Ariel looked at her watch. "I have to make dinner in about an hour, but I have a little bit of time."

As they turned to go, Mina noticed that Ariel and Dallas's faces were smeared with so much frosting they looked like Smurfs who got bleached in the laundry. And they were all sticky with sweat. She suggested they might get them to play in the pool in the yard.

"At least in my yard they can't go running off every two seconds," Mina added. She actually wanted to stay at the party, but there was a bounce castle in the playground area that had been set up for a different birthday party and Amelie would not accept that she wasn't allowed inside. She'd already had to run and intercept her eight times, and her feet were getting sore.

"Right," Ariel said, her voice still distant. Something about being married to Matthew had caused an emotional barrier that was hard to break with her. Or maybe she'd always been like that, and it was why the two of them had been able to stay married for so long. They'd been together even longer than her and Dima.

"Everything okay?" Mina asked, finally. Talking about sugar was getting tiresome. Perhaps if she asked her directly, they could talk about something real for once, instead of what brand of Pull-ups their kids liked or whatever new Facebook argument she'd gotten herself into that day. They began walking in tandem down the park's bumpy sidewalk, strolling past a family of geese that lived by the pond, ignoring the girls' squeals to get out and try to chase them.

"Oh, yeah, it's fine," Ariel said absently.

"Did something happen the other day?" The sun beamed down on them tyrannically. Mina had a sudden urge to pee, on top of everything else. She really had consumed a lot of alcohol. "When you wanted to get a drink?"

"Just Matthew being Matthew," she sighed.

"Which means…?"

She sighed again. "He's just been so out of it lately. He jumps down my throat about every little thing. I'm worried he's depressed again," she said.

"Again?"

"That's kind of why we moved from Oklahoma. He was in a really dark place. It's been really good for him to be here," she said. "Or I thought it was, anyway. And if not, then why the fuck did I leave all my friends and family to come here?" She shook her head. "Sorry, that's probably a little TMI."

"No, not at all," Mina responded. It was probably the most personal information Ariel had ever shared with her thus far, and they'd know each other for almost a year by then. "I can see why you'd be frustrated. You want to go back to Oklahoma?"

"I mean, yeah, or anywhere warm, really, but Matthew said he would never go back there, so that's that." She tried to shrug it off, but it was clear she was bothered by it. Mina felt a little bad that she was so unhappy here, and also that she didn't feel like they were good enough of friends for her to share stuff like that with her. She preferred this type of conversation far more than what Ariel usually wanted to discuss, which was always on the superficial side.

A lot of her mom friends were like that. So consumed with sleep schedules and play dates and plans that it seemed like their brains could no longer handle deeper thoughts. She had the opposite problem; her mind was so consumed with other thoughts it was hard to remember if she had fed Amelie any protein all day.

"I'm sorry," Mina said. "That sucks."

"No, no, it's fine. Forget I said anything," Ariel said. A look of regret took over Ariel's face, so Mina didn't pry any further. It happened sometimes, with new friends especially, that Mina got them to open up, but instead of feeling better after sharing their troubles, they felt naked and exposed, like Mina had stripped them of their armor. Talking about your feelings was too intimate for most people; even some couples avoided it. It was conversations like that with Matthew that had further confused her when they were still only friends talking after class. After he had consumed several beers, he could go on and on about his stresses at work in a way she knew he didn't do with Ariel.

"How's it going rearranging your craft room?" Mina asked, trying to move the conversation somewhere a little more neutral. She remembered her mentioning this project earlier in the week and talking about it at length.

"It's not," Ariel said. "It's a disaster in there."

"You need help? I love organizing stuff." She was happy for the change of subject, slurping on the remainder of her drink, despite her full bladder. Just the mention of his name had made her knees wobbly. And she didn't like knowing they were having more problems, especially since they were possibly her fault this time. At least Ariel didn't believe Matthew was having an affair. Or, had one, anyway.

"I just don't have anywhere to put anything," Ariel said. She raised her arm and wiped sweat from her brow. "I'll probably just have to put it all in storage. If we have another kid, we'll need the room."

Mina's heart plummeted, and she had to turn her face away. "You're trying to get pregnant?" she asked, trying very hard not to sound shocked. She had, wrongly it seemed, assumed they were only having one, due to their being both over forty. And the fact that he had slept with her many times in the recent past.

"Well, we're not *not* trying," Ariel said. This made Mina wonder if she was implying that their problems had not quite reached the bedroom yet. Mina let the comment float over her head; she was too drunk to consider what it really meant. She didn't know what to say. How could Matthew be off with her when he was trying to have another child with his wife? She really felt lower than dirt suddenly. She swallowed back the urge to puke.

Ariel looked at her with confusion, and Mina realized her entire face had gone pink. She sipped on her drink to relax. "Sorry, whiskey and this much sun just do not go together." This was true, but she knew deep down it wasn't the only reason her stomach had suddenly turned into knots. She was being reckless. And also she felt bad. It was true what she had said that first time: she was a bad, bad person. Not only was she married, but so was Matthew. That was two marriages being ruined at the same time because of her. Two families, with dogs and babies and mortgages, the things that added up to a life. Over sex. It was ridiculous and selfish and dumb on so many levels. She was glad she had put a stop to things. They needed to return to their spouses where they belonged.

"Oh yeah, I don't know how you do that," Ariel said. "That's why I stick to beer."

She swallowed back another bad burp. In her opinion, she and Matthew both drank too much beer and it was the reason they had an extra twenty pounds on them. Not that she would ever say that. In the Midwest, she was considered the weird one for avoiding any and all hops. "I can't do beer. And if I drink wine, I just pass out."

"I can see that."

Mina lived only a few blocks away from the park, and by the end of this conversation they were already back at the house. She unlatched the back gate, then went inside to let the dog out. Luckily, Ariel and Dallas immediately jumped into the large plastic pool, which was already filled with water from the morning rain. It quickly turned blue from all the frosting. Their faces still remained pretty Smurf-like, however, and they quickly lost interest in the pool.

Amelie, who was not yet potty trained, took off her sopping wet diaper and began to run around naked. Mina, not wanting to find another diaper at the moment, let her. It was still pretty hot. "Can I use your restroom?" Ariel asked. Isabelle was circling her and barking, which Ariel was used to, so she ignored it.

"Oh sure, go ahead," Mina said carelessly. "Dima's inside if you need help finding it. I don't think you've ever been inside our house, have you?"

"I haven't?"

"Pretty sure. We're always in the yard. Or at your place."

"Well, I'm sure I can manage," Ariel said.

Only after she had gone inside and this registered, Mina was struck with panic. She didn't think he had, but what if Matthew had left something there that would be incriminating? What if they hadn't been careful enough?

A few very tense minutes later, Ariel came back outside. Isabelle had relaxed and was chewing on some weeds in the garden bed as Dima followed her out, carrying something in his arms. A sump pump. Shit. She had totally forgotten about that. Behind her, Amelie squealed, then dropped something into the pool that she knew without looking should probably not be in the pool, judging by its weight.

"Thanks," Ariel said to Dima, looking a tad confused when he sit it down on the ground. "I had no idea Matthew even lent it to you guys."

Mina wiped her very sweaty hands on her jeans. She really, really wanted a cigarette suddenly. She had maybe never felt the desire so strongly in her life, even when she was addicted to them for years.

"Sorry," Dima said, looking at Mina with renewed annoyance. "I told Mina to call a plumber next time."

"Oh, yeah, Matthew's not really that great with plumbing. He broke our toilet at least twice." Ariel laughed uncomfortably, and

Mina had the strongest feeling that she was just registering the fact that she and Matthew had been alone, and she didn't know about it. What an idiot she was. She should have returned it right away. Or he should have told her he'd leant it. Now she would definitely find it suspicious. Ariel didn't let it show, but she also didn't look at her afterward.

"I'm sorry, I was panicking, the water was rushing everywhere, so I just kinda ran to the gym to see if anyone could help me," she mumbled.

Her heart was beating loud, terrified thumps in her chest, and she forced herself to take another sip of her drink, even though she already really had to pee. How long could she keep living this way? It was so stressful to have to wonder about so many things at the same time, while also watching a child. Amelie, who was still naked, was currently taking a tiny bucket with holes on the bottom from the pool to her bike, then back again. Dallas was drowning a toy in the pool.

"It's no problem, I'm sure. I mean, Matthew didn't even mention it, so..." Ariel trailed off, and luckily they were saved from more awkwardness by Amelie and Dallas, who had started fighting over one of Amelie's toys. A plastic baby soaked with blue pool water. That was the heavy object she'd heard being dropped into the pool.

"It's my baby! *It's miiiiiiine!*" Dallas screamed.

"No, it's not," Ariel said sternly to Dallas, walking over to her. "Give it back."

Amelie didn't really care either way, she was not a possessive toddler overall, but Ariel seemed to care a lot.

"My baby! *My babyyyyyy!*" Dallas continued. She dropped down on the ground and extended both arms and legs against the cement, writhing.

"Okay, we're going home right now," Ariel said, picking her up from the ground. Dallas began to kick and turn in her arms. Mina couldn't help but feel like them leaving had more to do with their conversation, but she couldn't exactly oppose. Ariel had said she couldn't stay long, and Dallas was in the middle of a tantrum.

"Thanks for having us," Ariel said, holding a still-kicking Dallas. She was still totally soaked with water, and holding onto the doll for dear life. "I'll have Matthew grab that sump pump later, if that's okay. My hands are kind of full right now."

"Oh, that's okay. I can drop it off," Dima told her.

"It's my baby!" Dallas continued to wail as Ariel tore the poor doll out of her little arms. Tears rushed out of her eyes, and she continued kicking and screaming against Ariel's chest.

"This is Amelie's baby," Ariel said, giving the baby back to Amelie. She gave her a wide-eyed look that implied *How did my life come to this?* which made Mina feel a little better about them leaving. Maybe she was being paranoid about the sump pump. Maybe it was only in movies where people actually noticed things, and Felix was a fluke. "You do not need any more babies, Dallas. You have enough babies."

"That's how I feel sometimes too," Mina joked, though it was partially true. She really could not imagine having another baby, especially once Amelie had turned two and began acting out all the time.

Amelie dropped the wet doll as soon as the gate had closed, then ran into the garden beds to pick cherry tomatoes and eat them. She was still without a diaper.

Dima stood outside next to her and began laughing about Dallas and the baby. "The drama! It was like a scene from a movie," he said. She couldn't look at Dima right now. Her bladder was screaming.

"I'm sorry, I have to pee so bad," Mina said, running inside. "Can you get her showered and dressed?"

When she returned from the bathroom, Amelie was no longer blue. Dima was cleaning her face off with a towel. Mina, still pretty drunk, was grateful for that at least.

She eventually sobered up and they managed to put Amelie to bed without too much fuss, but Mina couldn't help but feel like some grave error in judgment had occurred that she would not be able to take back. She even tried texting Ariel later, but Ariel didn't respond.

As she was about to fall asleep, she got a message from Matthew. It was pure luck Dima wasn't awake to see the notification, and still it made the panic rise from her belly to her chest. Before she responded, she turned off the setting that allowed notifications from social media apps to her phone.

Hey. We have a bit of a problem, it said.

She held her breath and wrote back *Ariel?*

Yeah, I think I talked her down but we should get our stories straight.

What is there to get straight? You lent it to me, and that's that.

Oh yeah? That's that?

Well, the sump pump part is true.

Like you said, details. She was asking exactly what time and how I happened to be over there. What did you tell her? he wrote.

That I ran to the gym to see if anyone was there and asked you for help.

There was a long pause after that. *Why would I be at the gym at fucking 12 o'clock?*

Noon class?

All she would have to do is check the calendar to see there's no noon class in Bridgeport on a Wednesday.

Did you tell her it was noon?

Yes.

She thought about it for a moment. *Okay. Say you were getting a private lesson from Felix. I doubt she would ask him. Do they know each other?*

Another long pause, then a reply came in: *Yeah, that could work.*

Sorry. We should have talked about it sooner. Or I should have returned the pump. I wasn't thinking clearly.

We need to start being more careful.

That will be easy since we're done with all that, right?

Right.

Mina could hear Dima stirring next to her, and panic shot through her body again. *I gotta go. I'll see you at the gym?*

Yeah. I'll see you Monday.

She reread their conversation two more times, then she deleted the messages from existence, like she had all the others. But the feeling of a storm brewing followed her into her dreams, turning them into nightmares, and waking her up several times in the night until she just gave up and made herself coffee. Then she sat in her office and played the saddest music she owned and let herself mope until the sun came up.

CHAPTER TWENTY-TWO

The problem with Mina and Matthew stopping the affair was that they couldn't stop. Sure, she could go a week without texting him, if she avoided drinking and hid her phone away at night. But inevitably she would end up seeing him at the gym, and they would flirt, or they would go out with everyone to the nearest bar, and suddenly it would be eleven p.m. on a Thursday and she would be fucking him in the back of his truck again. In the morning she would tell herself it was the last time. But it was never the last time. They would have long, drunk conversations about being together, followed by long, sober conversations agreeing to end things, and on and on it went for the entire season like a bad romance TV show stuck on repeat.

They were on one of their many hiatuses, perhaps their longest one, when, to celebrate the arrival of fall, the gym decided to throw a big party. Everyone was told to dress up, so Mina went out and bought a tight black dress and leather boots that accentuated all the right features. Realistically, Mina probably shouldn't have gone. Or Dima shouldn't have. Or Matthew. It was a bad idea for them all to be drunk together at the gym, and that was certain to happen. But Dima had insisted on getting a sitter and joining her, which meant she would have to spend the entire night in some combination of stressed out and wanting things she couldn't have. It felt pretty unlikely that it would just be another fun gym party. She knew this in the pit of her stomach. But when she tried to get out of it, Dima had started asking her too many questions, and she realized not going might be far more telling than going. Maybe she could just stop by and then feign exhaustion when she'd had enough. It didn't have to turn into a thing, she reasoned, even as her stomach turned in knots all day, too distracted to even play with Amelie.

The moment they'd put her to bed and let the babysitter in, she headed straight for the booze and took two shots of whiskey. It hit her right away, settling into her stomach and calming her nerves enough to get her shoes on and go. She brought a pack of cigarettes with her even though she didn't think she could really smoke them. She didn't want to do that in front of the Jiu Jitsu guys. Everyone was so obsessed with their health, despite the rampant overdrinking. Even the nicotine addicts chose to chew tobacco so it wouldn't affect their lungs. It was like something out of a 1940s baseball movie.

The gym was bright and loud, nearly overwhelming her senses the second they walked in the door. It was packed, and even though the temperature outside had started to cool to its normal mid-sixties September weather, it was sweltering inside. She sat down and wiped sweat from her brow, trying to get her bearings. The next thing she knew, someone was handing her a drink.

"What's this?" she asked, turning to whoever had brought it.

"Basically just whiskey," said Felix, sitting down next to her. "And Sprite."

"Oh. Thanks," she said.

"You look like you need one."

Well, he wasn't wrong about that. Felix was nursing a beer himself, with two unopened ones on the floor next to him, and she began half listening to him rant about media bias, one of his favorite topics. After she hadn't said anything in some time, he nudged her in the shoulder.

"You okay?" he asked.

She swallowed. No, she was not okay. She had been watching Matthew pound drink after drink, always aware of where he was in the room. She wanted to touch him so bad it almost hurt. She'd missed him that week. At the same time, she wanted to punch him. Neither of these reactions were healthy, she knew. She could barely make sense of it. But she had to ignore her feelings for Matthew. Dima was there, having a great time.

"I should have eaten dinner first," Mina managed to say finally. Someone had turned on The Cure, probably Felix, which didn't help her mood. Several small circles of boisterous conversations lingered around them.

"This is my dinner," Felix said, raising his Miller Lite.

"Healthy," she said with a nod.

"There's chips and stuff over there," he added.

"Yeah, I know," she said. "I just can't really stomach anything today."

Felix chuckled. "Uh oh. You pregnant?"

"No!" she said. "God, no."

"I'm just kidding. You're obviously having a midlife crisis over here. Last thing you need is to throw another human in there."

She turned to him. "Midlife crisis?" she asked.

He nodded towards Matthew. Her heart leaped into her throat. She had hoped he would have forgotten about that by now, considering how rarely she and Matthew had been at the gym at the same time recently. She couldn't even remember the last time they'd been partners.

"Not sure what you mean," she said, blushing. She and Felix had become pretty good friends, but he was definitely not someone she was willing to confide in. Her heart was bursting with the urge to tell someone, but it couldn't be another gym member.

Felix snorted. "Yes, you are."

She watched as Matthew pounded another drink, and he noticed her watching. They exchanged a very intense look for a moment that sent her mind spinning. She could hardly make out what it was he was showing her. Some combination of lust and sadness and anger.

He must have missed her too. Maybe that's what the look meant. She hadn't even texted him once that week, and they hadn't been alone together in more than two. Or maybe he was just drunk and wanted to have sex with her.

"You guys are fucking idiots," Felix said, rubbing a palm over his face. He'd seen the exchange. They were idiots, he was right about that. Couldn't they go one night without reliving this drama? Apparently not. "Tell me you at least stopped things."

Mina took a deep breath. Well, he knew, and what was the point of lying to another person, especially when lying would be totally fruitless? No point at all. And it felt good to be known, for at least one moment. That for a minute she could just be herself, not the person she was pretending to be.

She cleared her throat. "Of course we did."

Felix shook his head, downing the rest of his beer. She expected him to say more, but he stayed quiet, secretly judging her surely.

"What?" she asked when he continued to shake his head.

"It's none of my business," he said.

"Clearly, it is," she said in a more hostile tone than she intended. "Say what you need to say."

"You have children," he said. "I mean, you know I hate kids. They're stupid and they can't even read. But still. Why would you do that to them?"

Her face flushed red again. She had no response for that, because there was no response. She was selfish and so was Matthew. They were probably terrible people. They'd go to hell for what they'd done. But how could she stop an attraction so strong it had swallowed her up whole? It was like saying no to a whale.

"Not to mention the gym," Felix said, gesturing around them, where The Cure was still playing and drinks were still being swallowed at an impressive rate. The men there were expert borderline alcoholics. "Gyms have been closed over shit like this. It's always a shitshow."

"I don't see how what…I don't see how it has anything to do with the gym." She wasn't sure she believed it, but she still hoped it could all just stay separate. The gym, her marriage, and the thing with Matthew. When she thought if it all imploding, it made her heart shrink with hopelessness. But she also understood that one day, it would. How could it not?

"Of course it fucking does," Felix said, opening another beer and drinking half of it in one gulp. "You're a white belt, and there's the whole power dynamic of him being practically a black belt and we're supposed to be helping you. It's predatory. This is why I would never date someone from the gym."

"You never date anyone period," she said, rolling her eyes.

"That's because I'm always at the gym!" he said so loudly people turned and looked their way. Dima glanced at her questioningly, and she just shrugged, as if to say, *It's just Felix being Felix again.*

"Let's bring it down a notch, please," she said quietly. "Unless you want everyone to find out."

"That's the last thing I want," he said. "I actually like this place."

"I would really avoid talking to Matthew about it too," she added, suddenly worried.

"I'm not joining your idiot club," he scoffed. "I have enough problems of my own."

She finished her drink, telling herself it would be a good time to go home. Before anyone got any more drunk or did something stupid. But first, she would sneak off for a cigarette, because she literally couldn't not have one in that moment. She stood up, reaching into her purse.

"Great. Go smoke your little secret cigarettes, I'm sure that will help," he said. How did Felix know so much about her? She didn't think he'd given her any extra thought before. Now it seemed like he had been watching her.

"What's your problem?" she asked, sitting back down.

"Nothing, Mina," he said, finishing his beer and standing up.

"Nothing."

She watched him head over to the refreshment table and grab two more beers before she quietly exited the gym and walked around to the parking lot. She was about halfway through her Camel Light when she felt someone out there with her, getting closer. She turned to find Matthew. His face was flushed, and his eyes were lit up, the way they got when he was excited about something. Probably he was already wasted. Still, it felt good to be next to him again, wrong as it was.

"Can I have one of those?" he asked her.

"You should go back inside," she said, turning away.

"Give me a cigarette," he ordered. Then he stood so close to her she dug one out of her purse just so he would be forced to move away. She didn't want anyone to see them out there alone together, even if they were just smoking. And definitely not when they had such little space between them.

"Thanks. Was that so hard?" he asked.

"Are you mad at me or something?" she asked, inhaling a long drag.

"Why would you say that?"

"You've had very weird energy all night. And what was that look you gave me inside? Sloppy, Matthew."

"Yep, that's me, Sloppy Matthew," he said.

She shook her head. She should have gone home to smoke. But that was the addict in her; she couldn't even wait that long. "You're wasted."

"I cannot stop staring at your tits," he said. "Did you wear that dress for me?"

Of course that was the entire reason she had gotten this dress; she wasn't that un self-aware. But she only wanted him to want her from afar, their old game. Not blow up their lives right in front of everyone. "You shouldn't talk like that when anyone could hear us."

"So you did wear it for me," he said, his eyebrows raised.

"Of course I did," she replied quietly.

"Let's go somewhere," he said, inhaling the cigarette in one last drag and then throwing it onto the cement.

"We have nowhere to go, and I'm not fucking in your truck again. It makes me feel like a fifteen-year-old."

He reached for her, put his hands up her skirt, then down into her underwear.

"No," she said, but even she could hear that her voice was not very convincing. She pushed him away and tried to maintain distance.

"That doesn't really sound like a no," he argued, grabbing her again.

"We talked about this," she said, adrenaline pumping through her veins. She pulled her dress back down, moved away again.

"We talked about cooling off a bit, yeah. I think we've done a good job of that," he said, reaching for her again. She pushed him off her.

"Oh, is that what you heard?" she asked.

Matthew ran a finger up and down her arm, making her shiver, then grabbed her throat. Her adrenaline shot through the roof, but so did her sex drive. God, what was wrong with her? The harder he squeezed the more turned on she got.

"Just be a good girl, like you usually are," he said, his voice lowering. She caught his eyes, and they were hungry and violent, which only made her more turned on. But they were right outside the gym, both their spouses inside. This would be an epic disaster. She grabbed his wrist with both hands and pushed away. Surprisingly, he let her. He was definitely strong enough to keep his grip if he wanted to.

"You're being an idiot," she said, arms crossed over her chest. "Anyone could come out here."

"Mina," he said, pulling her back. "No one is coming out here. They trust us."

"Do you trust *me*? Because you shouldn't," she said. "I could blow up your whole life with three little words."

"You won't, though, because you'd be blowing up your own life too."

"Well, maybe you don't realize this, but sometimes that's exactly what I want to do."

"I do realize that, Mina. I'm not a fucking idiot. But you won't."

"How do you know that?"

He grabbed her by the throat again and squeezed. "Because you won't."

"Are you threatening me, Matthew?"

"Is that what you want me to do?"

"No," she said in barely a whisper. She didn't take her eyes off his as he put his hand back up her dress, sliding into her underwear. The edges of his mouth curled into a smile that was still part grimace.

"Then why are you so wet?" he asked, squeezing her throat even harder, so hard her lips went numb. "I bet you never get this wet for Dima." Just as she thought she might pass out, he let go. Her pulse raced as she pushed herself away from him.

"That was pretty fucked up, even for you," she said, catching her breath.

"I wasn't really going to let you pass out," he said, wounded.

"It wasn't the choking. It was the implication."

He watched her, brows furrowed.

"Sometimes I really think you could do it," she admitted quietly.

"Do what?"

She looked at him skeptically. He knew exactly what she meant. "Whatever. It doesn't matter. I told you the last time we talked, if you want to keep seeing me, we need to tell them. So, you want to touch me again, Matthew, then go inside and tell Dima about it."

Matthew sighed, sliding his hands into the pockets of his Open Guard sweatshirt. It was the only one she had ever seen him wear, just like his baseball cap. He was on Team Open Guard, that was clear. That's how she knew he would never let her tell anyone about them, because the gym was too intertwined in his identity; it wasn't even about Ariel, or maybe even Dallas, in the end. "I'm sorry. I'm wasted."

"I see that. Don't you think that's a bad idea right now?" She walked towards the door, then turned around to face him. "I'm going back to the gym, and then I'm going home. I'll make it easy for you."

"Nothing about you is easy," he muttered.

Mina sighed. "Yes, it is. You're just a coward." She pulled down her dress an extra time, just to be safe. She didn't turn to look at him again before she left, she just walked straight down the sidewalk and back inside. Dima was right by the gym entrance and her heart nearly jumped out of her chest. Had he been close enough to hear them? She really needed to go home. A person could only take so much.

"Were you smoking?" Dima asked.

"I was, sorry." She shrugged.

"Drunk already?" he said, smiling. "That was quick."

"Well, I did skip dinner," she said. "Anyway, I don't feel that well. I think I want to go home."

"Really? But you always skip dinner. And you love gym parties," he said, his smile turning into a frown. The music had changed while they were gone, and someone had put on an old-timey folk song. It really didn't match the energy of the room, which was loud and boisterous. She felt about as close to a panic attack as she could get without actually getting one. Everything in her body was telling her to get out of there, but Dima was holding her by the arm.

That's when Matthew came back inside, eyes glassy and dark. She wasn't sure what Dima had read on his face, but he suddenly began squeezing her arm tighter and tighter, watching Matthew walk across the room and then looking at her, then watching Matthew again. He seemed to be silently wondering if something weird had happened outside. And he wouldn't let go of her arm so she could leave.

"Hey," Mina said. "You're hurting me." She expected Dima would let go and apologize but instead he turned to face her, his eyes narrowed with something she couldn't quite place right away because she had never seen it on him before. It was suspicion.

"Anything you want to tell me?" he asked her, staring straight into her eyes, her soul.

She blinked. "What do you mean?"

He pulled her to the side and practically pushed her down into a chair. She wondered if anyone had noticed the change of energy in the room, and looked behind him. No one seem bothered. Only Matthew. He was surrounded by people, but she could tell he was watching them.

"I mean, what the fuck was that?" Dima said.

"What?" she asked, turning beet red. He had still not let go of her arm, merely switched his grip to hold her wrist more tightly. It was going to leave a huge bruise, she could already tell. It was a good thing she was already covered in them.

"You and Matthew."

She swallowed, hoping she could still get herself out of this mess. He didn't see anything, so there was no reason for him to be suspicious. If he'd seen something he wouldn't have been asking what happened. "We were smoking," she explained. "I'm not allowed to smoke with someone now?"

Dima's mouth tensed into a straight line, his eyes dark. "It looked like you had an argument or something. Did he try something with you?"

"No, Dima, of course not." He couldn't have really known anything, nor did he have proof, so he loosened his grip on hers and she finally tore her arm away, using a move she had actually learned in Jiu Jitsu, a basic wrist release. "I'm going to go home."

"Fine," he said without looking at her. His eyes had locked with Matthew's now, and she watched Matthew turn away and head to the men's locker room. "I'll see you later."

She took one last look around the room, part of her wanting to stay and enjoy herself, but she knew it would be impossible now.

She grabbed her bag and rushed out the door before anyone could notice. Once she was home in bed, she noticed several messages from Matthew, some apologizing, others telling her that he missed her. It took everything she had not to respond. She promptly deleted them all until there was nothing but a blank screen in front of her.

CHAPTER TWENTY-THREE

The problem was that once Dima had noticed, correctly, that he had something to be suspicious about, he began to hang around the house way more often. He traded shifts and began insisting they hang out or watch TV together, and he was always glancing at her phone when he thought she wasn't looking. After a few days of this, Mina started going crazy. She woke up early one morning, and while Amelie was eating breakfast, told him she was going to go visit her oldest friend, Lila, a bartender and mother of three who lived up in Rogers Park, just so she could have a few hours away from his obsessive eyes. She needed to talk to Matthew, to let him know Dima was onto them.

They hadn't spoken at all since the party. She hadn't wanted to risk texting him, with Dima watching her every move. So once she was on the train—she actually did intend to see her friend Lila, as she had been dying to tell someone what was going on with her, and she knew Lila could be trusted—she texted Matthew that they needed to talk ASAP.

A few minutes later, Matthew called her on Facetime; he was at home alone with Dallas that morning, while Ariel was at work. Mina put in her earbuds, moving to the back of the train car, where it was empty. "Hey," Matthew said. "What's up?"

"It's Dima," she said. "He's onto us. Or something."

"How do you know that?"

"He won't leave me alone since the gym party. He's always

checking my phone. He's been really weird."

Matthew sighed, licking his lips. In the background she could hear Dallas screaming, "Daddy! Daddy, come play with me!"

"Go play with your toys, Dallas. I'm on the phone," he said. Then he turned back to her. "Well, does he have proof? Did he see anything?"

"Just whatever look you were wearing on your face after you followed me out to smoke."

"I followed you out when you were smoking?" he asked, surprised.

"Jesus Christ, Matthew. You don't remember? You smoked an entire cigarette. Then you were feeling me up."

Matthew ran a hand across his face, blinking. "I do not remember any of that. Shit."

"How wasted were you?" Mina asked. She knew he drank a lot, but it still surprised her that he could just black out like that.

"I was annihilated," he said. He rubbed his face again. "I know. I really need to stop drinking."

"I mean, you don't need to stop completely, but maybe cut yourself off at, I dunno, ten White Claws? That seems like more than plenty."

Matthew laughed at this. Then she saw the top of Dallas's head come into the frame. "Mellie! I want to talk to her too!" she said.

Dallas still didn't know Mina's name, so she just called her Amelie too. It worried her that she saw them talking. But everything worried her these days.

"Dallas, go back to your room. I'll be done in a minute," he barked. Dallas left, but Mina could hear her whining the entire way.

"Is she going to tell Ariel you were on the phone with me?" Mina asked.

"No. She won't remember this in two minutes," he said.

"Are you sure?" she asked.

"Yes. I know my daughter," he said. It brought an ache to her belly, him talking about Dallas like that. They so rarely saw each other with their kids now, she sometimes forgot he was a father and husband, one that did not belong to her, one that she was in fact stealing away, bit by bit.

She took in a deep breath, trying to shove the thought out of her mind. "Okay, back to the problem at hand. Should we maybe try to avoid being at the gym together, or something? I'm just not sure what to do here."

"I mean, I don't know how that's going to be possible without switching gyms. I'm not gonna start missing classes. Are you?"

"I would rather not."

"Maybe just don't go if Dima is going. You're not usually there at the same time."

"Yeah, but that might change, now that he's so paranoid."

Matthew let out a long groan. "I should have just called that nurse who was into me," he said. "So much less drama."

"Yeah, you really should have. This is all the stress without any of the fun," she said, trying to say what they were both thinking.

"Well, I still really want to fuck you," he said. "That part hasn't changed."

She covered her eyes with a hand. Now instead of guilt, her stomach burned with desire. It was always one thing or the other lately. Sometimes she wondered if it was connected in some horribly disturbed way, because it really had become a cycle. Like the guilt was too much to bear so it turned into lust instead, only to turn back into guilt if the lust waned.

"I mean, it hasn't changed for me either," she said. "But we really can't do that again. Especially now."

Dallas was back on screen, trying to grab the phone from Matthew.

"I'll just let you go. This hasn't exactly been a productive conversation anyway," Mina said.

"Yeah, thanks. It's been real fun for me too," he said.

"I'll see you at the gym later. Just…" She paused. "Just be careful around Dima. But don't avoid him or anything, that would just prove his point."

"Okay. See ya later."

Mina spent the rest of the day stressing out about all the ways things were bound to go wrong, now that Dima was picking up on her transgressions. She would need to be extra careful at the gym, no lingering smiles, no long conversations in the parking lot, nothing. Just in case people were watching and Dima was asking. In case he decided to just show up. In fact, maybe it would be better to skip a few classes, she decided. It was definitely the least risky option.

When she got home, she told Dima she wasn't feeling up to going, and let him go. For the rest of the week, she stayed home, thinking and thinking and thinking herself into a complete state of panic. But by the weekend, Dima had stopped suffocating her with attention and began leaving the house again, so she started to feel better. Her life was far more manageable without Matthew in it, without the gym. Maybe she should just keep it that way. For a while, anyway.

But then he texted her one morning when she was feeling depressed, and she had nothing better to do, so she went to his house and they had sex two more times. She didn't even bother to stay and have another conversation about how it was the last time. Having had that discussion at least four times in the past several months, it was starting to feel pointless and redundant. Clearly, they couldn't stop themselves; the only thing that could stop them was getting caught. And it didn't seem to work like the movies—no one was showing up out of the blue catching them, even if Dima had become a little jealous lately. He had no proof. It would be annoying if it wasn't so damn lucky.

That night, she felt comfortable enough to go back to the gym. Class started out normally; they did warmups and she followed the rest of the gym members as they ran in a circle around the mats, then practiced shrimping and back rolls, which was usually what they did for the first five minutes of class before Jonah picked the highest belt to use as a dummy for the new move they were going to learn.

That day, he used Matthew to demonstrate. She slowly made her way across the back of the gym towards Violet, so that when it was time to partner up, she could go with her instead. It was hard enough to focus on Jiu Jitsu when she wasn't thinking about Matthew's dick in her mouth that morning. This new move involved spending a lot of time in mount, which meant someone sitting on top of the other person, and that would definitely not help get the images of all they'd done earlier out of her head. She was so busy thinking about it that Violet picked up on Mina's lackluster attempts at drilling, so they took a break and began talking instead.

"How's it going, girl?" she said cordially.

Mina shrugged. "I've been better," she admitted, looking at the floor so she wouldn't look at Matthew. Her butt was so sore from how hard he'd spanked her that she had to sit on her legs or her side, and from the expression she'd caught earlier from across the room, she could tell he knew this and was enjoying it too. He really was a tad fucked up in the head. And so was she, for liking it. "Sorry I'm so distracted."

"I keep meaning to ask you, what's the deal with you and Felix?" Violet asked.

"Felix?" She frowned, both perplexed at the question and relieved that it wasn't about Matthew at least. "What do you mean?"

"Oh, maybe I'm overthinking it. He just seems super into you or something."

"Oh, that," Mina said with a shrug.

Violet wasn't the first person to bring this up to her, and Felix wasn't making it easy by being unable to go an entire class without touching her in some way; sometimes he would flick her in the head, other times he would pat her on the back. Once in a while he even put his arm around her shoulder in what he probably imagined to be a friendly manner, but always made her nervous because she would then have to figure out a way to get out of his grasp. Not because she particularly hated being touched by Felix; he wasn't terrible looking, and they were friends. But she had enough to deal with, and the optics, publicly, were bad. "It's fine, I'm dealing with it."

"So there is something?" she asked.

The door opened and closed, and Mina was so surprised to see Dima walking in she didn't answer Violet right away. She thought he would be home with Amelie, and hadn't mentioned bringing over their niece to babysit. She waved at him, but he ignored her, facing the window and getting his belt tied.

"I mean, he probably just has a little crush," Mina admitted absentmindedly. "I don't think it's even related to me as much as the fact that I'm the only woman who talks to him regularly."

Still keeping an eye on Dima, Mina was starting to get a bad feeling; a premonition that things were all about to collide or collapse on top of her. Right as she let this feeling wash over her, and dismissed it as paranoia, Dima got a message on his phone, and turned his back to the mats again in order to look at it. He stood there a very long time, not moving or saying anything, and before she could ask what had happened, the buzzer started, indicating it was time to roll. It was possibly the worst roll of her life, the first three minutes she went with Violet. She was so busy trying to watch Dima and Matthew that she had to apologize afterward. But at least Violet was too polite to tell her how bad she was.

Violet took out her mouthguard and shook her head. "Girl, don't even worry about it, you're fine," she said, catching her breath, her chest rising and falling with exertion.

Mina stood up, intending to sit out a round, but Dima came over to her before she could. She didn't really want to roll with him in the moment, seeing he was already in an aggressive mood from whatever bad email he'd gotten as he walked in the door, or perhaps just being around Matthew had made him annoyed, but there was no way out of it that she could think of. The next thing she knew she was on the ground; Dima had tackled her with one of the takedowns he knew. She landed so hard everyone around the gym looked over at them, but only momentarily; unless someone tore an LCL or passed out and started shaking from a strangulation choke, Jiu Jitsu people generally ignored what was going on around them. It certainly wasn't that unusual for someone to be loud during a breakfall, as anyone falling to the floor at full speed would make some noise. It could be dangerous if you didn't know how to fall properly, which was why beginners spent a lot of time practicing the art of the breakfall; how to land properly so you didn't injure yourself was an important skill to learn at the gym. But it was usually the men, with much higher belts, who started standing, if they ever did at all. The gym was usually too crowded for that.

Her back vibrated from the collision with the mats, but she made herself sit up, putting her legs and arms into a defensive position, close to her body. Dima passed her guard right away and baseball choked her from side control; she tapped out, then moved away from him.

"Hey," she said, rubbing her neck. Her lips felt numb, he'd choked her so hard. "Can you take it down a notch?"

He didn't respond, just passed her guard again and got into mount, trying to isolate her arm for an armbar. She managed to get out of it, but it took all the strength she had, and by the time she'd caught her breath he had control of her shoulder, moving off her and onto the mats to get her caught in an arm triangle, which was a way to choke someone with their own arm. It was one of the only submissions she was decent at finishing so she knew it was coming and managed to block it at the last moment with her hand.

Mina stood up. "What the fuck is your problem?" she asked, although of course she knew. She knew exactly what his problem was, and that was because it was her problem too. It was the dark pit at the center of her, eating everything around it. Her sadness and her lust, intertwined into one horrible black hole.

Whenever she had been sad in the past, sex was always her body's answer to it. It was the reason for many of her past bad decisions. Now it was like she was reliving her troubled youth in real time. But she couldn't, not really. She had a house and a mortgage and a child. Responsibilities. She had never allowed herself to really sit in the sadness, because she couldn't. Unlike when she was in her early twenties and had no obligations, she now had to get through very long, busy days, keep another person alive and healthy.

By the time she could get enough air to tell him she was going to go take a break, Dima had swept her back down to the floor with a De La Riva, then mounted her and went straight for an Ezekiel choke. This was a fast choke, impossible to defend if you didn't see it coming, which she did not. She tapped out right away, before he could finish it. But Dima didn't release his hold on her. She was starting to see little yellow lights in the side of her vision when someone suddenly pulled him off of her. She sat up to see Matthew standing over them.

"She was tapping out," Matthew was saying, angrily. "I saw her."

"She didn't," Dima explained.

"Yes, she fucking did," Matthew said.

"Why don't you mind your own fucking business?" Dima asked, in an uncharacteristically rude tone.

"Dima!" she said, her brows furrowed. Was he still that mad about them talking outside the party? It was just a passing glance in the darkness, whatever had made Dima suddenly jealous; it seemed like a bit of an overreaction, especially with how drunk everyone was.

Matthew and Dima continued to glare at each other in silence; it was awkward enough that a few people looked over at them, which was starting to stress her out. She wasn't good under pressure.

"Look. I'm fine," she said, standing up. "Let's move on."

Violet looked at her with her eyebrows furrowed. She had been rolling with someone right next to them and had overheard the whole thing. "Did you tap out?" Violet whispered.

"Of course," she said before she could stop herself. Maybe she should have lied. People would not like someone choking his own wife out at the gym. Matthew and Dima looked like they were about to get into a fight. An actual fight.

"Is there a problem here?" Matthew asked, still looking at Dima.

A few people had gotten off the mats by then, and were sitting down in chairs, taking a break. Felix and another friend of his, Steve, were both looking at their phones. A moment later, their heads bobbed up and they exchanged glances; then they both seemed to look right at her. What was going on? she wondered. So many weird vibes were bouncing around all at once.

"I don't know, Matthew," Dima said. "What were you doing this morning at, oh, I don't know, nine thirty this morning?"

Matthew frowned. "What?"

"Yeah. Nine thirty a.m.," Dima repeated.

"What are you talking about, man?" Matthew asked. He finally turned to see the now-growing group of people sitting out and looking at something on their phones. Perhaps because what he had been do-ing at nine thirty a.m. was her, instead of answering Dima, Matthew walked over there and grabbed Felix's phone right out of his hand.

"What the—?" Then he stopped, his face falling. He looked up at Mina for a moment, then back down at the phone, which he then threw across the room.

"Who the fuck sent this?" he asked Felix.

"Uh…" Felix stammered. "It just showed up in the gym group text."

Mina finally forced herself to get up and go over there. Whatever it was, it seemed to have something to do with her or Matthew. "What is it?" she asked Matthew. Her heart dropped into her stomach. She knew it had to be pretty bad to make him as pale as he now was.

"The area code is, like, foreign or something," said Steve, trying to help. "It's got a plus sign and some weird numbers..." he started, reading out the entire phone number.

Matthew's status as a cop combined with his aggressive nature made certain people at the gym a little afraid of him, including both

Felix and Steve. Mina wasn't though. She grabbed Steve's phone.

"Don't look at that," Matthew told her, trying to get the phone out of her hand, but she walked off in the opposite direction with it. "All of you, don't fucking open any video from the group chat."

Mina clicked play on what appeared to be a black-and-white video attachment. She gasped and dropped the phone when she saw what it was; it was Matthew. And her. A grainy video of them having sex, a clear view of her breasts right there for anyone to see. It looked like…one of those motion cameras, the kind she used in Amelie's room. It was obviously them, and there was no doubt about it, and no reason to even try to deny what they were doing.

They'd been caught.

In a way, she had wanted to get caught. Or at least she had wanted the secret to no longer be a secret, for the weight of it to stop making everything in her life feel so heavy and difficult. But she did not want to get caught on camera, and she did not enjoy the fact that Ariel had sent the video to literally everyone on the Open Guard text message list. She couldn't be mad at her, of course, but Jesus Christ, it was possibly the worst way for all of this to come out. She had assumed it would start with a rumor, and maybe some suspicion, or maybe someone would see the two of them leaving a room together when they shouldn't have been. Not this. Not irrefutable evidence that was also basically porn that now lived on the internet forever.

While Mina knew she was very lucky in the chest department, she was not a person who enjoyed that kind of attention from strangers. She didn't even like going to the beach in a swimsuit. She didn't own shorts for most of her adult life. And now everyone was staring at her naked chest, and they were staring at her, in her bright blue Gi, her face redder than a tomato. Mina's legs nearly gave out under her and she carefully sat down into a chair, her face so hot it felt like it could melt. She covered her face with a hand and sat there, frozen. Time seemed to have stopped; all she could hear was a blur of indistinguishable noise.

It felt like an hour had passed before Jonah broke the silence, when it was probably only a few minutes that all of this had been transpiring over. She finally opened her eyes and looked up.

"What the fuck is going on here?" Jonah asked, standing between Matthew and Dima, who were once again facing off on the mat. He was blinking, bewildered.

Dima nodded towards Matthew. "I guess someone's not as good at covering his tracks as he thinks he is."

Matthew shook his head. "Dima, listen—"

"Oh, you're going to tell me that wasn't a video of you fucking my wife?" he said. After that, the entire room went quiet. No one was rolling anymore, and someone turned off the buzzer. "Or, what, that it was the only time? It was a mistake? Which lie you gonna go with?"

"Dima, please," she started, but she didn't know what to say. Nothing she could say would change facts. On top of her fear and shame, she also felt like she deserved it all. In fact, in a way, she had been waiting for this to happen.

Dima turned to look at her. "What, Mina? It was an accident? You went to his house after dropping our daughter off at school and his dick just, what, fell in there?"

She closed her eyes and shook her head. "Of course not."

"That's what I thought."

"Dima. Let's go. This is not the place—"

"Isn't it the perfect place, though? It's what started your whole little romance," Dima said. "So, what, Jiu Jitsu is like an aphrodisiac for you?"

"Enough," Matthew ordered. "That's enough." She turned to him, but he didn't meet her gaze. His jaw was clenching, his eyes stony. He had gone to his dark place, she could tell. Even she felt a little scared of him now.

"Or what? You'll choke me?" Dima barked, moving closer to Matthew, trying to get into his space. "Maybe I'll like it. My wife certainly does."

Jonah stepped between them again, attempting to be the keeper of peace. "Why don't we all just take a breath. We can walk down to Bernice's, get a drink…"

It was gallant of him to try, but there was no getting off this train, Mina thought.

"How many times?" Dima asked. She stared at him blankly. Was she really supposed to answer that? "Five, ten?"

She shook her head, unable to answer. God, she couldn't even guess. It could have been fifty times, for all she knew. A hundred, even. The look on her face must have given it away, because she saw Dima's face fall. "That much, huh? Wow. I'm a fucking idiot."

A moment later she saw Dima's arm go up and, winding his way around Jonah, he landed a punch across Matthew's face. Someone gasped; it might have been her. The air seemed to get totally sucked out of the room. Matthew nearly toppled over, then caught his balance; he touched his lip, which had started to bleed. Then he tackled Dima onto the mats.

No one moved, unsure what to do. Matthew was better at Jiu Jitsu, and he had Dima pinned, but Dima used to box in Russia, and he managed to punch his way out fairly quickly. She had never seen Dima behave this way and was suddenly afraid of him too, of what he could do. Ten years of marriage, and turns out you never really know another person. Maybe you couldn't really know a person until you did the worst thing you could possibly do to them.

Matthew trapped him in a triangle with his legs, but Dima stood up and pushed himself out of it, climbing on top of him and slamming him in the face again with his bloody knuckles. Hitting was not allowed in Jiu Jitsu, not even a little bit. But this was no longer Jiu Jitsu; it was pure violence. By then, Felix and Jonah had woken up enough to rush in and grab the two men. Eventually others joined them, until they were several feet apart. It was an entire gym of people who were very good at fighting. They had to stop it before it got out of control or who knew what could happen. There were chokes in Jiu Jitsu that could really knock a person out, maybe even kill them. At the very least, limbs could get destroyed.

"You both need to go," Jonah ordered. "Right now."

Everyone was staring now, shocked into silence, unsure what to do when two members of the gym were actually trying to hurt each other. Sure, they practiced martial arts there every day, but no one ever really tried to injure each other. It was for fun. A game. The only people who used this stuff outside of class were the cops and security guards, and those were a small minority.

"He punched me, Jonah," Matthew said. For his part, he was not fighting to get out of his arm hold. Felix had his arms pinned behind his back, but he could have easily gotten out of it. He looked calm.

"Like you don't fucking deserve it," Dima said, spitting in his direction.

Her vision blurred, and she had to blink profusely to focus on the scene in front of her. She could see Felix shaking his head at her, even while pinning one of Matthew's arms back. Matthew may have looked a bit sheepish, but he didn't say anything, and he looked way too calm. But she knew inside he was likely fuming.

Dima stepped forward again, but Jonah pulled him back with a firm grasp of his elbow.

"Dude," Felix said. "Just don't."

Dima inhaled deeply, then turned away. Jonah let go and stepped around to face him, putting an arm around his shoulder. "Dima, I love you, man, but go home. Or go to a bar. This cannot happen in my dojo."

Dima looked at Jonah, taking a deep breath, then, following his instructions, turned to go. He wasn't about to say no to Jonah; no one said no to Jonah. It was perhaps why half the gym had such serious drinking problems. He was the kind of leader you wanted to follow, the kind you wanted to be in the presence of. He had a very magnetic personality, and the man liked to party, so they all partied. And when he told someone to go, they went.

Once Dima left, without a second glance in her direction, she felt a hand grasp her arm. Jonah's. "Mina, let's go outside for a minute," he said softly.

She nodded, feeling oddly numb. It was all so mortifying she could hardly focus enough to understand what was happening, so she just froze completely. She'd had nightmares about Dima finding out, and none of them were as bad as the reality. She had never imagined there being a video of them. To everyone else, Jonah said, "Class is over early, guys. Let's get this place cleaned up, all right?"

She noted a few of the guys following Dima out of the gym. She tried not to make eye contact with any of them; she knew what they were all thinking. She was a slut. A whore. They always blamed the woman. A man, well, he could hardly be blamed for thinking with his penis. But a woman should know better.

"Mina," Jonah said again, nudging her forward. She followed Jonah outside, where Matthew was leaning against the wall, smoking a cigarette she had no idea he had. She hadn't even noticed him leave the gym, but now, she took the cigarette and inhaled a long drag before giving it back.

"Oh good, you're here too," Jonah said. He stood across from them with his arms crossed and just stared at them in silence for a while. It felt like they'd been sent to the principal's office. Was she supposed to say something? Was he? It was not like they needed to explain; it was very, very clear, even without the video in his hands.

"Matthew, we've been friends for ten years," he said. "Ten fucking years. Isn't that right?"

Matthew nodded, still quiet.

Then Jonah slapped him upside the head. "What the fuck is wrong with you?" he asked. Matthew rubbed his head with a palm. He looked devastated more than pained. Like his whole life was over. And it might as well be. "Fighting in my gym?"

"Jonah…" he started.

"No, Matthew. Don't start apologizing to me. This is a real

damn shitshow."

Matthew nodded, swallowing his words. Jonah ran a palm over his half-shaved head, then over the tiny blonde ponytail in the back, then his mustache, curled on both sides with wax. She had never seen him so uncomfortable.

"It's not all his fault," Mina said. "It's mine too. And Dima shouldn't have punched him. I'm sorry he did that."

"I mean, I can't blame the guy. If that was me, I would have done worse," Jonah said, still looking at Matthew. He couldn't seem to face her.

"Jesus fuck, you two," Jonah said, shaking his head. "You're even stupider than I thought." This comment made Mina feel, for a moment, shred of hope; Jonah was always calling everyone stupid, and meant it as an endearing term. If he was saying it now, then maybe he wasn't going to ban them from the gym forever after all. It also sounded like maybe he had already had some suspicions. "You have beautiful families. You need to make it right with them."

"I don't think that's possible," Mina said. A cold wind began to blow past them, making Mina shiver. She wanted so badly to be at home, in her bed, hugging Amelie. Now she wondered if that would ever happen again. Her home was no longer home. Jonah put his head into his hands, letting out several more swear words. He seemed at a loss of what to do. Several long moments went by before he spoke again.

"Of course it is. Unless…You weren't stupid enough to fall in love, were you?" Jonah asked.

"No," they said in unison.

Mina looked at Matthew, and he caught her eye for a moment before looking away again. She realized only then that maybe they had been that stupid. From the way Matthew could no longer look at her, he may have been realizing it too. This gym really was like a church, after all; and Jonah, the hippie tattooed killer, was like their preacher.

"I won't train here anymore, I get it," Matthew said, looking sadder than she had ever seen him.

"Yeah, about that," Jonah said. "For now, yes, definitely stay away. Let things die down a little, then I don't know, maybe we can think about you coming back. Both of you."

"I can never show my face here again, Jonah. Come on," she said, shaking her head.

He sighed deeply. "I get why you might think that, but I care about both of you, and I don't want you to quit Jiu Jitsu over this. You're gonna need it now more than ever."

She kept shaking her head. "Everyone thinks I'm a slut. They love Dima."

"They'll get over it. The dojo is neutral ground. You leave your shit at the door."

Judging from Matthew's face, he didn't believe this. But she chose to accept it as an option. Because without hope of some normality returning, she didn't know how she would ever be able to wake up in the morning again. She didn't want to take Jiu Jitsu away from Matthew, even if she might have to give it up herself.

Jonah ran his hand over his lean face one more time before sighing. "You two probably need to talk. I'm going to go deal with the gym now."

And then he was gone, and it was just Matthew and her, standing alone in the dark parking lot, like they had so many times before.

CHAPTER TWENTY-FOUR

Mina sat down, despite the ground being dirty and covered in burnt wood from the last fire they'd had out there. She lit another cigarette from the pack she found there and gave one to Matthew, who was still silent, brooding. "Okay, that was pretty bad," was all she managed to say. He shook his head, lighting the cigarette.

"You need to tell me what you're thinking now," Mina said. "I don't do this whole brooding silent vampire thing anymore, okay?"

Matthew shook his head again. "I don't even know what to say."

"Your life isn't over," she said, putting a hand on his thigh. He just looked so damn sad. But it felt weird keeping it there, so she took it off. "Just please remember that."

"Oh yeah? It isn't?" he asked with a mean chuckle.

"No. It isn't," she said.

"I have to go talk to Ariel now," he said, standing up.

She nodded. "I know. I can't believe he hit you," she said. She touched his face, wiping the blood from his lip. "I'm sorry."

"Nah, I deserve it. But you..." He paused, shaking his head. "He's ten times stronger than you. You're a woman. It's not cool."

"Well, maybe. That whole scene was really fucked up."

"It was embarrassing, Mina. Fucking embarrassing."

"For who?" she asked. "I think you got off just fine. It's me who can never show her face around here again."

"For me too. Trust me, they are not going to be cool with this."

"Who cares about them? What about Ariel?" she asked. "Why would she even put a camera in the bedroom like that?"

He looked at her with fury in his eyes. "I don't know, Mina. Why would she?"

Mina was bewildered by this response. "Are you trying to say that it's my fault?"

"Well, I certainly didn't tell her about it," he said.

"You think I told her and then she planted a camera in there? Why would I do that?"

Matthew shook his head. "I don't know. Maybe you have a death wish," he said.

Mina stood up, embarrassment now washed out entirely by furious rage. "Oh, so now you're going to kill me?" she said. "That's great. Such a healthy response."

"Fuck you," Matthew said. He shook his head again and started walking towards his truck without even looking at her. She didn't know why she expected more from him; it wasn't like he ever treated her like someone he cared about. But it still hurt.

"Fuck you too. Maybe you're just not as good of a liar as you think," Mina yelled to his back. "Have you ever thought of that?"

Matthew ignored her and got in his truck and left. That was possibly the most surprising thing of all. She thought at least they could talk about what they were going to do next, how they would handle this. But maybe she hadn't really known Matthew as much as she had thought; maybe he wasn't the type to look at the fire and not turn away after all. Maybe it depended wholly on what kind of fire it was. Or maybe he was just incapable of caring about anyone other than himself, and she had been deluding herself all these months when she thought they might have something, something fucked up, surely, but still something good.

Mina stayed outside the gym for a long time, long enough for her butt to get sore again from the hard ground. She was unsure what to do with herself, with the rest of her life. She couldn't go home, but she didn't know where to go. Lila had three kids and no space for her, that was for sure. Her family was either dead or lived too far away. Her total isolation was half the reason she'd started this thing with Matthew in the first place, and why Open Guard had become such an important part of her life. If there were other people around to care for her, she might have not needed any of it. There was a cost to normalizing the nuclear family; it turned everyone into tiny little planets merely orbiting each other, not a connected network, like it had always been before. People tried to replace that feeling with social media, but social media wasn't real, so it didn't really work.

She lit another cigarette and leaned against the building for a while, lost in thought. Eventually, Felix found her out there and handed her a hard seltzer.

She took it gratefully, without meeting his eye. She was dying for a drink, and one with alcohol was even better.

"Well, that was quite a show," he said, opening another one for himself.

She nodded dumbly.

"What are you going to do now?"

"I really have no clue," she said. "Find a new gym, I guess. Probably get divorced."

"Well, I assume you got what you wanted then," Felix said.

"What do you mean?"

"You must have known that was the most likely outcome," he said nonchalantly. He said everything nonchalantly. Like he couldn't care less. But the more she got to know him, the more it seemed the opposite was true, and this was just some kind of defense mechanism. "If you wanted to stay married, you wouldn't have done that."

She swallowed. There was some truth to that. She did love Dima, but for a long time it had felt more platonic than anything, like they were roommates who shared a child. It was probably a common enough problem, and yet, she hadn't wanted to work on it, she had just thrown a bomb into her life instead. She really was an asshole. "It wasn't that bad," she said. "It just wasn't what I wanted anymore, I guess."

"Probably better ways to handle that," he said with a snort, finishing his drink.

She took in a large breath, inhaling the newly cool Autumn air. "I don't know. Maybe I was just bored. Is that possible?"

"Sure," he said. "Life is pretty dull. Doesn't mean you have to go around hurting everyone who cares about you to make it exciting again, though."

"Thanks, Felix," she said, shaking her head. "Like I don't feel bad enough as it is."

"You should feel bad," he said. "That was a shitty thing to do."

"I know that. Don't you think I know that?"

He frowned. "I thought you said it was over."

"We're both not good at endings, I guess."

"Yeah, no shit. I've read your books."

This surprised her so much she found herself laughing, in spite of everything. "You have?"

"Yeah," he said, looking at her shocked face. "What? I read."

"I didn't know that, Felix. That might be the most surprising thing I've heard all day."

"Everybody in there just saw your tits and that's the most surprising thing you've heard today?"

"Yeah, kind of." She sighed, looking towards the gym. "What are they saying about me in there anyway?"

"Nothing," he said flatly. "Not out loud, anyway."

"Can you please, please delete that video?" she asked, covering her face with her hands. "I mean, I'm not, like, insecure about my body, but that's not really an image I want out there in the world."

"Already did," he said, surprising her.

"Thank you." She threw out her cigarette, finishing the rest of the seltzer in one quick gulp. "Do you want to go to Bernice's and get really fucking drunk?"

Felix shrugged. "Sure."

Later, she would bathe in self-pity and remorse, and maybe she would come out of it a stronger person, or maybe she would come out of it a weaker person, but at least she would come out knowing the worst had already happened. She didn't need to worry about it anymore. But for now, she would try to erase the memory of what had just happened by drinking herself into a stupor. She might even let Felix kiss her. Why not? It wasn't like Dima would stay with her after what had just happened; and Felix had wanted her since the day she'd joined the gym. While he was far too much like her father, a depressive with a more-than-borderline drinking problem, for her to ever date—he wasn't unattractive, and sometimes when she saw him beating every guy in class with what seemed like no effort at all, she had felt fleeting moments of attraction for him.

So when Felix stood and reached out his hand to her, she grabbed it and pulled herself up. Then they got in his car and drove down to Bernice's, where they proceeded to get very drunk, and she proceeded to make bad decisions.

MARCH

CHAPTER TWENTY-FIVE

"What do you mean, they found his car?" Mina asked, grabbing a hold of Matthew's shoulder. It was like the man was speaking a different language, that's how difficult it was to get this information into her head. She just kept blinking and staring at him. "Was he not in the car?"

Matthew ran a hand over his head again, and stared ahead at the dashboard. "He was not."

"What does that mean?" she asked. "Is he dead?"

Matthew sighed. "Not necessarily," he explained. "But his phone and wallet were inside."

She let go of his shoulder and sat back against the seat. As a mystery writer, and a person who had watched far too many detective shows growing up—possibly this had something to do with her attraction to Matthew, and cops in general—she understood that an abandoned vehicle was never a promising sign. And no one these days left their phones unless they were forced to. Matthew once told her that ninety percent of the domestic disputes he got called to had to do with phones; someone taking or losing or breaking their significant other's tiny window to the world. Of course, if people realized that window was also a prison, maybe they would be happier to let it go. We were not meant to have access to so much. Violence, sex, every hobby and piece of information to have ever existed could now all be found in a tiny box that sat in your pocket all day. How could one ever be present in the moment, or give another person their full attention, when turning on a device could provide everything you thought you ever wanted? You'd have to be a monk to avoid the temptation.

And it was, in so many ways, a temptation. On top of being a constant distraction, and a recipe for mob mentality, it also made certain things too easy, including infidelity. Before Instagram and Facebook, it was a lot harder to have a one-on-one conversation with a married person of the opposite gender. Now all it took was a click of a button.

Mina turned away from him. "That's not good," she managed to mumble.

From the corner of her eye, she could see Matthew shake his head. "It's not," he said. "They want to talk to you. I'll just take you over there."

Mina nodded at him, suddenly unable to speak; all she could do was stare at the tiny cluster of freckles on the side of his neck as he drove, until finally she leaned her head back against the leather seat and closed her eyes. She didn't say a word the entire drive through downtown, which at nine in the morning had so much traffic she probably could have biked there faster. Sometimes she fantasized about leaving Chicago, she really did. Maybe she could move to some mountain town out west and just start over. It was possible, right?

"I can't go in there again," she said when she felt the truck stop moving. She opened her eyes to see they were at the station. The straight gray angles cutting across the dark gray sky, the lines and lights of CPD stripes, all of it made her want to throw up, cry, and-scream, maybe all at once. It was a feeling she was getting far too familiar with lately.

"You can do it," he said with a short nod. She saw him place a nicotine pouch in his mouth and hold it in his cheek; not the gum this time, which revealed to her his stress level more than what he was saying. "This is your problem in Jiu Jitsu too, by the way. Your attitude is the only reason you don't have your blue belt."

"No, you're the reason I don't have my blue belt. I stopped going to Open Guard because of you."

"Oh right, that's the other reason," he said, now chewing. "Blaming other people for your own shit."

"Fuck you, Matthew."

"I'm trying to fucking help you," he said.

"Oh yeah? Is that what you're doing?" she said. "Because, to me, it just looks like you're being a dick, as per usual."

"That's literally what you say every time I'm trying to help you. Do you want me to lie?"

"No. You know I don't," she said. "We spent enough time lying."

"Well, then quit being so soft," he said.

"Soft?" she said.

Matthew sighed and turned off the car. "Yeah," he said. "All these feelings, with you."

"I barely have feelings, Matthew," she argued. "That's what happens when your life goes to shit."

"Well, the ones you do have are soft," he said.

For whatever reason, this sounded so absurd it made her laugh. "Okay. Sure," she said, when she caught her breath.

"Mina. Come on," he said. When she didn't move, he reached over and unbuckled her from the seat. She probably should have stormed off and never talked to him again. That was always the dichotomy of her feelings for Matthew; a furious desire to push him away and an uncontrollable, urgent need to see him were constantly fighting each other inside her brain. Had he left her there, she may have been able to actually do it this time, actually stop talking to him. That's what she assumed he would do. But he surprised her again by waiting there for her, and she didn't say no, because she always felt so much more relaxed in his presence, and underneath it all, she wanted him there, even if he didn't want to be, even if he wanted to be as far away from her as possible. He wasn't. He was in Chicago, and he was next to her.

Deep down, she understood his meanness for what it was, and that was why she could never really cut him out of her life. It was pretty psych 101, really—being mean was his defense mechanism. It was possibly even his love language. She knew this because most of the time his words didn't match his actions. He would be saying fuck you and she knew what he really needed was some attention. He wasn't the only one who behaved this way, especially at the gym. Perhaps she understood this now because she had a toddler, but it seemed more and more like everyone still had a scared, excited, easily wounded little three-year-old inside them no matter how old they got.

"Mina," he repeated. "Fuck this little pity party. Let's go."

Matthew looked like he would carry her out of the truck if she didn't move, so she forced herself to get up and jump out into the brittle winter air. She took in a deep breath and walked slowly across the icy parking lot, following Matthew into the crowded police station. She wouldn't have had a clue where to go if he hadn't been there to guide her, despite having been there before. The place was like a maze, and she was so out of it she could hardly tell right from left. It wasn't until they were right outside the detective's office again that she could finally think. Mina leaned against the pale, yellow wall, closing her eyes for a moment before opening them again. Dima couldn't be dead. She really didn't believe that. But where the hell was he? And why had he left his phone?

Their marriage hadn't worked out, but she still loved Dima, he was still family. He was still Amelie's dad, and a great one. Mina had never lost sight of that, even at the peak of their marital problems, the fights in mediation, the battle over the house. In the back of her mind, she was still comforted to know he would always be in her life. She still held out hope they might one day become friends, despite his insistence this could never happen.

Matthew sidled up next to her, then waved his hand towards the detective's door, as if to tell her to go in. Well, she was here; she might as well go get it over with. She inhaled another long, deep breath to calm her nerves, and headed straight inside the overheated room.

As she sat down in the hard wooden chair across from Detective Conner's desk, the pale gray office with its flickering florescent light made her feel like she was in a movie. A bad movie, the kind where too many horrible things happened so she would just turn it off. She wanted to go home and sleep until summer, but instead, she hung her head, waiting for the mustachioed detective to speak. She could hear her heartbeat in her ears, that's how nervous she was, but she kept her face neutral. After all, she was pretty used to it now—being two different people. She just had to turn off the nervous one and be the confident one.

"Morning, Ms. Banksy. Thank you for coming here so quickly," he said.

"No offense, but I was kind of hoping to never see you again," she said, sitting up straight now and trying to make light of the mood.

"You'd be surprised how many times I've heard that," Conner said. He let out a stiff chuckle, then stood from his desk to open the door, where his partner was waiting. Detective Miller circled around her to join him, leaning against the front of the desk as Conner returned to his chair. They were both perspiring profusely, which made her wonder why they didn't just turn down the heat.

"Just tell me what happened," she said, watching the two of them stare at her. She couldn't make out the expressions on their faces; it wasn't neutral, exactly, but some sort of forced politeness. They both seemed rigid and possibly uncomfortable. "Please."

"That's what we're trying to figure out," Detective Conner said. "There was no evidence of a struggle, but considering the recent death of Mr. Elliott, and that we have been trying to get a hold of your husband for several days now, we have to treat this disappearance very seriously." He took a folder from Detective Miller and placed a giant stack of papers on the table in front of them. It must have been hundreds of pages. He began talking again, but she interrupted him.

"What's that?" she asked, pointing to the stack of pages. It was covered in text, but not like a book, in paragraphs and justified in the margins. They were just lines, an endless poem. And there were little colored flags poking out of several portions.

"Ah," he said. "Yes. This is…well, here. Why don't you take a look?" Detective Miller pushed the pile forward, and she picked up the top page. It looked like one of those old chat room screens. Messages back and forth. She wasn't sure she wanted to see what they were, but her curiosity got the best of her. She was a writer after all. She picked up a page at random and began reading.

```
I've had some very naughty thoughts today. You
should probably arrest me.

I think I will need do that, yes. Then I can
get those pesky hands out of the way and you
can get the punishment you deserve.

Good. I need to be punished.

I know you do. You've been a bad girl. You made
me wait all week to cum on you.
```

She was so confused at first that it took her a minute to understand that these were messages, ones that she and Matthew had sent to each other. Once this knowledge spread to the rest of her body, it felt like she couldn't get enough air.

"Oh my God," she said, her face burning hot. She pushed the pile of papers aside. "What is that?"

"You really need me to answer?" Detective Conner said.

She swallowed, trying to calm her face, which she could feel getting redder and redder by the moment. Her heartbeat was back in her ears, even louder than before. She put her head in her hands, temporarily unable to look at the men. "Did you read these?"

Detective Miller cleared his throat. "Uh, yeah. Pretty spicy stuff, there."

She took a few deep breaths, then placed her hands on the desk and raised her head. "These are private messages," she said. "Private, deleted messages. Why on earth do you have them?"

"Anything that is relevant to the case is no longer private, ma'am," Detective Conner said. He couldn't even look her in the eye, she realized. He'd been looking around her and behind her since she'd walked into the room. That was why it had felt so uncomfortable from the moment she arrived.

She inhaled sharply, her embarrassment quickly getting replaced by righteous anger. How was this anyone's business after all these months? No one could leave it alone. First the video, now this? "Okay. Matthew and I had an affair. You figured that out already, I'm sure. So what? What does this have to do with Dima? Or Dylan?" she asked.

"We don't know that yet," Detective Miller said, leaning back into the desk. He took off his thin-rimmed glasses and wiped them off with the edge of his shirt before replacing them on his head. "But the one thing everyone here has in common is you. So yes, I would say this is relevant."

"That's just a coincidence!" she exclaimed, louder than she had meant to. Her head went back into her palm again, her breath catching. "God, I'm just never gonna live this down." She almost started crying right then and there, but she could feel the two detectives rustling above her, uncomfortable, like men who had daughters and could not bear to see them cry, so she sucked it up as always, because that was what a woman—especially a mother—did. Men could leave, men could blow off steam. They could sleep with their secretaries and at worst be called a cliché. But women had to suck it up and deal. If they liked sex too much, then they were sluts. If they didn't, they were prudes, a ball and chain. And on top of it all, they were always expected to do the majority of the childcare and house maintenance, even if they had jobs too. There was just no winning sometimes, if you were a woman.

"Sorry. But I just don't see what any of this has to do with Dylan's murder. Or Dima's disappearance." She forced herself to take another deep breath and focus, allowing her fingernails to dig into the fists that had formed at her sides. "We all belonged to the same gym once, but it's just a coincidence."

Detective Conner looked at her with what seemed like pity. "Ms. Banksy," he started. "I'm not so sure that's true. In fact, I think it's unlikely to be a coincidence."

They sat in silence for a moment as she tried to process what they were saying. They really seemed to think this had something to do with her, or at least her affair with Matthew. But how was that even possible? "But why?" she said.

"Well, we don't know that yet. But every road leads back to you," Detective Conner said. "We're not saying you're responsible. You're, what, a hundred and thirty pounds? No one thinks a tiny girl like you strangled a felon who spent four years in prison and who knows how many years doing Jiu Jitsu and left him in an alley."

"Of course not. Dylan was a purple belt, and I'm terrible at Jiu Jitsu. Plus, we were friends," she explained.

"But," Detective Miller interjected. "You probably do know who did it. Even if you don't realize you know."

"But I don't! I swear I don't!" she said. Then, realizing how shrill her voice sounded, she stopped talking. Eventually her glance turned from the two serious men and fell back to the stack of pages in front of her. "Where did you even get these?" she asked again. "These were deleted. I know that for a fact."

Detective Miller cleared his throat. "There was a file on your husband's phone."

She nearly coughed with surprise. "What? On Dima's phone?" she asked. "How?"

Detective Conner shrugged. "The email came from an untraceable account. Someone who knows his way around computers."

"Uh, isn't kind of hard to get deleted messages recovered?" she asked.

"If you're not in law enforcement, it can be quite difficult, yes," Detective Miller said.

"Matthew's wife was CC'd on the email," Detective Conner said. "And it was flagged. That's why we noticed it. It was sent back in September."

Her body turned ice cold. "Who would do that?" she asked. She really had no idea, but it did explain, she supposed, why Ariel had decided to tape them that horrible day in the fall. Sometimes it kept her up at night, wondering how far the video had gone, and who had seen it and how many times. At least the cops didn't have that.

"We wanted to ask you that same thing."

She stared at them blankly. "I have literally no idea." She really didn't, either. She could not even guess who might be out there possibly trying to destroy her life, or if it was the same person as the murderer. Detective Conner took the stack of papers back and opened to a red-flagged page, skimming over what was sure to be a horribly embarrassing conversation, before swallowing and looking back up at her.

"It's a bit odd that since Officer Stone has come back to Chicago, one person you had a relationship with has died and the other is missing," Detective Conner said, making her cough again. "Two men, to be specific."

"Excuse me?" she asked.

"You have to admit the timing is odd," he said.

"I mean, yeah, this whole fucking week is definitely odd," she said. "I'm sorry. Excuse my language. But I didn't have a relationship with Dylan. We were just friends. It was platonic." When she noticed the disbelief in their eyes, she had to continue, even though it was probably pointless. "Look. I'm sorry I fell for a married man, but I'm not the gym bicycle you think I am."

"No one is calling you a bicycle, Ms. Banksy." Detective Miller frowned, then looked to his partner, who pointed to a highlighted section of a page and pushed it in her direction. She really, really did not want to read it, but forced her eyes to focus on the words.

I'm not sure how I can stay married after this. I'm really not.

Well, that's up to you. It's your marriage. But please do me the courtesy of leaving me out of it.

You don't understand how hard this has been for me. Every other day it just feels like it's about to pop out of my mouth.

Mina, don't even start with that shit again. I'd end up living in my truck.

I would have to live there with you then I guess. I doubt I'd get the house.

More reasons to keep your mouth shut, then.

What are you gonna do about it, huh? Kill me?

You really want to find out?

Mina looked up from the page, closing her eyes. This really felt like torture, having to relive the entire affair with Matthew in front of two detectives and these flickering lights and the smell of death still hovering in her nose. She put her head in the palm of her hand. "Okay. I know this looks bad."

"It looks like Officer Stone threatened to kill you," Detective Conner said. "In fact, he threatens to kill you more than once."

"Look, he didn't really mean it," Mina said. "That's just how we talked. We were mean to each other, I don't know why, it was just fun like that."

"It sounds like he got pretty violent with you, Ms. Banksy," Detective Conner said. "You can imagine why it might draw some suspicion in a murder investigation."

"It was consensual," she explained.

They both looked at her like she had said the sky was orange. "It was consensual," she repeated. "What, you've never met a woman who liked to get spanked? Come on."

"Can it really be consensual when a man has that much power?" Detective Conner asked. "Mr. Stone is a law enforcement officer, and he's got nearly a hundred pounds on you. If you had said no, would he have listened?"

"What is this, a gender studies class?" she asked, leaning forward in her chair. "You ever stop to think maybe the power is what attracted me? It's really infantilizing when you start telling me that I can't make my own decisions, okay? I'm a grown woman. Please, let's move on."

Detective Conner looked back down at the stack of papers, flipping through to another marked page, and pushing it over for her to read.

```
We really need a safe word, because I just
really want to go to town on your face later.

Safe words are dumb. Just don't leave any marks
and we're good.
```

She sighed. "Like I said. Consensual," she said. She crossed her arms over her chest. "Are we just gonna sit here all day reading old sexts? Because I need to pick up my daughter soon and tell her that her father isn't coming to get her today."

"We don't mean to embarrass you, Ms. Banksy," Detective Miller said.

"I'm not embarrassed. I think this is a waste of time, though," she said. The heat had left her face, and she really meant it. Everyone had kinks. What was there to be embarrassed about? "There's some deranged killer out there and my husband is who knows where and you're here reading erotica."

Detective Conner sat up in his chair, crossing his hands on the desktop. "Look, we aren't sold on Matthew as a suspect. And, obviously, that would be terrible for the department, so it's not really a tree we want to be barking up. But we have no choice," he explained. "We have to bark up that tree."

"What, you think Matthew killed Dylan in a fit of jealousy or something?" she asked, frowning. "You obviously don't know him at all. He couldn't care less who I sleep with." She took another deep breath, trying to calm herself down. "Plus, Matthew has an alibi. I'm his alibi. He was at my house."

"Yes, we are aware you are each other's alibis," started Detective Conner, in a slightly disbelieving tone.

"You can go ask Ariel about it if you don't believe me," she said.

"And why's that?" he asked.

"Because she came over to tell him he can't live at their house," she explained. Detective Miller, to his credit, wrote this down in his notepad. "That's the only reason he ended up staying over."

Detective Conner leaned back in his chair, crossing his arms behind his head. She could see little pools of sweat under his ironed blue button-up shirt, and the strap that must have been holding on to his pistol. "Okay. Let's step back a bit here. Can you think of anyone who might have wanted Dylan or Dima dead? Maybe another lover, or a boyfriend?"

"No, I can't," she said. "There's no other boyfriend. Like I told you before, Dylan and I were just friends. Why aren't you looking into the whole drug trafficking thing? Isn't that more relevant than this dumb old love triangle?"

"We are looking into that, ma'am," Detective Conner said.

"And what about Dima? What was he doing if not going to work all these months? Maybe that has something to do with it."

The detectives exchanged another look. "Yeah, we checked on that. It's unlikely. After he quit his job, he started doing Uber."

"He quit his job? To do Uber?"

"Seems so."

She shook her head in disbelief. She felt suddenly exhausted. Not that she could be mad at Dima for not telling her about quitting his job after all the lies she had told him in the last year; she just didn't get why he would do that, let alone not tell her about it. There were way too many difficult, unanswerable questions spinning around in her head. Mina could have probably collapsed right then and there, if not for the intensity of the room. She'd had enough for one morning. If it was Jiu Jitsu, she would be tapping out.

"Can I please go now? I've told you everything I know," she said, stifling a yawn.

"For now," Detective Miller said. "But if you think of anything, please call us right away."

"We're going to put an unmarked car outside your house as well," said Detective Conner. "Until we find this person, your safety is of concern."

"Fine." She didn't have the energy to argue. And she was starting to get a little scared herself, so maybe it would be a good thing to be watched. She stood up and turned to leave, then turned around again. "Wait. Is Matthew in trouble?" she asked. "For the ... well, you know."

"If you say everything was consensual, and he was not involved in either of these crimes, then he should be okay," Detective Conner said.

"Okay, good," she said. "I just messed up his life enough. I would feel bad if he couldn't go back to work."

"Matthew is a grown-ass man," said Detective Conner gruffly, looking her straight in the eye. For a moment, it seemed like he was angry with Matthew. She glanced at his desk and noticed a picture of him with his arms around three little girls, probably his daughters. "He made his own bed. Now he has to lie in it."

"Not that it's any of my business," Detective Miller began, opening the door for her and eying her with pity. He clearly didn't like what he'd read in all those texts either. But they were different than her. Normal. How could she make them understand? It took her thirty-two years to figure out what she liked in bed, and she wasn't about to let it go, or feel ashamed about it either. Whatever other things Matthew had done, at least he had opened her eyes to some important information about herself. What they'd had was transformative, to say the very least. "But you shouldn't let him talk to you that way, ma'am. You shouldn't let anyone talk to you like that."

"You're right. It's not your business," she said, and walked out the door.

CHAPTER TWENTY-SIX

When she left the police station, the sun had come out, and the snow was starting to melt. Matthew was nowhere to be found, so she walked down the block to catch the Red Line, switching at Roosevelt to the Orange Line. Once she sat down across from the sliding doors, she checked her phone—it was almost eleven, and she still hadn't written a word. But she understood in that moment, as the sun burst in from the windows and warmth cut briefly across her face, that she would probably not be writing today, or any day in the near future; this was real life bursting in. There were times in life to write and there were times in life to live, and this was one of those times.

She needed to do some of her own detective work now. She was tired of being a passive participant. It was one thing when Dylan was found murdered, especially after she'd learned he'd been using the van to smuggle drugs. That was so outside her realm of knowledge and experience that leaving it to the police to figure out had been the only option.

But Dima, well, that was something else entirely. She could at least try to find him. She could try to understand what had been going on with him the last few months. And once she did, she would bring that information to the police, and they could stop focusing so much on Matthew. It wasn't that she didn't believe Matthew was capable of murder. He probably was. She had seen the look in his eye when he would squeeze his hand around her neck. But he would never kill someone out of jealousy, that was for sure. And definitely not jealousy in regards to her; he didn't even want to be with her. He'd had the chance and had chosen to stay with Ariel. That told her everything she needed to know. Hopefully the cops would eventually catch on too, because looking at him was a total waste of time.

Mina swallowed her pride and took a lot of deep breaths as she got off the Orange Line at Halsted and walked down the slippery steps to get onto Halsted Street, because the first place she would need to go was unfortunately the last place she wanted to be. But then again, maybe it was good to face her fears. Wasn't that what exposure therapy was about? If something caused you to have panic attacks, she'd heard, back when she was still doing therapy, one way to resolve your fear was to face it a little at a time.

So, with this in mind, she forced herself to walk carefully down the icy sidewalks until she got to the door of Open Guard. No one had pointed or yelled at her when she was there last time. What was she so nervous about anyway?

"Mina!" she heard Jonah yell from the back of the gym the moment she entered. She hadn't been sure anyone would be there yet, so she was surprised to find the door unlocked. It was empty except for Jonah, who was digging through a box in the back, wearing a tank top and board shorts despite it being ten degrees out. She took off her wet boots and slid across the mats in her damp socks.

"Hey, Jonah," she said.

"I'm so glad you decided to come back, but class doesn't start for another..." He looked up at the large clock on the far wall. "Thirty minutes, or so. I'm just here early trying to tidy up."

"Oh, I'm not here for class," she said, attempting a polite smile. His version of tidying up almost made her laugh; it seemed even messier than the last time she was there. "I came to ask you something."

"Oh!" Jonah said, standing up. He reached for a hard seltzer that had been sitting on a nearby shelf and took a long sip. "What's up?"

"Well, it appears that Dima is...missing?" she said.

Jonah's deep blue eyes widened. "Missing? Like *missing* missing?" he said.

She swallowed a dry lump in her throat and nodded. "I just came back from the police station," she said. "I mean, it's probably just a misunderstanding, but…I don't know, I'm worried."

"Fuck," he said, shaking his head. He offered her another seltzer that had been sitting next to his own. She took it. It was all she could do not to drink it all in one gulp. "How can I help?"

"I was just wondering, have you been in touch at all recently?" she asked. "I know you hate to gossip, but we really need to find him. The cops…I don't know, they're not really of much help. All they do is ask me about Matthew." She rolled her eyes, then took a long sip of the seltzer.

"Matthew? Isn't he in Arizona?" Jonah asked, surprised.

"No, actually, he's back now," Mina said.

Jonah's forehead scrunched up in confusion. "Oh. And they think, what, that he's involved somehow?"

She rolled her eyes again. "Yeah. Even though he has an alibi, so I don't know why they're wasting their time."

"Wow," Jonah said, looking around the gym, his brows narrowed in thought. "Wow. That's a lot."

"Yeah. It hasn't been the best week for me," she said, finishing her seltzer. He handed her another right away, and opened one for himself too. "So, have you? Heard from Dima? I know you guys are still friendly."

Jonah nodded absently, his gaze focused on the bright yellow of the sun in the windows, as if trying to decide what to tell her. It was a problem with divorce, she knew, that everyone had to take sides. And Dima had known Jonah longer than she had, plus they were both men. It wasn't like she spent a lot of time alone with Jonah, like Dima had. He was far too proper for that, and he was too popular. Everyone always wanted a piece of him, being the magnetic leader that he was. She had seen people literally walk into a frozen lake just because he decided to do it; if he asked them to jump off a bridge, they might do that too.

"Jonah, please," Mina asked. "His life might be in danger."

"Honestly, Mina, I wish I could help, but I don't really know anything," Jonah said, turning his attention back to her.

"Do you know if he and Dylan were hanging out? I heard he was dealing again. Maybe Dima got involved somehow?"

Jonah placed a hand over his tattooed chest, which was visible under his flimsy Open Guard tank top. "Honestly, I didn't know Dylan was doing that. It really breaks my heart what happened to him."

She sighed. "Yeah. I didn't know either," she said. "Some people are just better at keeping secrets, I guess."

"The only thing I can tell you is that…" Jonah paused, and finished his seltzer. "Well. He is seeing someone. Dima, I mean."

"He is?"

"I don't know how serious it is, but I saw him with her one night at this bar in Pilsen. Skylark?"

"Well, that's good! I'm glad for him," she said, and really, she was. He deserved to be with someone who was less fucked up than she was, someone who could appreciate him for all his positive attributes, which she had all but forgotten toward the end of their marriage, but slowly remembered after they'd separated and things had calmed down. Someone who didn't mind doing all the housework and never having enough money to go on real dates. Maybe that's all his disappearance was; maybe he'd been so mad at her he just decided to sneak away with this new woman. She could hardly blame him. Though it didn't explain him leaving his car like that. "Did you know her, by chance?"

"I do, actually," Jonah said, staring at the floor by her feet.

"Really? Who was it?"

"Meghan," he said.

"Dylan's ex-wife Meghan?" she asked, her eyebrows raised.

Jonah nodded, unable to look at her. "Small world, I guess."

She blinked, a bit surprised by this information. Not that she could be upset by it, after what she'd done. It was just odd. Meghan had purple hair and piercings and cut hair for a living, and didn't seem like Dima's type at all. Then again, she didn't really know what his type was, other than her. He was shy and hadn't really dated anyone before they'd met, having spent his first few years of adulthood in the army, and the next few in a truck.

"I mean, she's very pretty," Mina said. "And I think she goes to the same gym. I get it." She finished her drink and then shrugged.

"Sorry I can't be of more help," Jonah told her as she turned to leave.

"Oh, that's okay, Jonah, really," she said. "I'm sure it's all a big misunderstanding."

Mina slid back across the mats and put her boots back on with a disappointed sigh. She really thought Jonah might know something useful. People were always telling him things. Although now that she knew Dima was seeing Meghan, she could message her and ask if she had heard from him lately. Mina dug into her coat and found her name in her Facebook Messenger app, then typed out a message she hoped wasn't too awkward. Meghan probably hadn't mentioned that she was dating Dima for a reason. Mina had just opened the door to the vestibule of the gym when Felix walked inside, sunglasses on and bag swung over his shoulder. He stopped when he saw her, a smile starting on his face before quickly disappearing.

"Hey," he said. "You finally getting your lazy ass back to the gym?"

Mina rolled her eyes and sighed. "I'm not lazy."

"Yes, you are," Felix said. He lifted her arm up loosely. "I don't see any muscle here, do you?"

Mina pulled her arm back and crossed it over her other arm. She stepped backward, into the gym, to let him through and inside. "How can you tell that when I am wearing a coat?" she asked, good-naturedly. She had sort of missed their banter over the last few months. And he was probably right anyway, about her lack of muscle. Since she could barely ever get to the new gym she had joined, most of the exercise she'd been doing involved using her rowing machine for thirty minutes after Amelie went to bed. It was decent cardio, but nothing compared to Jiu Jitsu.

"I just can," he said. "X-ray vision."

"Huh," she said. "You have X-ray vision and that's what you waste it on?"

Felix chuckled a little as he took off his shoes, leaving them by the door. "It's not the only thing."

Before he could disappear into the changing room, she asked, "Hey, Felix! You haven't seen Dima lately, have you?"

He turned back to her, his expression blank, sunglasses still on. "Uh, no," he said. "I mean, a couple days ago I saw him by your house when I was walking to my car."

"Really?" she asked. "What was he doing?"

"Maybe it was more than a couple days ago. Yeah, it must have been Monday, because I left early to meet Steve in the West Loop," he said, then began going into unnecessary detail about the traffic and how drunk they'd gotten later that night in Logan Square. Mina stepped forward to interrupt him.

"Okay, whatever day it was, was he acting weird at all?" she asked.

Felix shrugged. "What would you consider weird?"

"I don't know."

"I wasn't close enough to see anything, weird or unweird. I think he was on his phone."

"Did you hear what he was talking about?"

Felix shrugged again. "No. Like I said, it was too far away. Why?"

Mina exhaled a long breath. "No reason." She turned again to leave, but Felix stopped her, pulling on her shoulder, and leaving his hand there for a moment too long, which reminded her why she'd been avoiding him in the first place. She moved backward a little.

"Stay for class," he said. "Just watch at least. I know how much you hate to actually put in effort."

"I put in effort, I just suck."

"You suck because you don't put in effort. You roll at, like, twenty percent effort on a good day," Felix argued.

This was a conversation they'd had many times before. And they both knew it wasn't effort as much as insecurity; on the mats, she still lacked confidence in what she was doing, to the point where she would let people win before attempting a move she wasn't one hundred percent sure she could finish. It was the same exact reason she could never pick up another language. When she'd first started dating Dima, she'd spent a year trying to learn Russian, but gave up after too many failed attempts to talk to his elderly grandparents at family functions. "You're already here, just stick around."

"Yeah, I second that," Jonah said, walking past them with a pile of new Gi belts that were wrapped in plastic, a combination of blue, purple, and brown.

"Oh. Is it promotion day?" she asked, looking at the belts.

She loved promotion days. They always came as a surprise to everyone involved. At the very end of class, Jonah would throw the few people who were getting promoted to the next level into a "shark tank." It was nonstop takedowns and submissions for nearly thirty minutes. Everyone would be dead tired after, but because it took years of dedication to get a new belt, there was such a feeling of camaraderie during the ceremonies. People were so excited for each other in a genuine way you didn't see much of in real life, outside of weddings and such.

"Shh," Jonah said, confirming her suspicion. He held a finger up to his lips before setting the belts down into a box under the table by the door and returning to the men's locker room.

"Oh. Well, I don't have my Gi anyway," she said, biting her lip.

"There are a few in the lost and found you can borrow," Felix said, sliding his sunglasses over his head so she could see his eyes.

He looked hungover, as usual. And like he had just woken up, which was also per usual. Clearly, he had still not found a new job, all these months later. At this point she'd even forgotten what he did for work before.

"I don't know if that's such a good idea," she said. She blinked, getting sad enough to cry again, before pushing the feeling away. Being in the gym now, when it was just the three of them, wasn't so bad. It was actually nice. But she didn't think she could face everyone else, let alone go to class and act like everything was as it was before. Even now they weren't addressing the elephant in the room. And there was clearly a very large one there.

"Why?" Felix asked.

She shook her head again. "I can't."

Then Mina heard a voice behind her, and turned abruptly. "You say that one more damn time today, I'm gonna double armbar you and then put you in a body triangle." She turned to look at who it was, even though her heart already knew, because she would recognize that voice anywhere. It was Matthew. A smile spread across her face before she could stop it.

"You can't do that at the same time," she said, then started laughing.

"Don't know till ya try," Matthew said, raising his brows.

Felix rolled his eyes, looking annoyed at both of them. "Matthew, didn't realize you were back," he said in a flat, even tone.

Mina was surprised as well. Not that he was back, which she obviously knew already, but that he was at the gym. He had told her so many times he would never go back to Open Guard. "Are you rolling?" Mina asked.

"Yes, and so are you," he ordered, kicking his dirty checkered Vans to the floor. "Go get a fucking Gi on."

God, she loved it when he ordered her around. Her insides went all fluttery, and it almost made her forget where she was, where they both were, and why. They hadn't been at the gym together since the video. Neither of them wanted to face the looks they might get from everyone. She still didn't feel ready for that, even now. It was the main reason she didn't want to stay.

"Matthew, you know I can't. I need to find Dima," she said, lowering her voice.

"Let the cops do their job, Mina," he told her. "You're not one of the crazy chicks in your books who goes around solving crimes. Real life doesn't work like that."

"I can't just sit here while he's out there missing or dead or whatever," she said in a whisper. "The cops don't even know he's dating someone."

"Yes, they do," Matthew said. He began pushing her towards the mat, then onto it.

He knew she couldn't say no to him, and she hated proving that to him yet again, but he was sort of right. She'd be better off here at the gym than pacing around her house until pickup. Plus, maybe she could ask around to see if anyone else had seen Dima recently. Mina sighed and slipped off her coat, draping it over one of the empty black stools near the windows.

"Jesus Christ, is that you, Matthew?" she heard Jonah say before coming across the mats and tackling Matthew to the floor so hard it made a loud thud when they landed. He slid his arm around his neck and squeezed, then rolled forward into a standing position. Matthew laughed and stood up too, then Jonah gave him a big, back-patting hug. "It's good to see you, man."

"You too, Jonah," Matthew said sheepishly.

"I had no idea you were back," Jonah said. "I would have called you up."

"Yeah, I've been keeping a low profile," Matthew said with a glance in Mina's direction.

"Do you have more of those seltzers?" she asked Jonah, finding she could no longer stand there, the four of them like that. It reminded her too much of that horrible night in September. And all the nights before, when they'd drink there together until she was so tired she had to go home and go straight to bed.

Jonah gave her an exaggerated snort, still smiling and keeping a hand on Matthew's shoulder. "Where do you think you are?" he said. "We're a drinking club with a Jiu Jitsu problem. Check the fridge."

Mina headed back there, then took her seltzer with her to search through the lost and found, trying not to overhear their now-hushed conversation by focusing on the noise of the fan, which was on the other side of the box. At the bottom, she actually found her own Gi, a bright blue one that she must have left the last time she was there. Somehow it didn't smell, which meant it had likely been washed during the time it had been at the gym. As she took it out, she stepped back right into Felix's chest, who was coming out of the men's room. He smelled like a distillery, her nose instantly noticed.

"Sorry," she said.

"Whatever," he mumbled, walking past her to sit on the mat. His total reversal in mood wasn't even strange for him, so she thought little of it; she had enough to deal with at that moment. Part of why she had never wanted to date Felix was his mood swings. They reminded her too much of a toddler, but in a far more unattractive manner than other people's inner toddlers. One second, he would be fine, the next pissy. His happiness only showed up in short spurts, usually when he was pretty drunk, and the rest of the time he was kind of a downer. Just like her dad.

That's why, after she had made the mistake of drunkenly sleeping with him, she had stayed away from him for the last six months. It wasn't like the sex was bad—it was fine, at least what she remembered of it—she just felt awkward afterward. She had enough problems at the time, and couldn't add another, which he was surely to become. It was easier to ignore him, and the entire gym, for that matter. Better for her mental health, too.

Mina went into the girl's room and put her Gi on. Once she was dressed, she felt at home again at the gym. It was an instant change.

People started slowly trickling into the room, and she was so relieved that most of them were new or hadn't been around when she was rolling last year that she allowed herself to go sit near Matthew, who had also changed and was relaxing against a wall. The only odd look she got was from Violet, who raised her eyebrows when she saw them together, but then hurried to the changing room and didn't say anything to her about it once.

"Is this super weird?" she asked Matthew.

"Oh yeah. It's fucking awful," he said, staring ahead at the bright red mat. He put one knee up and rested his elbow on it, and she could tell he was sucking on a piece of Nicorette gum.

"Then why are we here?"

"Well, I realized that I was doing the same thing I was giving you shit for earlier," he said. "That, and if I don't roll, I'm gonna actually fucking kill someone soon. This is more time off than I've ever had in my life."

"Oh yeah. When are they letting you go back to work anyway?"

"No clue," he said.

"Maybe they're waiting to see what is going on with people from the gym disappearing first."

"Nah," he said. "It's the government. Everything takes forever."

"Well, good thing you have an alibi," she said, bumping his shoulder with hers. "They're really up in our business. Kept asking me if I ever felt unsafe around you."

Matthew let out a disgruntled laugh, letting his other leg relax onto the mat. "Oh, I know. I was there all fucking morning."

"Did they show you the texts?" she asked, her eyes raised.

He nodded, still staring blankly ahead. "Uh, yeah. Was really a challenge looking at those things while they sat there. My pants were getting real tight." He shook his head and laughed. "Damn, I love how dirty you are, though."

"Who do you think sent them? I don't even know who would want to read them, let alone send them to our spouses."

"No fucking clue," Matthew said.

"Well, at least you can stop blaming me now," she said, bumping him again, this time with her knee. Touching in public still felt so strange so she moved down the wall a little. Not that anyone was looking at them; everyone was in their own worlds, stretching, getting dressed, or huddled in small groups and talking. "God, I really missed this place," she said happily.

"Me too," Matthew said. "I'm going to destroy you in class, though. You really fucking pissed me off today."

She snorted. "Everything pisses you off, Matthew," she said. "Have you ever thought about going to therapy? There is some really disturbing stuff going on in your head."

Matthew shook his head and laughed. "Says the girl who can't come without a hand around her throat. Maybe you're the one who needs therapy."

Well, she couldn't exactly argue with that.

"All right, let's circle up," she heard Jonah say from the center of the room, and then class was starting, and it was the happiest she'd felt in a while, despite everything. It wasn't until they had rolled several rounds and she stopped to take a breather and check her phone that she remembered this was no fairytale. Things didn't just blow up and then settle into normalcy, at least not for her. Like an earthquake, there were shockwaves, and hers were still coming.

Mina, Dima is with me, said a message from Meghan. *You need to stay away from the gym. And call me.*

CHAPTER TWENTY-SEVEN

Mina stared at her phone for a moment, frozen. Her temporary relief about finding Dima was quickly destroyed by the more pressing issue of why Meghan told her to stay away from the gym. She must have known something, maybe about Dylan's murder. If anyone knew anything, it was probably her. But why hadn't she told the cops she was with Dima? There was no way she could wait to talk to her until after class. Mina took her phone and ran outside without even getting her coat or shoes on. She called the number Meghan had sent along with the message, her feet instantly cold on the icy ground.

"Mina?" asked the voice on the other end.

"Is Dima okay?" she asked Meghan without preamble.

"Yeah, he's fine," Meghan said. "Someone kept trying to run him off the road so he just got out and walked here."

"Jesus," Mina said. "Did he see who it was? Why didn't he call the cops? They're looking for him."

"He did. It just took him a long time to get here because he left his phone and wallet in the car," Meghan said. She sounded short of breath. "He had to borrow money from some stranger to finally get on the train out here, and my apartment is pretty far from the station."

"Oh. But he's okay?"

"Yeah, he's okay," she said. "And hey, look, sorry I didn't mention that we—"

"Meghan, please. Don't even worry about it," Mina interrupted.

Who Dima was dating was really the least of her concerns. And frankly, she was glad he had someone. "I just need to know why you said to stay away from the gym. I'm here now. I was looking for Dima."

There was a rustling in the background, and then Dima's voice was in her ear. "Mina," he said. "Get out of there."

"Why?" she asked. "Do you know something? Did you see who was in the car?"

"No," he said. "But there was an Open Guard sticker on the car. I saw it when the guy was trying to run me off the road. Anyway, the cops are here, I have to go. I'll call you as soon as I can, just go get Amelie early and go home. There's still an unmarked cop car out front right?"

"I think so," she said, looking down the block and noting that, yes, the unmarked police vehicle was still indeed there. Before she could tell him, though, he hung up.

Mina stood frozen on the pavement for another few seconds, trying to wrap her head around everything they'd just said, but then her feet began to feel like they might fall off, and she didn't want to get hypothermia on top of everything else, so she went back inside.

She only meant to go get her stuff, but before she knew it, Jonah was pulling her back onto the mat and forcing her into the middle of the room. Then he called out Carrie, an older blue belt covered head to toe in tattoos, and two purple belts, and soon they were all standing there and she realized in a panic what was going on.

He was promoting her. It could not have happened at a worse time—there was no way anyone was letting her out of that gym until the shark tank was over and Jonah had fake-choked them all out. The whole gym would have dragged her back inside if she tried to leave, and she could hardly fight one of them, let alone all twenty-three. She looked to Matthew, her eyes large with panic, but all he did was cross his arms and smirk at her. She shook her head and turned to Jonah.

"Jonah, seriously?"

"All right, guys, you know what to do," he said, ignoring her.

"Everyone get in a line, and let's start with the takedowns."

Mina swallowed. She was so rusty she could barely remember if she still knew any takedowns. But, luckily, in a shark tank they were only done to her, she didn't need to do them back. This was followed by endless attempts to pass her guard. Twenty torturous minutes later, they were taking pictures against the wall. Mina felt like she was going to collapse from exhaustion. She'd wanted to get her blue belt for so long, and after everything that had happened with Matthew and Dima, she had assumed that would never happen. But she could hardly enjoy it when there was some murderer out there trying to run her ex-husband off the road; especially when whoever it was could be there in the room with her.

Normally, this would be the perfect excuse to drink and hang out with everyone, but she merely chugged the seltzer Jonah brought her and then ran to the changing room to get back into her street clothes. On her way out, people stopped to congratulate her and shake her hand, and then Felix lifted her up and nearly dropped her before setting her down on her feet.

"God, you have to stop doing that," she said.

"See, I knew you could do it," Felix said. "Look, you're actually sweating."

"I really have to go. I need to pick up Amelie," she said, gathering up her dirty Gi.

"Fine, whatever," he said, walking off, looking a little offended. But she didn't have time to banter with Felix right then.

She looked around the room for Matthew, and saw him in the back, downing a beer with a few of the upper belts. She wanted to tell him what Meghan had shared with her on the phone, but she wasn't about to go over there in front of everyone and interrupt their conversation. He looked so happy there, back in his element. They may have made it through class without any weirdness, but that could have just been luck, or the distraction of promotion day. Plus, she was scared. She wanted to just be home with Amelie until they knew what was going on. She put on her boots and coat and left without saying another word to anyone and practically ran to the train.

God, she was happy to see her daughter's daycare, knowing she was in there, safe. As much as she had screwed up, as much as she didn't know who she was most of the time, she knew one thing for sure: she was still a mother, at the very least. Overwhelmed with the urge to hug her daughter, she opened the slate gray door and ran inside the vestibule of the colorful daycare at full speed. When she arrived, she spotted the back of Amelie's head in the three-year-old room, looking through a picture book by herself. It made her heart surge with love in such a way it nearly knocked her over.

She never knew it was possible to love something so much, so much it could actually hurt at times. She had made this beautiful little person; at least that. Of all the things she had fucked up, having Amelie could never be included in that list, and really, it kept her from drowning in self-pity most days. At least no matter what she would always be her mother.

"Amelie!" she cried, and watched her daughter turn to see her there, a smile spreading across her face. She jumped to her feet and ran in her direction, nearly falling over with her desire to reach Mina. That kind of pure love and joy was so rare to see it filled her up completely, whereas she'd felt so empty just moments earlier. Mina caught her and squeezed her so tight that Amelie said, "Ow."

"I'm sorry, baby. I just love you so much."

"I not baby," Amelie argued. In the past half year alone, she had made so much progress, and still, the fact that she could say a full sentence made Mina's eyes tear up. Such a simple thing, but it meant so much after everything they'd been through.

"I know," Mina said. "You're a big girl. Sorry."

"Movie?" Amelie asked.

"Sure," Mina said. "As soon as we get home."

Later, she and Amelie were walking back to the house when she noticed Matthew's truck was still parked next to Open Guard.

Were they all still drinking in the middle of the day? she wondered. Not that it would be a first, by any means. But it had been at least an hour since she'd left.

Mina, feeling better now that Amelie was with her and she was only a block away from her house and could see the unmarked cop car still parked just a few houses down, decided to go back in the gym for a minute to see if Matthew was still there. She wanted to tell him what Dima had said about the car running him off the road.

When she found the door locked, she dug around for her keys, which she still had even though she hadn't been a member there in a while. Jonah had never asked her to return them, and she liked having them in her possession as a reminder that once she belonged to a place that had made her feel so welcome; and maybe she might belong somewhere like that again one day. Maybe she could even belong here again one day, if she was really lucky. And maybe she might even learn to appreciate the things she had for once in her life.

Mina grabbed the keys and opened the door, expecting to find the place empty and dark, but the lights were still on. Had they forgotten to turn everything off before they left? But no, it sounded like someone was still there, in the back. She thought she heard a noise near the rear exit, like a weight falling off the shelf, and put Amelie down on a chair with a bag of Cheetos so she could go back there to follow it. And that's when she saw Felix, still wearing his Gi, wrenching Matthew's neck in a rear-naked choke. Matthew's face was turning purple, like he'd just passed out, and he even started shaking a little, but Felix kept his arm over his neck.

"Felix!" she said, so shocked that she wasn't entirely sure what she was witnessing. Were they just fooling around, or was he really trying to choke Matthew out? They must have been at it for a while to have let it go this far, as they were nearly equals in Jiu Jitsu; Matthew was a brown belt with two stripes and Felix was a brown belt with three stripes, though he could have probably been a black belt if he hadn't been kicked out of two gyms before joining Open Guard.

"What the fuck!"

Felix, his face red and his hair dripping with sweat, glanced up, an expression of panic washing over his face, before letting go. The look was clear enough to her that she could make an educated guess that they had not been messing around at all.

Matthew fell to the floor in a heap, his face still purple. When he didn't immediately get up, she reached for her phone, but before she could get it unlocked, Felix had it in his hand and had her down on the floor, her hand bound behind her back. Amelie, she thought then. Amelie was in the other room. She would be walking back there any second. Her heart began pounding so loudly you could practically hear it, the thumping spreading to her ears, the way it used to do when Matthew would choke her hard enough and her body would fill with adrenaline. Except now, she didn't like it. Not at all.

"Felix," she said, taking short, panicked breaths. At least she had a lot of practice with being able to breathe without getting enough oxygen. "Please. Let go."

Felix dragged her arm even further across her back, then took the other hand too, so both of them were crossed behind her. Then he lifted her up to her feet. She had done Jiu Jitsu with him long enough to know there was no reason to try to fight him. He always won, he won against everyone, even some of the black belts. She stared at Matthew on the floor, then looked to the mats, trying to find Amelie. She could still see her on the chair eating Cheetos.

"Felix. What is going on?" she asked. Talking was her only way out of this mess. She had to at least try. Maybe those cops waiting down the block would find it odd she was in there for so long and come check it out. Or Matthew would come to and run for help. Something. In a movie, the girl would reach into her soul to discover some hidden inner strength and fight her way out of a man's grasp. But in the movie, the man wouldn't be a brown belt in Jiu Jitsu with at least a hundred pounds on her. That would never work here. Even if he wasn't it probably wouldn't work. Men were just stronger, that was a fact. It was an advantage she had to constantly work around while rolling, using her flexibility or core strength to try to defend submissions rather than strength. "What are you doing?"

"You know," Felix said.

"I really don't," she said. She thought she could see Matthew's arm move. Was he waking up? If he was, she just needed to keep Felix talking a little longer. "Please explain it to me."

"He was in the way," Felix said, like it was an obvious fact. "Now he's not."

"In the way of what?" she asked.

Felix let go of her arm, only to spin her around to face him. He still had a tight grip around her and she couldn't move. "You and me," he said. "I thought once he'd left, and Dylan was out of the equation, you'd finally realize it. Your husband you at least managed to get rid of all on your own. Well, I mean, with some help. But then this douchebag had to fucking come back."

She blinked, horrified. "Realize what, Felix? That you're crazy?" she said.

Felix shook his head with disappointment. "I thought you of all people wouldn't call me that. After everything."

"This is crazy, Felix. Come on," she said. She had to keep him talking longer, because she could see, and he could not, that Matthew was starting to regain consciousness. His foot moved first, then his arms. She must have gotten there just in time to keep him from doing real damage. But by saving Matthew she had just put her own life in danger. More importantly, her daughter's. She took in another shaky breath and forced herself to talk. "Did you—kill Dylan?"

"The guy was a criminal, Mina. He was using your van to deal drugs, and your idiot ex was helping him. The world is a better place without him, and you really need to get better fucking taste in men, Jesus Christ."

"I'm not disagreeing with you on that," Mina said, slowly, watching as Matthew finally got up from the floor and silently sat in a crouching position behind them; he caught her eye, placing a finger in front of his mouth, his gaze furious but sobering. She looked back at Felix, finally admitting out loud what she hadn't wanted to deal with for nearly a year. "But... You and me? No. That's just... not happening."

Now, she understood that it had been weak and shortsighted to try to ignore his feelings for her, just as it had been weak and shortsighted to ignore all the other problems she'd had too. Everyone was right about *Turn and Face Your Problems*, how it was necessary both on and off the mats. But who honestly did that in life? She surely hadn't; not until she'd been forced.

"Why not?" Felix asked. "Because you don't want to be with someone who actually treats you well?" He finally let go of her arms, placing a hand on her shoulder, freeing her. "You know I can be that guy. Don't you remember that night?"

"Barely," she said. "I was wasted. It was a mistake."

"It was the best night of my life."

"Felix, that's just—really sad," she said.

And it was sad. As much as she was currently terrified for her life, and Amelie's, and even Matthew's, she couldn't help but feel pity for the guy. Which was maybe why she didn't immediately kick him in the balls. Instead, she stepped back a little, and it was enough for Matthew to jump up and tackle him. She didn't stay to watch them struggle, she just ran to the mats and grabbed Amelie, carrying her out the door without even getting her shoes or coat on. She put her down once she got outside, trying to flag down the unmarked police car, but it was impossible to tell if they saw her or not.

"Amelie, baby," she said, taking a big chance here, but it was the only thing she could think to do in that moment. "I need you to go down the street. You see that car right there? The black one? Go there and tell them Mommy gym bad guy, okay? Anything like that, just go get them," she said, and to her utter shock and relief, Amelie actually listened to her. She saw her running down the street, long brown hair bouncing, and before she even got to there, two uniformed cops had already exited the car and were running towards them down the icy sidewalk, picking her up as they ran.

Knowing they were on their way, she went back into the gym where Matthew and Felix were still wrestling. It looked like Felix was about to break Matthew's arm. It was past the point where people would normally tap out, his rotator cuff probably already sprained at best, broken at worst. "Felix, stop it!" she said.

"Why should I?" he asked, leaning over Matthew, who he had in side control. His side control was more difficult to get out of than anyone else's at the gym, so it worried her.

"Because I'm asking you to," she tried.

"This is the only thing I'm good at," Felix said. "Why not just finish it?"

"Felix," she started, but then Matthew shrimped out and got his arm back. Her being there had distracted Felix enough that Matthew was able to get his knee on Felix's stomach. Matthew was still red, his sweat dripping so profusely she could see it landing on Felix.

"He doesn't give a shit about you, Mina," Felix said from beneath him. "When are you going to see that?"

Matthew turned to look at her, his hands gripping Felix's Gi tight around his neck, jaw clenched in an expression she was all too familiar with—murderous rage. It was not even close to the look she'd witnessed when they were in bed and he was choking her. He truly wanted to kill Felix.

"Time to go to sleep," he said, walking his leg around Felix's head and then choking him out from the North-South position. Just as the cops had run through the door, one carrying Amelie, the other a gun, Matthew leaned back and fell onto the mats, trying to catch his breath so hard it turned into a coughing fit. Mina grabbed Amelie and then ran to him, sitting down. Amelie climbed Matthew and gave him a hug.

"Are you okay?" Amelie asked. Mina almost wept hearing it

come out of her mouth at an actually appropriate moment. For a moment she thought about Dima, how happy he would be to know that Amelie had actually communicated properly, before she realized how unhappy he would be knowing why, once she told him everything that had occurred. But she felt grateful too, so grateful that any depression she had still been feeling was suddenly gone, completely vanished from her body. She was alive, and so was Amelie, and so were the two men she cared about most. Even if she wished she could stop having any feelings at all towards both of them.

When Matthew didn't answer, Mina repeated the question. "Matthew, are you okay?" she asked, grabbing his shoulder. He winced, but then he nodded, grabbing Mina's thigh with one hand. Felix had woken up already, and Mina could see one of the cops putting handcuffs around his wrists and reading him his rights.

"You know I fucking hate liars," Matthew grumbled, trying to stretch out his shoulder and then stopping when it hurt too much.

"Aw. Does that mean you do give a shit about me?" she asked, almost laughing at the absurdity of it all.

"Shut the fuck up," Matthew said, closing his eyes. She stood up and held Amelie to her hip, then reached out a hand to help lift him up. When he opened his eyes to take it, looking relieved to see her still standing there, she knew what he really meant was yes.

"God, I'm never fucking coming back to this gym again," he said, slowly getting to his feet while holding his shoulder with the other hand.

"Yes, you are," she said, looking around the brightly lit room, now filling up even more with cops and a pair of EMTs, one of whom was a member there and recognized them both. For a moment, even in the chaos of almost dying, it felt like they had escaped a treacherous ocean to find their own perfect little island. "You'll be back here tomorrow."

"Yeah, you're probably right," Matthew said. Mina turned to watch them take Felix away in handcuffs, but he didn't even look up at her.

"Oh! I finally remembered what Felix did before he was unemployed!" she said. "IT or something. Computer stuff." Matthew looked at her, understanding at the same time that it must have been Felix who sent their deleted texts to Ariel and Dima that day in September.

Matthew shook his head. "See? What did I tell you? Where there's Mina, there's drama."

"Hey. I saved your life," she said.

"Whatever. We all gotta go sometime," he said. "If I'm gonna die, might as well be here."

Mina punched him in the shoulder, forgetting it was injured.

"Ow," Matthew said. "Jesus."

"Sorry," she said. "Habit."

"Oh no! Ouchie!" Amelie said, looking at him and pointing. "Ouchie band-aid!"

She moved Amelie from her hip and hugged her to her chest. "Yes. Matthew probably *does* need a band-aid." Before Amelie could go digging through Mina's purse looking for *Frozen* band-aids, a current obsession of hers, both the movie and the idea of band-aids, Mina began walking towards the exit. From across the room, she turned and told Matthew, "See ya later?"

"Yeah. I'll see you later," he said, his head covered slightly by an EMT's back.

"Hopefully no one tries to choke you again on your way out," she joked.

"Hey. Leave the choking to me," he said, with a wink.

So she did.

z

ABOUT THE AUTHOR

Zhanna Slor was born in the former Soviet Union and moved to the Midwest in the early 1990s. She has been published in many literary magazines, including *Ninth Letter, Another Chicago Magazine,* and *Michigan Quarterly Review,* as well as contributing to the popular news publication *The Forward.* Her debut novel, *At the End of the World, Turn Left,* was called "elegant and authentic" by NPR and named by *Booklist* as one of the "Top Ten Crime Debuts" of 2021. She lives in Milwaukee, WI.